WILD WOLF CLAIMING

RHYANNON BYRD

Published in Great Britain 2015
by Mills & Boon, an imprint of Harlequin (UK) Limited,
Eton House, 18-24 Paradise Road, Richmond, Surrey, TW9 1SR

© 2015 Tabitha Bird

ISBN: 978-0-263-91826-7

89-1215

Harlequin (UK) Limited's policy is to use papers that are natural, renewable and recyclable products and made from wood grown in sustainable forests. The logging and manufacturing processes conform to the legal environmental regulations of the country of origin.

Printed and bound in Spain
by CPI, Barcelona

Rhyannon Byrd is an avid, longtime fan of romance and an author of more than twenty paranormal and erotic titles. She has been nominated for three RT Reviewers' Choice Best Book Awards, including Best Shapeshifter Romance. Rhyannon lives in the beautiful county of Warwickshire, England, with her husband and family.

For information on Rhyannon's books, visit her website at www.rhyannonbyrd.com or find her on Facebook.

To everyone who hoped that Elliot would one day have a story of his own. . .

This one's for you!

Prologue

Nine years ago

Elliot Connors was in a shitty situation. One he'd been putting off for too long.

A week had passed since another human life had been lost because of his mistakes, and he knew he should have dealt with this reckoning, or confrontation, or whatever you wanted to call it long before now. But he hadn't, because he suspected he knew *exactly* how this meeting would go.

Standing at the far end of the dining room table in his parents' house, he watched as Jerry and Miriam Connors digested the confession he'd just made to them. A dark, ugly confession, full of blood and sin and evil. And in their eyes, no doubt, embarrassment—at least as much as they were able to process. He didn't for a moment think they would mourn the loss of the human life he'd taken, or the one that'd been lost because of him. No, compassion for humanity wasn't in their makeup. Hell, compassion for anything was beyond them.

But his lack of control would be the thing that proved difficult for them to face. To Jerry and Miriam Connors, control meant everything. There was nothing, nothing in this entire world, that they believed in more.

As pure-blooded werewolves in the Silvercrest Lycan pack, Elliot's parents could have easily been one of those arrogant, racist couples who despised anyone and anything they deemed beneath them. Humans, the half-breed Bloodrunners who protected the pack, and any Lycan who mated with a human. For most purebloods, these groups were not only deemed inferior, but often abhorrent.

His parents, though, were different. The thing they hated most in this world was emotion, in any form. As orphans who had been raised with foster families, his parents had suffered for lack of attention and he'd always wondered if that had forged them into such cold, calculating adults. But, in truth, he didn't honestly know. The only certainty he had when it came to the two Lycans who had given him life was that emotion in their eyes meant weakness. And what was a loss of control but the absence of logic in the face of extreme emotion? Passion, love, devotion. The concepts were no doubt as foreign to them as guilt would be to a sociopath.

God, no wonder he'd been so attracted to Marly, with her kind smiles and her natural warmth. She'd been the kind of girl who could make even the shyest introvert feel welcome, and he'd been drawn to the warmth of her human soul like a moth to a flame. Only...Marly hadn't been the danger. Elliot and the world that he came from had. And now it was too late. Marly was gone, his seventeen-year-old soul was blackened and there was no one to blame but himself.

From the look on his parents' faces, he knew they blamed him, too.

Reaching for the cup of coffee that sat before him, his father took a sip of the steamy beverage, then lowered the mug. His dark eyes, so like Elliot's own, narrowed with decision, and in a calm voice, he said, "You made mistakes that could have easily been avoided had you been willing to control your more primitive urges, and then you took refuge with the Runners. It seems logical that your place is with them now. We'll expect you to have your things out of the house by the end of the day."

Well, that was no fucking surprise. And yet, he couldn't quite swallow down the lump that had just lodged its way into his throat. "Yeah?" he choked out. "So that's it?"

His mother's tone was as bland as her expression as she turned her attention from his father to him. "What more did you expect, Elliot?"

A husky, bitter laugh left his lips before he could stop it. "I suppose a heartfelt 'We love you and will stand by you' would be asking a bit much, huh?"

"And what place does love have in this life that you've chosen for yourself?" his father asked. "How can love exist for something as ill-disciplined as you?"

He kept his gaze focused on his mom, feeling like an idiot for hoping for something that would never be there. A flash of regret. A flicker of guilt. Instead, she was like a beautiful china doll, and just as lifeless. He idly wondered if she would shatter like dropped porcelain if that wide mouth of hers ever tried to curl in a smile or a sneer...or an impassioned defense of her only child. But she simply sat there, like a statue, and he forced himself to turn away before he made a fool of himself in front of them.

Heading upstairs to his bedroom, he could only give another hollow, gritty laugh when he found the stack of moving boxes they'd left on his bed. He told himself that a lot of people left home at seventeen, and that he'd be fine. But it didn't make the ache in his gut hurt any less, or the anger firing through his veins burn any colder.

It took him little time to pack his things, his need to be gone from that place more important than organization. He shoved his crap into the boxes in huge armfuls, only taking his clothes and books and leaving the rest behind.

His parents still sat at the table, both of them reading the paper in icy, sterile silence, and Elliot didn't even slow his steps as he made the last trip past the dining room archway and out the front door.

Climbing into the truck the Runners had let him borrow, he started the engine and got the hell out of there. The back of his throat and nose burned, but he sniffed and tightened his jaw, refusing to shed any tears over the couple who had given him life.

Not. A. Single. Damn. One.

Chapter 1

Present day
December

So this is Charity, Pennsylvania, Elliot thought, casting a long, dark look down the wide street that ran through the center of town. *What a screwed-up name.*

Despite the beauty of the state, this particular place was a shithole, and that was putting it nicely. In Elliot's opinion, there didn't seem to be a single *charitable* thing about it, its only redeeming feature the fact it was surrounded by thick, lush forest. As a Lycan, or werewolf, Elliot craved the scent and feel of the woods the way a baby hungered for mother's milk. So in his eyes, the surrounding forest was the only saving grace to good ol' run-down, seen-better-days-decades-ago Charity.

Not even the haggard Christmas lights flashing down the sides of the street could make the place look cheery.

"Dude, what's up with the look on your face? You step in some yellow snow, or just thinking about how long it's been since you actually made an effort to get laid?"

The questions came from the pain in the ass standing beside him, his Bloodrunning partner and best friend, Max Doucet. The two of them had met nearly a decade ago, at the lowest points of their lives, and somehow found their way through the nightmare together. Max had once been human, before he was attacked by a rogue wolf and turned. And Elliot... Elliot's nature had been forged in the jaws of hell itself.

And now they worked as Bloodrunners alongside the men and women who'd saved them all those years ago. Max had been fortunate to have the Runners' support because he was an innocent who'd been caught up in the pack's troubles, and Elliot because he'd acted on instinct and saved the life of Torrance Dillinger when she was attacked by the group of rogue wolves he'd been involved with. Her husband and mate, Mason, had told the frightened, traumatized young Lycan Elliot had been back then that they'd helped him because they could tell he had a good heart. Such simple words, and yet, he knew it was their faith in him that had made the difference. That had kept him in the light, when he could have easily slithered into a cold, emotionless existence that would have been too much like his parents' way of living.

Thanks, but no thanks.

Given a second chance, he'd held on to the Runners' belief in him with a white-knuckled grip as the years went by, while still holding himself back from the things most men craved. Holding back, until he finally reached a point where he'd started to believe he could trust himself as much as they did. And it was then that he'd started to let his body and mind want *more*.

And, yeah, by more he meant a woman.

He might not have any experience, save that one hellish night all those years ago, but he'd learned physical control. You couldn't be a Runner without it, and he was one of the best. Elliot could say that without being cocky, the work he and Max did more than worthy of their positions within the group.

But he refused to let his hard-earned control over his body bleed its way into his emotions. He might be more subdued than Max, but he still felt things deeply… strongly. Probably a hell of a lot more strongly than even those closest to him knew.

So, yeah, he lusted and hungered for the pleasure that could be found in the soft, tender clasp of a woman's body. And yet, when he'd finally allowed himself to want more, there'd been no one he knew who'd captured his attention. He'd tried dating within the pack a few times, but as badly as his body craved release, he hadn't found a woman who was *the woman*. The one he wanted so badly he ached with it. And if he'd waited this long, Elliot figured he might as well make it worth it.

Despite how long he'd been alone, he wanted a lover. Someone he could lose himself in; someone he could *learn*. Learn to please. To make moan. Even to scream.

But with pleasure. *Only* ever with pleasure. So much pleasure that he would be the only thing she craved. The one thing in the world she needed above all others.

So I'll wait as long as it takes, he silently growled, hoping that all the hours he spent hunting for the scum of the earth in shitty towns like this one would pay off for him one day. That his years of sacrifice would lead him to something good. Something that was damn well worth the wait.

Tired of being ignored, Max suddenly stepped in front of him and arched a raven brow. "Since you've gone mute on me, I'll take your crabby expression to mean that you want out of this shitastic place as badly as I do."

He jerked his chin up in response, glad that Max was on the same page with him.

"So how are we gonna do it?"

"We could always flip a coin," he murmured with a smirk, since it was one of the tamer ways they divvied up jobs when they didn't have a preference. "I don't think the cops around here would appreciate it if we tried to see who can howl the loudest."

Max gave a rough bark of laughter, then pulled a shiny new quarter from his front pocket and rubbed it between his fingers. "Heads, you get to go inside and risk food poisoning while waiting for the waitress to show. Tails, you get to haul your ass over to the apartment complex and scout out the other one."

"Vivian, right?"

"Yeah, and this one is Skye, with an *e*." With his free hand, Max pulled his phone from his other pocket, and flicked a look down at the screen, where the info that had been emailed to them by Jared Monroe—a Fed who was friendly with the pack—was displayed. "Skye Hewitt."

"What kind of person names their kid Skye?"

Max snorted. "Probably some nature-loving hippy who wears daisies in her hair."

"Yeah," he murmured distractedly, his thoughts already drifting back to the hunt that had brought them there, and away from the human's unusual name.

For the past three weeks, he and Max had been hunting a...puzzle. A monstrous one, but a puzzle no less. One they wanted solved so badly they could taste it.

It had all started with a string of missing persons' reports that Monroe had asked them to look into. Some unusual happenings around the disappearances had caused Monroe, whose sister was married to a Lycan from the Silvercrest pack, to suspect that there was more to the case than his human agents would be able to handle. Something dark and sinister and predatory—like an animal on the hunt for its prey—and Monroe had been right to be suspicious.

When Elliot and Max had worked over the crime scenes, their sharper-than-human senses had picked up clues that the FBI had failed to notice. Things like the faint, musky scent that clung to the locations where seven different women had simply vanished.

That was the killer part of the case right there. All of the victims were female...and human...and exceptionally beautiful. And now they were just gone, with no trace of them left behind for their loved ones to cling to.

There had been no bodies recovered, which meant that if the psychopath responsible was killing them, he was smart enough to hide the victims where they were difficult to find. But Elliot didn't think that was the case, and Max agreed with him.

Instead, they believed the women were being kept. Imprisoned. And undoubtedly *used*. Though at this point, they couldn't be sure of anything. All Elliot knew for certain was that he and Max planned to find those women, set them free and make the one responsible pay. With blood and pain...and ultimately death. That bastard deserved no less, and he sure as hell wouldn't be shown any mercy.

"Okay," Max murmured, drawing Elliot from his thoughts. "Let's do this thing."

The late-afternoon sun glinted against the shiny metal as Max tossed the coin into the air. It spun, then fell into his waiting hand. Max flipped the coin onto the top of his other hand, then revealed the outcome.

"Congratulations!" the jackass said with a smirk, knowing the noisy diner would grate on Elliot's nerves. "Looks like you get to go in and meet the mysterious Skye."

Shaking off the cold chill that had started to settle over his shoulders, he jerked his chin toward the front of the retro-styled diner. "Guess it's a good thing it takes a hell of a lot to poison our guts, huh?"

"Hey, you never know," said the guy with a cast-iron stomach. "It might taste freaking fantastic."

"Or like shit."

"That, too," Max agreed with a laugh. "But look at it this way—at least you get to relax for a while, while I'm off to venture even farther into this shit-stain of a town in search of her friend."

"Just hurry and get back here," he murmured, shoving his hands deep in the pockets of his jeans. "I don't want to be waiting all night. We don't know how much time we have before they try to take them, and Mase'll kill us if we have a showdown in the middle of a human town."

"Mase would understand."

This time, Elliot was the one who snorted. "After he kicked your ass."

Max laughed as he pulled out his crumpled pack of cigarettes. "The old man could try."

"Yeah, right," he muttered, enjoying ribbing his friend. "Even you're smart enough to know not to mess with those guys." At twenty-seven and almost twenty-nine, he and Max were by far the youngest of the Runners. But while Mason and the other guys were into their forties now, they were in their freaking prime. As lethal and powerful as they'd ever been, and some of the dirtiest fighters Elliot had ever seen.

Which meant Max would undoubtedly get his pretty ass handed to him, seeing as how the guy's conscience was still a bit more human than wolf. He could be just as deadly as the rest of them, but there was always a subdued edge to Max's brutality. A sense that he was doing what his head told him had to be done, rather than his heart. It made Elliot worry that his friend might hesitate a second too long one day, instead of fully trusting the instincts of his wolf. And those types of delays could be costly…especially when dealing with the kind of monsters they came across.

They chatted for a few more seconds, while Max lit his smoke and took a deep drag. Then they said their goodbyes, and Max turned to head back to his truck.

Unable to shake the sense of foreboding that was climbing up his spine, Elliot shouted, "Watch your six!"

"You, too, man," Max called back over his shoulder, before disappearing around the corner.

Instead of heading straight into the diner, Elliot decided to stay outside for a while, where it was quiet. He propped his back against one of the gray lampposts that ran down the snowplowed street, content to simply have a few moments to himself while he watched what was going on in the place through its massive front windows.

There were three waitresses working the floor, but none of them matched Hewitt's age or description. Not that they had all that much to go on. He and Max caught a lucky break back in Philly, where the last abduction had taken place. A drug addict, who had been sleeping under some cardboard boxes in an alley behind the club the victim had been taken from, had listened to a group of what he described as "big, badass-looking men" as they'd discussed their next "targets." The jackass hadn't done a goddamn thing to help the woman who was dragged into the alley, bound and gagged, and tossed into the back of a white delivery van. But he'd at least been able to tell Elliot and Max fragments of the conversation he'd overheard.

According to the addict, who had never come forward to the police officers who had canvassed the area, the men were meant to drop off the woman they'd taken from the club with their employer, and then head to Charity, where they would track down two young roommates by the names of Skye Hewitt and Vivian Jackson. And while Vivian certainly seemed to be in keeping with the employer's taste—lean and brunette and exotically beautiful—Skye was the exact opposite. A so-called "wholesome, pudgy blonde." She sounded more cute than drop-dead, in-your-face gorgeous like the other victims had been. But Elliot didn't give a crap what she looked like. He just wanted to find her, and protect her, while hopefully getting a lead on where the other women were being held.

With Skye and Vivian's names, as well as the town they lived in, it'd been easy for Monroe to track down their current address and places of employment. A few carefully worded phone calls, and the Fed had even managed to get the Runners both of the women's schedules, which was how they knew Skye's shift would be starting any moment now.

As if he'd managed to make her appear by simply thinking about her, the swinging door that Elliot assumed led to the kitchen was pushed open, and a woman walked through, coming into view. A young woman who looked to be in her early twenties, with thick, lustrous hair falling down past her shoulders, a curvy body and a smile that made him suck in a sharp breath, just before his body jolted like he'd been kicked in the stomach.

Son of a bitch, he thought, pressing his hand against the center of his chest. The sight of her smiling face had just knocked the air out of him so hard that it hurt.

Elliot narrowed his eyes as he stared at the woman, eating up every detail like his wolf with a bone. With his keen eyesight, he could see the letters on her nametag: *S-K-Y-E.* It was really *her*, Skye Hewitt, and Jesus, she was…different. But in a good way. In an "I can't stop staring, would probably kill to get closer to her" kind of way. And, um, yeah…that was unexpected.

As Elliot stood there like a friggin' statue and watched her, it became easy to see what—beyond her physical beauty—had captured the interest of the man responsible for the kidnappings. She was…soft. Soft and sweet and inviting as hell. Standing outside in the chilly evening air, shrouded by the deepening darkness, the faint flicker of the scattered Christmas lights too weak to reach him, Elliot couldn't take his damn eyes off her as she started serving the tables in her section. There was an addictive, undeniable warmth in her gaze, and in the bright smile she gave to those around her, even while working her ass off. It was completely out of place in the dingy town, and impossible to resist. A lure…and it was calling to him, making him want, when he hadn't wanted anyone in what felt like forever.

Not since Marly. And never... *Shit*, never like this.

When he glanced down at the thick watch on his wrist and saw that nearly an hour and a half had gone by since she'd walked through that swinging door, he cursed under his breath. What the hell? Had she put some kind of spell on him? Then he lifted his head, catching sight of her as she playfully stuck her tongue out at a toddler who was giggling and doing the same, and Elliot found himself giving such a loud bark of laughter that it made the old woman shuffling past him on the sidewalk jump.

"Sorry," he murmured, when the old lady huffed at him. He gave her an apologetic grin, then glanced back into the diner, and instantly scowled at the sight of some jerk checking out Skye's ass as she bent over to clear a table. The bastard. Thinking it was time he finally went inside, he pushed off from the lamppost and walked over to the door.

The first thing that hit him when he walked into the diner was the scent of the place. It was strong, especially for someone with his heightened sense of smell. A heavy mixture of greasy food, strong coffee, even stronger perfume and an underlying layer of whatever cleaning products they used. He was trying to search out Skye's scent in the midst of all those odors when an older woman chewing bubble gum and sporting an actual beehive hairdo popped up from behind the hostess's station.

"You want a table or a booth, pretty boy?" she asked, coming around the side of the station with a plastic menu in her hand.

"Whatever you have free in Skye's section."

The woman gave a low, knowing laugh, and started leading him over to an empty booth. "Skye's slammed at the moment," she told him, handing him the menu as he sat down, his long legs barely fitting in the cramped space under the table. "But she'll be over to take your order in just a few."

"No problem," he murmured, barely aware of her setting down a bowl of peanuts, his attention already captured by Skye. She was delivering food to a table only about ten feet from his booth, and he couldn't look away. The damn building could have caught fire, and he would have still been sitting there, completely mesmerized by her.

She was even more beautiful without the distance between them, though he would have preferred to have her right there with him, *in* the booth. Or even better, straddling his lap, polyester skirt tugged up around her generous hips, and his hardening cock pressed tight against the warm seam between her legs, while he shoved his hands into all that thick, wavy hair and kissed the hell out of her. She had the figure of a 1940s pinup girl, all lush curves and feminine swells that were making his mouth water. She looked vibrant, even in the ugly pink uniform, her skin all creamy and flushed, and those green eyes flashing with her emotions, constantly shifting from humor to kindness as she talked to her customers. Each feature of her beautiful face intrigued him, from her full, succulent mouth to the cuteness of her nose.

And then were the freckles. Tiny, dark little pinpricks scattered over her nose and cheeks. Christ, he wanted to touch his tongue to each one of them, then strip her beautiful body bare and search for more. Wanted to learn this woman's taste and scent and the kinds of sounds she made when she came. He didn't know her, beyond her name and the fact that he was there to protect her from an evil they knew far too little about. But he wanted to.

He wanted to know every goddamn thing there was to know about Skye Hewitt. Including what it would feel like to drive himself deep inside her, and lose himself in her soft, sexy body, until their skin was slick with heat and their throats were raw from the husky, unrestrained sounds they were making.

He wanted to fuck her. And he wanted to fuck her hard.

"You need anything, honey?" The question came from the skinny waitress who'd just stopped beside his table, blocking his view of Skye. The woman's perfume was so heavy it almost made his eyes water, the hungry way she was looking him over so blatant he was surprised she didn't lick her lips. "Because I'm willing to offer you something a heck of a lot better than anything you'll find on that menu."

"I'm good, thanks," he said in a low voice, just wanting her to move on so that he could keep watching Skye.

She instantly scowled. "Your loss," she muttered, before cattily adding, "Especially if you're saving it for Skye. That girl wouldn't know how to please a man even if she had a sex manual for fat chicks."

Elliot had to bite back an angry, snarling growl as the waitress flounced away, his protective instincts shooting straight into overdrive. He knew it was pure, seething jealousy that had the woman mouthing off, but he hated the idea of Skye ever having to put up with those kinds of bitchy remarks from her coworkers.

As if she knew he was thinking about her, she looked over from where she was standing, about two tables over, her hand busily jotting down a family of four's order. She gave him an apologetic smile, misreading the anger in his expression as frustration that he was having to wait for her to take his own order. Forcing himself to relax, he shot her a lopsided grin as he leaned back against the booth, his grin widening when her full lips parted with a gasp. She blinked, as if the sight of his smile had left her feeling a bit dazed, and he couldn't help the surge of hot, masculine satisfaction that swept through his long frame, tightening his muscles.

That's right, beautiful. You've hit me exactly the same way.

Looking adorably flustered, her cheeks bright with color, she shook her head a little as she turned her attention back to the family. Elliot took a handful of the roasted peanuts from the red bowl the hostess had left for him, and absently chewed as he continued to watch the delectable Skye. Deep inside, he could feel his wolf slowly stretching its way into awareness, curious about what had snagged his attention so thoroughly, while his brain finally kicked into gear, trying to figure out what the hell was going on with him.

He'd never reacted this strongly to a woman—not even with Marly—and the logical side of his nature wanted to know why. Why her? Why now? But the rest of him was simply too buzzed to care. His blood pumped heavily through his veins and his cock was as hard as a friggin' rock, as he fought the instinctual urge to go and toss her over his shoulder, carrying her off—caveman style—until he could get them away from the crowded diner and he could have her all to himself.

The bell that signaled that an order was up dinged, and she hurried across the restaurant, collecting the plates of burgers and fries. Elliot found himself nearly panting as she headed toward him, or rather, the booth right beside his. She was coming so close, that sexy lower lip caught in her white teeth as she blushed and avoided his gaze, and he swore he could feel the searing attraction between them actually sizzling on the air. He growled low, tossing another couple of nuts in his mouth so he hopefully wouldn't look too threatening. God only knew what kind of expression he had on his face. Then he caught a hint of something unbelievably mouthwatering on the air, and he sucked in a deep breath through his nose as she drew closer, only to find himself rocketing into a ground-shaking, mind-shattering state of shock.

Holy...shit! Just, um, yeah. He couldn't... He didn't... *Shit!* He didn't know anything in that moment but one blinding, brain-melting fact:

She. Was. *His.*

This woman... Skye... She fucking belonged to him. With him. She was his life-mate! The one person in the entire world who was meant to be his and his alone.

Jesus, he was so stunned that he sucked in an even deeper, hungrier breath of her sweet, telling scent, this time through his mouth, his wolf ravenous for the smell of its mate, and that's when it happened. The peanuts he'd been getting ready to chew lodged deep in his windpipe, making him choke.

Son of a bitch! Here he was, a powerful, deadly Lycan who had survived harrowing situations, and he was choking in the middle of some god-awful diner, right in front of the woman nature had chosen as his perfect match. It was like some twisted cosmic joke. After everything he'd survived, he was going down because of some stupid salted nuts!

With his beast howling in his ears and his lungs burning, Elliot was about to hurl himself against the table, hoping to expel the little demons, when someone suddenly whacked him hard on the back. He coughed so violently the peanuts shot from his throat, clear across the table, where they pinged against the opposite padded seat and scattered over the floor.

Heart pounding, Elliot sucked in a much-needed breath of air, and turned his head to thank whoever had helped him.

Then he wished he'd just choked on the damn nuts.

It was Skye. She was the one who'd hit him on the back—saving him when he was there to fucking save *her*—and he felt the heat rise in his face. Christ, he was blushing like some gangly teenager!

"Hey, are you okay?" she asked in the sweetest, huskiest voice he'd ever heard, before giving him a shy smile.

Elliot opened his mouth, ready to say a million things at once. But nothing would come out. Despite his embarrassment over looking like an idiot, he was stuck on one short, simple phrase that kept looping its way through his head, like something set on continual repeat. Something as shocking as it was… Hell, he couldn't even think of any other way to describe it.

All he knew was that his world, and hers, had just been hit by a supernatural lightning bolt. One that was going to change them both. Change their lives. Their future. A shocking, cataclysmic event that was going to alter every goddamn thing they'd ever known about hunger. About desire and craving and lust…

And what it was like to need another person so badly you'd not only die for them, but they were the very reason you *lived*.

Chapter 2

When Elliot failed to give a verbal response to Skye's question—just sat there staring back at her with what was no doubt a poleaxed expression on his face, his head jerking in a stiff nod—she gave him another one of those sweet, shy smiles. Then she turned and hurried back over to the kitchen window, where another one of her orders was waiting. He watched her carry the heavy tray over to one of the nearby tables, and tried to get his damn head on straight.

He'd always wondered how his life-mate's scent would hit him, when he finally found her. *If* he ever found her. Had always wondered what it would *feel* like, when it hit him.

And now he knew.

It felt fucking incredible. Unbelievable, yeah, but so good it was about to kill him. His pulse raced, heart ham-

mering in his chest like a drum, beating double time…
triple time. Beating loud enough he wouldn't have been
surprised if the entire diner could hear it.

In that moment, he wanted so many things from her…
with her. He wanted to taste her full, pink lips. Wanted
to bury his face against the tender side of her throat and
breathe that heady scent deeper into his lungs, getting
drunk on it. Feel her plush, soft curves pressed tight
against the hardness of his body.

Was it wrong that *Mine, mine, mine,* was still playing over and over in his head, like those goofy seagulls
in *Finding Nemo*? It was one of Katie Dillinger's favorites, and since the little girl was like a sister to him, he'd
done his duty and watched the animated movie with her
more times than he could count. The other guys ribbed
him like hell about it, but he didn't care. If Mason and
Torrance trusted him to watch their son and baby daughter—an adorable little moppet who seemed to think Elliot was the best thing in the world—then he was going
to enjoy every moment of it. He owed those two everything, and the fact that they treated him like an important part of their family had always been the best thing
in his world.

Until now.

Until the moment he'd realized Skye Hewitt was his.

Maybe another male—a *better* male—would have
felt bad for the girl, given how twisted his past was. But
Elliot was simply too grateful to have any doubts that
he could hold it together. Because he *would* be good for
her…and with her. Jesus, this was his life-mate. He'd
chew off his own goddamn arm before he hurt her.

But there is *someone out there who wants to harm our
woman,* his wolf snarled, and he slowly curled his hands

into fists under the table. Christ, he couldn't even think of a word to describe how furious that made him. Deep inside, he was burning with it, and he knew that when the time came, and he had the bastard responsible for this shit under his claws, he would be ready for blood.

With all her other orders delivered, she'd finally worked up the courage to approach him, and he didn't miss the way the pencil in her hand was shaking with a slight tremor. Her breathing was accelerated, as was her heart rate, the dark of her eyes dilated with desire. Something about the situation had her rattled, but she *was* attracted to him. As a human, she wouldn't feel the pull of the life-mate connection in the same ways as Elliot, but there would definitely be a *pull*. An instinct that told her to get close to him, because that was where she belonged. And if she desired him, then that instinctive need to be with him would be even stronger—*Thank God.*

"Um, hi," she whispered, the huskiness of her voice sliding over his skin like a sensual touch.

"Hi," he rasped, still clenching his fists to keep himself from grabbing her and pulling her closer.

"I'm sorry about the wait," she said in a rush, all breathless and beautifully flushed. "It's, um, kinda crazy in here tonight. What c-can I get you to drink?"

You, he thought, rubbing his tongue against the roof of his mouth. He'd never done it before, but he wanted to sip from Skye Hewitt's beautiful body. Wanted to lay her down, push her legs wide and lick his way inside her. Penetrate her pink, drenched sex with his tongue, fucking her with it until she came against his face in a hot, sweet rush. And then he wanted to *drink* from her, savoring her orgasm as he swallowed her down, drop by decadent drop.

As if she could read his carnal thoughts on his face, she blushed a deeper shade of pink, and he had to fight back the low, excited growl that was rumbling deep inside him. They were both eating the other up with quick, heated glances. An appreciative visual sweep over her thick-lashed eyes, while she took in the corded length of his throat, his Adam's apple moving beneath his skin as he gave a hard swallow. The sounds of the busy diner faded away as she took in the bold shape of his nose and the angle of his stubble-covered jaw, his own gaze hungrily locked on her pink, bee-stung lips. She had the kind of mouth that women paid crazy amounts of money to try to replicate, but never actually looked real unless it was.

It all took less than a handful of seconds, and yet, each moment in time felt like a piece of sun-warmed taffy being stretched out as long as it'd go.

It was maddening to think that if she hadn't been noticed by some evil asshole intent on making her a part of his unwilling harem, Elliot might have never found her. The idea of never coming face-to-face with her made his insides churn with dread, and yet…wasn't that wrong, seeing as how he was here because she was in *danger*?

Unless… Was she meant to catch the kidnapper's eye all along, just so Elliot could walk into this greasy diner and find her? Was that how fate worked—one shitty circumstance for an amazing one? It seemed twisted and wrong to him, and he hated that her entire world was about to be turned upside down. But part of living with his past was to always be brutally honest with himself, and he knew there wasn't a chance in hell that he would change the connection between them. Even if he had to give his life to get her out of this situation, he would take the deal, just for this opportunity to meet her. To be close to her.

But, God, he hoped it didn't play out like that. He wanted this moment with this woman, and then a thousand more. A lifetime of them, as they learned each other and grew together. And maybe, just maybe, he would be lucky enough to one day earn her heart. He didn't have the slightest idea how that could be possible, given…given everything that he'd done—but Christ, it would be sweet.

Shifting from one foot to the other, she finally cleared her throat and gave him another shy smile. "So, um, do you know what you'd like?"

You, deliciously naked and needy, desperate for me to please you, he thought, while his wolf rumbled in approval, completely on board with that idea. But to Skye, he simply asked, "What do you recommend?"

"You look like you're a pretty healthy eater." She tilted her head a bit to the side, a teasing look in her eyes as she added, "But even though they're a far cry from nutritious, our chocolate milk shakes are to die for."

Elliot watched her flick a quick look at his dimple as he smiled. "Then definitely bring me one of those."

She bit her lip and lifted her brows, big green eyes full of warmth and humor. "The cold should also feel pretty good on your throat."

He smirked as he slowly shook his head. "You'll never let me forget that, will you?"

"That I saved your life?" she asked with a cheeky grin, before softly laughing. "Heck no. It's not every day that I get to feel like a hero."

Thinking she was completely charming, even if she was teasing him, Elliot lowered his voice and leaned forward on the table with his arms crossed. He'd slipped his jacket off when he'd come inside, and he couldn't help but notice that her attention had shifted to his biceps as they pressed against his black Henley. Lowering his voice, he said, "I guess I should say thank you, then. You know, for saving my life and all."

She brought her beautiful gaze back to his, and smiled again. "Anytime."

"Wanna share my milk shake with me?" he asked, enjoying the way his head went a little fuzzy as he pulled in another deep breath of her incredible scent. With Skye Hewitt around, he wouldn't ever need alcohol to get a buzz. He could just bury his face in the tender curve of her shoulder and breathe her in, so warm and sweet and delicious.

She blinked a few times at his question, and then blushed a little brighter. "Um, that would be lovely, but we're too busy for me to take a break right now."

"Maybe later, then," he murmured, knowing damn well that he was going to have to sit her down and explain why he was there before too long. Max could be back with Vivian at any moment, and it was probably best if he talked to Skye before they arrived.

Softly, she asked, "Do you want anything to go with the shake?"

"A bacon cheeseburger and fries?"

"Good choice." Then with another shy smile on her lips, she turned and headed back to the kitchen service window, where she pinned his order to one of the silver clamps. She cast a quick glance over her shoulder, and it looked like she gave a small laugh when she caught him staring right at her. Her blush bloomed brighter, and then her attention was drawn away by one of the other waitresses who came up and started talking with her. Elliot kept a careful eye on them, relaxing only when it became obvious that Skye and this woman were friends, unlike the scrawny bitch who had been so rude about her.

When a plate of potato skins was suddenly set in the window, Skye grabbed it and carried the order over to one of the tables that were closest to the door. Though Elliot was dimly aware of the chime that signaled the door being opened, he didn't pay any attention to whoever was coming inside. He was too preoccupied with watching Skye share a laugh with an elderly man at another table, before putting her arms around the old guy's shoulders and giving him a gentle squeeze.

The girl…yeah, she was something else. Watching her, he wouldn't have been surprised to learn that half the people there came in simply to be around her, and his mouth had just started to twitch with another appreciative smile when reality came crashing into the moment with the blunt force of a hammer.

"I want everyone to fucking stay where they are!" a harsh male voice suddenly shouted from near the entrance, causing the entire diner to fall silent in fear. "Just dump your cash on your tables and keep your mouths shut!"

Son. Of. A. Bitch! Elliot blinked as he shifted around a little more in his seat, taking in the asshole standing by the hostess's station with a deadly, narrowed gaze. *Damn!* He'd been so drunk on Skye, he hadn't been paying proper attention to his surroundings, which was unacceptable. He'd been doing this job for too long to let some jacked-up junkie in need of his next fix sneak up on him.

"I mean it!" the guy yelled, waving his gun around

with a trembling hand. "Any of you even think of giving me any shit, and I *will* pull this trigger!"

Sliding out of the booth and to his feet, Elliot held up his hands as he took a step toward the pale, twitchy male whose angular face had probably been handsome before it'd been ravaged by drug abuse and hard living. "You don't want to do this," he said as calmly as possible. "Trust me. Your best option is to just turn around and get the hell out of here."

"Not a step closer," the robber snarled, suddenly reaching out and snagging Skye's upper arm. She cried out as he yanked her against him, while keeping the gun pointed at Elliot.

"Skye, look at me," Elliot demanded, his low voice vibrating with rage. It took everything within him not to release his fangs and claws in front of the frightened humans and tear this dude's throat out. But one of the founding tenets of his pack was that their species never be revealed to the masses—*ever*—under any circumstances.

"Shut up!" the guy yelled, but Elliot ignored him.

"Will you trust me and do what I say?" he asked her, flicking his attention back and forth between the junkie's wild gaze and her frightened one.

"Why?" she mouthed, and he knew she was asking him why she should give him her trust. Why he was helping her.

"Because I know how to handle these types of situations."

"Are you a cop?" the robber shouted, wrapping his arm around Skye's throat. She reflexively reached up and curled her hands around the guy's forearm, the panicked look on her face making Elliot ache.

He shook his head in response to the asshole's question, but kept his sharp gaze locked tight on Skye. Then, for the second time, he asked, "Will you trust me and do what I say, baby?"

Her eyes went wide at the husky endearment, and he kept his focus on her as he directed his next words to the bastard trying to use her as a human shield. "You so much as cause her even one second of pain, man, and you're going to be dealing with me," he warned. "And you really don't want that."

"Fuck you!" the guy spat.

Elliot felt his wolf seething just beneath his surface, and knew he needed to end this quickly. Any hope he'd had that the idiot would rethink his plan and run was gone, and now his time was up. "Wrong answer," he scraped out in a voice that was more animal than man, his hard gaze still locked tight with Skye's. "The instant I get my hands on him," he told her, "you drop and crawl away."

"Are you fucking crazy? I swear I'll shoot you, you stup—" was all the robber got out, before Elliot went into action. He was not only stronger than a human male, he was faster than one. It took him no more than a second to charge the asshole, knocking the gun out of his shaking hand and squeezing the wrist of the arm he'd wrapped around Skye so strongly he felt the bones crack. The asshole screamed as Elliot jerked his arm up with enough power that it dislocated his shoulder, allowing Skye to drop away from him and quickly crawl across the floor, exactly like Elliot had told her to do. Then he pulled back his free arm and knocked the bastard out with a single punch.

"Yes!" the older woman working the hostess's station shouted, coming around the podium and kicking the junkie in his ribs with the pointed toe of her shoe. "And you stay down, you slimy jerk!"

All of a sudden, a great roar of cheers exploded across the diner, and Elliot found himself being hugged by one human after another. The mother of the family Skye had been waiting on even planted a kiss on his cheek before bursting into tears of relief that her children and husband were safe. It was a surreal moment, and all he wanted was to find Skye and get the hell out of there before someone called the cops and he ended up having to deal with the local PD.

He searched the crowd for her, worried when he couldn't spot her, a raw sound on his lips when he finally caught sight of her coming through the swinging door that led to the kitchen. For a brief moment, he wondered what she'd been doing back there. Then he forgot all about the question as their gazes locked, the grateful look on her face making him feel like he'd just saved the friggin' world.

He began making his way through the crush toward her, and she did the same. "Are you all right?" he asked, the moment they reached each other. The question felt heavy on his tongue, his arms aching with the need to pull her close and wrap her up tight against him. But he hadn't earned the right to touch her yet, and he didn't want to frighten her.

"I'm fine, thanks to you," she said with a soft smile. "That…what you did…it was amazing."

"You don't need to thank me." *Not for protecting you, baby. It's what I was born for.* "You sure you're okay?"

"Yeah, I'm good." She stepped a little closer to him, the difference in their heights making her have to tilt her head back a bit to see his face. "I just… I can't believe you came at him like that when he had a gun."

"He wasn't going to shoot anyone." And if he had, Elliot would have survived the shot. As a Lycan, it was damn difficult to kill him with a bullet. "I was more worried about you. There was no way I was letting him keep his hands on you a second longer."

She blinked up at him, and he thought, *Because you're mine,* doing his best to appear like a normal guy so he didn't scare the hell out of her. But inside, his wolf was seething with fury, prowling like a caged beast, with only one thought churning through its mind:

No matter what it takes, we protect what's ours…

Chapter 3

Skye Hewitt stared up at the gorgeous, dark-eyed stranger standing in front of her, and couldn't help but remember how he'd called her "baby" when the robber had been using her as a human shield. She'd been so stunned by how hearing that word on his lips—in reference to *her*—had made her feel, she hadn't been able to find the words to answer him to save her life. Literally. Lucky for her, though, he'd trusted her to do as he'd said anyway.

Now, with another one of those sexy, kind of crooked smiles that he'd given her earlier curving his lips, he shook off the visceral tension that seemed to be coiling around him, and said, "I guess we haven't really been introduced yet, have we? I'm Elliot Connors."

Elliot...mmm. The sexy name fit him, because...like, seriously. This guy was by far the sexiest freaking thing she'd ever seen. Tall and lean and muscled in that way that didn't come from being a gym rat. No, this guy looked like a soldier. Someone who did brave, dangerous things for a living, and he had the body of a god to show for it.

It no doubt made her a hussy, but she couldn't stop herself from imagining what he would look like without the black Henley, worn jeans and kick-ass black boots. Just thinking about him in the buff, with all that dark golden skin on display, stretched tight over rippling slabs of muscle and masculine cords of sinew, had her pulse roaring in her ears, while lust poured so thickly through her veins it was probably written all over her face.

Heck, from the way he was looking at her, it had to be. Because he definitely looked like he was trying to figure out what she was thinking.

Then she realized that he was still waiting for her full name, and she laughed as she shook her head at herself. "I'm Skye. Skye Hewitt."

"It's lovely to meet you, Skye."

"You, too, Elliot."

He grinned in a way that had his dimple showing again, and she was pretty sure her ovaries spontaneously combusted. Holy freaking cow, was he hot. And nice. And, oh…not to mention brave as hell, going up against that guy the way he'd done. It was like he hadn't even cared that the junkie had been pointing a gun at him. He'd only seemed to be worried about *her*, and that little fact was dangerously close to melting her into such a huge, embarrassing puddle of *I'm crushing on him so bad and seriously want to have his babies* it wasn't even funny.

When she heard the sirens in the distance, she cleared

her throat a little, just in case her voice came out all rough with lust, and told him, "I called the cops as soon as I got away from him. That's what I was doing in the kitchen."

She could have sworn she heard him mutter "Shit" under his breath, but when she looked up from his broad chest to his face again, he didn't look angry or upset. She honestly didn't know what to make of him, her emotions all in a jumble where he was concerned. Desire, gratitude, awe and no small amount of disbelief. The guy could have any freaking woman he wanted, and yet, he was looking at *her* as if he wanted to pull her into his powerful arms and kiss the ever-loving hell out of her.

"Come on," he said, jerking his chin toward the door. "Let's go outside and talk to them where it won't be so loud."

Skye went and grabbed her purse and coat from the break room, then had a quick chat with her manager. When she came back and joined Elliot near the booth where he'd been sitting before all the madness had started, she saw that he'd pulled on a black jacket that looked incredibly good on him. He gestured for her to take the lead, and she purposefully didn't look at the jerk-off that was still passed out on the floor, a couple of the younger male customers keeping watch over him until the cops arrived. Elliot opened the door for her, then followed her outside, the chilly December air making her huddle deeper into her coat. They stood together on the sidewalk in front of one of the diner's massive windows, and she was about to ask him what he was doing in town, curious about what had brought him to a place like Charity, his accent making it clear he wasn't a local, when the first cop car pulled up in front of them, parking at the curb on the far side of the road.

This time, she was the one who muttered "Shit" when she caught sight of the stocky, good-looking policeman climbing out the passenger-side door. She blinked as he made his way toward them with an arrogant stride, hoping her vision might clear and the guy would suddenly morph into someone she didn't want to kick in the balls every time she ran into him. But no such luck.

This cocky jerk wasn't just a cop. No, coming straight toward them was one Officer Derek Carlton—her freaking ex-boyfriend from hell!

At that moment, Skye kind of wished there was a hole in the ground that could just conveniently swallow her up. The last thing in the world she wanted to do was talk to Derek, and especially not in front of Elliot.

Please, God, don't let him be an ass. If he embarrasses me, I'm going to kill him. Or castrate him.

Seriously, what next tonight? Maybe it would start raining a little fire and brimstone. Or a tornado would sweep through the center of town. Who knew? They might even be attacked by a deranged, ax-wielding Santa. That certainly seemed to be where her luck was headed.

"Hey, what's wrong?" Elliot asked in a low voice, shifting a little closer to her side.

She gave a tired sigh. "The cop headed toward us— he's my ex."

"You were *married* to that guy?" His deep voice was all rough with shock, and she could feel the heat of his stare burning hot against the side of her face.

"God, no." She shook her head, and shot him a look that no doubt said *I'd rather be anywhere but here right now.* "Ex-boyfriend. We went out together back in our senior year of high school."

He grunted in response, and a heartbeat later, Derek reached them, looking as smug and as full of himself as he always did. Before he could get a word out, Skye said, "Elliot, this is Officer Carlton. Derek, this is Elliot. He's a customer at the diner."

Neither man said anything, since they seemed to be too busy staring each other down, and she ended up just rambling on. "Elliot is the one who saved the day. He disarmed the robber and made sure no one got hurt."

Derek slowly brought his gaze to hers, and she could tell by his tone that he was going to be a dick. "How do you know him, Skye?"

Crossing her arms over her chest, she spoke through her gritted teeth. "I just told you, he's a customer."

Derek cocked one pale brow. "A regular?"

Skye rolled her eyes. "What does that have to do with anything? You should be thanking him for doing your job for you, not asking stupid questions."

Derek glared, and she drew in a deep breath to keep going, only to stop short when she felt Elliot place his big, strong, deliciously warm hand on her shoulder. He gave it a comforting squeeze, letting her know in a supportive way that she needed to calm down.

Right, she thought. *Okay, I can do this.* She could be calm…and civil. It just meant burying the hurt she felt every time she came into contact with this jerk.

It seemed so bizarre now to think that there'd been a time when she'd thought Derek was the hunkiest, greatest, most awesome guy she'd ever known. She'd secretly crushed on him for months her senior year of high school, and had nearly died from excitement the day he'd come up to her after math class and asked if she wanted to go out with him on Friday night. It'd been like a dream, the star running back of the football team asking out the poor, chubby girl who only had Vivian for a friend. And he'd been so sweet and persistent, she'd found him impossible to resist. So much so that she'd ended up giving him her virginity when they hit their four-month mark, only to find out the next week that he'd been banging five cheerleaders from three other schools the entire time they'd been together.

She'd learned a hard lesson from the experience, and it wasn't one she ever planned on forgetting.

Stepping a little closer to her, Derek lowered his voice. "I'd like to talk to you alone for a minute."

She shuddered, and knew that Elliot must have felt it, because he moved his hand off her shoulder and pulled her into his side instead. And, oh geez, did it feel good to have this gorgeous hunk's arm wrapped around her waist. She'd have preferred to stay right where she was, but from the look on Derek's face, it was clear he was going to cause a scene if he didn't get his way. And Skye had already had enough drama for one night. So with a muffled curse, she pulled away from Elliot, giving him an apologetic look. "I'll be right back."

He didn't argue with her—but he sure as hell didn't look happy about it, either. "You sure?"

She nodded, and couldn't help but smile at him. "Will you wait for me? I don't want to miss being able to say goodbye."

Something warm and delicious began to smolder in the depths of his dark, hooded gaze. "I'll be right here. I won't take my eyes off you."

She caught her lower lip in her teeth as she stared up at him. "Thanks."

Derek muttered something under his breath, and she quickly walked a little farther down the street as he followed behind her, just wanting to get this over with.

"You really going slumming with that guy?" he demanded, as soon as she turned around to face him.

"First of all, *that guy* happens to be awesome. So stop sounding like a jealous douche."

"Jesus, Skye." His lip curled as he sneered at her. "I thought you were different."

"From what? What does that even mean?" she demanded hotly. "And who are you to judge me? You're a cheat and a liar! And I'm…" She suddenly broke off, shaking her head as she laughed. "Oh, God, why am I even having this conversation with you? We have *nothing* to say to each other."

She started to walk around him, when he quickly blocked her path. Giving him her best go-to-hell look, she growled, "No, Derek. I'm done talking to you."

"You're done when I say so," he snapped, sounding like a petulant child as he puffed up his chest.

She blinked, wondering when he'd gone and lost his damn sanity. And then every single thought was shoved from her mind as Elliot's tall, powerful body suddenly pushed between them. Peering around his side, Skye watched in shock as he stepped up to Derek, towering over him, his low voice cut with anger as he growled, "The lady said no, jackass. So get the fuck away from her."

Derek's blue eyes went wide with outrage. "Who the hell do you think you are?"

Elliot shook his head and smirked, as if he found Derek's posturing a little funny. "I'm someone who's not afraid of you, even with that shiny badge you're wearing. So. Back. Off."

Oh, man. Skye could tell that Derek was seriously pissed…as well as embarrassed. And she'd have so been lying through her teeth if she'd said there wasn't a tiny bit of her that freaking loved it. If Elliot Connors hadn't been her hero before, he most definitely was now. She felt like she'd found her own personal guardian angel, and she had to bite her lip to keep from smiling when Derek took a couple of steps back and shot her a furious scowl. "We're not done, Skye."

Using her best bored tone, she told him, "We were done years ago, Officer Carlton. Let it go."

Rage made him red in the face, the blue of his eyes burning with it. "Don't go anywhere," he bit out. "I'll need to talk to both of you before we leave."

A piercing wave of relief spread through Skye's chest as she watched Derek turn and stalk away, and then she stepped in front of Elliot, tilted her head back and gave him such a wide smile that it hurt her cheeks. "You are like the most freaking awesome person ever!" she gushed, not even caring that she was making a fool of herself. "Thank you so much for standing up for me. For helping me."

He gave her a look that somehow seemed both hungry *and* tender, his voice a deliciously husky rasp as he said, "You never need to thank me for that either, Skye."

"Okay," she breathed, feeling her face heat despite the cold wind whipping around them. "But, just so you know, you…you're not like any other guy I've ever met."

He gave a quiet, sexy bark of laughter, and she had a feeling there was a joke somewhere in there that she didn't get. And now she really felt like an idiot. "My manager said that I could go ahead and take off, since they're going to shut the diner for the night, and I really don't want to stick around to chat with Derek again. So I, uh, guess I should get going," she rambled on, burrowing down deeper into her coat, kind of wishing she could disappear in it. "I mean, you probably have somewhere you need to be, right?"

Without a word, he put his hand against the small of her back and pushed her along beside him as he headed down to the corner, then around it, until they were out of sight of everyone gathering outside the diner to talk to the four policemen who were now on the scene. Then he moved until he was standing right in front of her, in the low, colorful glow of the town's ancient Christmas lights. His face was tilted down so that he could look into her eyes, and she froze as he lifted his hand toward her, only to pause for a moment, as if unsure he should do it. Then he reached up and gently pushed her hair back from her cheek, tucking it behind her ear. Her breath sucked in on a shallow gasp, desire pumping so heavily through her body she felt filled with it, the lush sensation only growing as his hooded gaze got darker and he cupped the side of her face with his big, masculine hand.

His lips parted, and he made this wonderfully low, rumbly sound deep in his chest that made her shiver. And even though Skye knew it must be a trick of the light, his dark eyes suddenly looked as if they were glowing with a thin ring of gold around the outer edge of his irises.

Oh, God, was he...was he going to kiss her? Or...was she just imagining it? After all, guys like Elliot Connors didn't get all hot and bothered over girls that looked like her. So, um, yeah...like what was her problem? Seriously? She normally wasn't this crazy, but this whole night so far had been a giant case of bizarre, and now she was projecting her lust onto this poor guy who had done nothing but help her.

"Skye," he whispered, and though she'd just scolded herself for letting her imagination get away from her, it sounded like he *wanted* to kiss her. Like he wanted to take her into his arms and kiss her until she forgot her freaking name!

"Yeah?" she breathed, loving the way his smoldering gaze followed her tongue as she nervously licked her bottom lip. Sure, she didn't know this guy from Adam, but she…she *wanted* to know him. And strangers or not, she already trusted him. Hadn't he earned that when he risked his life to save hers? And when he'd stood up for her to the guy who'd once broken her girlish heart?

Do it…yes…please, she begged with her eyes, her lips trembling with anticipation.

They swayed a little closer together, and it was like some invisible line between their chests was drawing tighter…pulling them in. She made a soft, needy sound, and his eyes went so bright they burned, just before he squeezed them shut and lowered his head, pressing his forehead against hers. His warm breaths pelted her parted lips, and she was ready to grip him by the shoulders, press up on her toes and do it herself. Just rub her tingling lips against his, kissing him as she gasped for air, desperate to sate this aching need that was growing inside her, making her dizzy with want. With emotions she'd never felt in her entire life—not even at the height of her infatuation with Derek.

"Christ," he rasped, his thumb sweeping across the corner of her mouth, and she started to lift her hands, only to have the moment broken when his phone suddenly started buzzing in his pocket.

Nooooo! she wanted to scream, as he shifted back from her and reached for the phone. He grimaced as he read the text on the screen, and she knew that whatever it was, the news wasn't good. He typed in a quick response, then shoved the phone back in his pocket, his beautiful gaze shadowed with worry as it locked with hers.

"Where are you parked?" he asked, looking down the mostly empty street, as if he would be able to tell her car just by looking at it.

"Why?" The cold wind howled around them, and she huddled deeper into her cheap coat. "Do y-you need a ride?" She normally wasn't in the habit of offering rides to men she didn't know, but this one…well, he'd saved her life. It was the least she could do for him, right? Especially when she'd only been a second away from shoving her tongue in his mouth. "Because I can drop you off somewhere if you need me to," she added lamely, feeling like the world's biggest dork.

He stabbed his fingers back through his short, caramel-colored hair, and released a sharp breath. Then he slid his dark gaze back to hers. "We need to talk, Skye. And this isn't the place to do it."

It didn't make any sense, but something in his stark tone made her believe him. And with the belief came a churning sense of dread. "Why? What's going on?"

"You and your friend, the one you live wi—"

"Wait!" she gasped, cutting him off. She grabbed his arm, and knew that at any other time, she'd be melting over how hard his muscles felt under her touch. But right now she was too worried to appreciate it. "How do you know that? Have you... *Ohmygod*, have you been watching me?"

"No. I'm one of the good guys, Skye. I swear," he said in a deep voice that was low, urgent and full of conviction. "But you and Vivian, you're both in trouble."

"Trouble?" she whispered, covering her mouth with her fingers. "Oh, God. Does this have anything to do with Viv's new job at that club? You're not here to try to make her strip there, are you?"

His eyes went comically wide, and she would have laughed if she weren't so freaked out. "No. You've got it all backward. My partner and I, we're not here to cause trouble for the two of you, and we don't have anything to do with the club where your friend works. We're working on a criminal case, and we're here to make sure that both you and Vivian stay safe."

"What?" she breathed, thinking she had to have heard him wrong.

"Think...think of me and Max like bodyguards. Because that's essentially what we are." His chest lifted as he pulled in a deep breath, and then her freaking heart was in her throat as he took her hand in his, gave it a gentle squeeze, and told her, "Baby, I'm here to protect you."

Chapter 4

Glancing at his watch, Elliot swore under his breath. It'd taken a good ten minutes to persuade Skye to trust him enough to lead him to her car so they could head to her apartment. In the end, it was the PI license he always carried with him that had convinced her he was telling her the truth, and using it was definitely going to come back and bite him hard in the ass. The damn thing was a forgery, and based on the argument he'd heard between her and the cop, Skye Hewitt had a thing about cheats…and liars.

It felt all kinds of wrong to trick her that way, but what choice did he have? It sounded like Max had somehow lost track of Vivian, and he had a feeling this night was going to get a hell of a lot worse before it got better.

"Sorry, but it's kind of a piece of crap," she said, as they neared a beat-up-looking, powder-blue VW Beetle.

"Naw. It's cute."

"Thanks." As she opened the driver-side door, she gave him a brief smile that damn near buckled his knees. "I thought so, too, when I bought her."

Elliot waited until she'd climbed behind the wheel, then somehow managed to fold his six-three frame into the cramped confines of the car.

"Um, before we go," she murmured, sounding adorably rattled as she watched him from the corner of her eye, "you should know that I carry a weapon in my purse. And I'm...I'm not afraid to use it."

"That's smart. You should always be ready to protect yourself. But I swear, Skye, you don't need to worry about my intentions. I only want to help you."

She gave him another brief, but strained smile. Then she started the engine, and he tried not to wince at how awful it sounded. Someone needed to put this poor car out of its misery.

"So, you aren't nervous about letting a girl drive?" she asked, looking into her rearview mirror as she reversed out of the tight space. It was kind of a weird question, but he figured she was trying to keep herself from freaking out about what he'd told her, and he couldn't help but think she was adorable.

"Nope, I'm not worried at all. I trust you not to wreck my body."

She glanced his way, flicking a quick look over his torso, and he wanted to growl with satisfaction when he saw that she had that glazed look of lust in her pretty eyes again. Her smooth skin was flushed pink across her cheekbones, that full lower lip caught in her small white teeth, and he had to bite back a smile. She was so easy to read, it was like words on the page of a book that'd been written especially for him. *Only* for him.

There wasn't much traffic in the town, since it was nearing eight, so they made their way easily onto the main road. She didn't say anything for the first few blocks, and he was grateful that she wasn't grilling him about what was going on, since he wasn't sure what he was going to find once they reached her apartment. Max had just sent him another text, and all it had said was: It's bad. Hurry!

And, yeah, there was definitely a part of him feeling like a total jackass for being so excited about finding his life-mate—and her turning out to be someone like Skye—when there was no telling what had happened to her best friend.

"Will you please tell me what's going on?" she suddenly asked, exhaling a shaky breath. "I know you said your partner was making contact with Vivian, and that we'll talk at the apartment. But I'm worried about her, and I know she won't be able to call me if something goes wrong because my stupid cell phone is broken. The battery finally gave up today, and I didn't have time to get it replaced before my shift."

"Let's just get to your place, and then Max and I can explain everything. It's going to be a lot to take in."

"You're scaring me," she whispered, chewing on that lower lip so hard he was worried she was going to break the skin.

Knowing it needed to be said, he murmured, "I'm sorry, but you need to be a little scared, because it will keep you sharp. But not of me, and not of Max. We'll do whatever it takes to keep you both safe."

It was dark inside the car, but his wolf's eyes could see

her clearly in the dim glow of the lights on her dash. Her brows were drawn into a deep V between her delicately shaped brows, her big eyes shadowed with concern and confusion. "So you're here because you're working some kind of case?" she asked him, taking the next right. "You and this Max guy?"

"That's right," he replied, wishing he could just take her into his arms and tell her everything was going to be okay. But that would only freak her out even more.

"And Viv and I are involved? How is that even possible?" Before he could answer, she smacked the flat of her hand against the steering wheel and growled, "It has to be connected to that strip club where Viv took a job last month. I told her not to do it, that it wasn't the kind of scene she needed to be a part of, but the sleazy owner just kept offering her more money. He's paying her way more than she could make anywhere else." Flashing him an angry look, she added, "Viv is gorgeous and the ass likes her serving drinks to his clients, even if she refuses to strip or go topless like the other girls. This is because of him, isn't it? Does it have to do with drugs? Or something even worse?"

"I know this club owner seems like the logical explanation, but it's got nothing to do with him, Skye. He's not a part of it."

"But nothing else makes sense!" she argued, smacking the wheel again.

"I get that." He gave a frustrated sigh, knowing damn well that they couldn't get into this while she was driving. "Just…give me a little time. Please."

She chewed on that gorgeous lower lip again, then muttered something under her breath that he couldn't quite make out. "We're here," she said a moment later, turning into the parking lot of one of the most run-down apartment complexes he'd ever seen. What. The. Hell? He couldn't believe this was where his girl had been living. How was that even possible?

Jesus, there were so many things wrong with the place, he didn't even know where to start. For one, there didn't seem to be a single light anywhere, though there were plenty of liquor bottles scattered across the asphalt and snow-covered patches of dead grass. And there seemed to be more broken windows than whole ones, many of them either covered with pieces of cardboard or doctored with silver strips of duct tape.

Then there was the group of men huddled around a flame-filled trashcan at the far end of the parking lot. They looked like a rough group, and though he was the last one to pass judgment based on a person's appearance, Elliot still didn't like the idea of Skye and her friend walking past those men at night, with no one there to protect them. Didn't mean he thought she was weak or naive or in any way less capable than a man. This was an issue of numbers, and he knew firsthand how twisted a pack mentality could become under the wrong influences.

Hell, he lived with the internal scars from that very thing every goddamn day of his life.

She drove around the back of the complex, and pulled into a parking space that was only three down from Max's truck. Elliot did a quick visual sweep of the area, but didn't see his partner. Then he turned his head toward Skye, who was turning off the engine.

"How long have you been living here?" He winced at the guttural sound of his voice, noticing how she flinched, but there was no masking the way he felt at the moment. His protective instincts were in full Lycan mode, and it was all he could do to keep from throwing her over his shoulder and getting her the hell out of there.

"Just over a year." She had an embarrassed expression on her face as she turned to look at him. "The last place was even worse, if you can believe it."

"Skye," he said carefully, trying to keep his voice calm, though he was seething inside at the thought of his mate living in this dump. And how in the hell did she give so much comfort and happiness to the people at the diner when she had *this* to come home to every night? "Honey, this isn't a safe place."

Her chest lifted, heavy breasts pressing tight against her pink uniform as she drew in a shaky breath, then slowly let it out. "I know, but it wasn't this bad when we moved in. Then, three months ago, the owners went bankrupt, and it's all pretty much fallen apart. But they won't allow us to break our lease, so we're stuck here for another two months."

"That's bullshit."

"I know," she said again, sounding defeated, and he knew this was a situation neither her nor Vivian wanted to be in. "But I always have a can of pepper spray in my purse, and I pay attention to my surroundings. Viv and I know how to be careful."

Fuck, he hated this. Hated knowing she walked around in fear, always looking over her shoulder. Where the hell was her family? Why wasn't someone helping them? Where in God's name were their dads? Uncles? Cousins? Weren't there any males in their lives looking out for them?

And, yeah, he knew that if one of the women back at the Alley ever heard him say something like that out loud, he'd get ripped for it. But from the age of seven-teen, Mason and the others had ingrained in him what it meant to be a man—and first and foremost, being a man meant protecting a woman when she needed it.

They climbed out, and the moment they reached the front of her car, Max stepped out of the shadows near the apartments, looking more furious than Elliot had ever seen him. There was a hard, aggressive energy rid-ing his partner, the lines of his usually easygoing face drawn tight with strain.

"What happened?" Elliot asked, hoping Max wouldn't say anything in front of Skye that he shouldn't. It wouldn't normally have been a concern, but with as raw as Max looked, there was no telling what might come out of his mouth.

"I completely fucked up, that's what happened."

Elliot gave him a sharp what-the-hell look, and Max sighed, shoving both hands back through his short, black curls. "I..." He lowered his arms, and his hands tight-ened into fists at his sides. "It's bad news, man." He took a shaky breath, then slowly let it out. "I'm afraid it's the *worst*."

Shit, he thought, praying that Max was wrong.

"What's happened?" Skye suddenly cried, fighting against Elliot's hold when he caught her as she tried to rush past him.

"Skye, just hold on a second. Let me—"

"Damn it, let me go!" she screamed, tearing away from him. He was right on her heels, but Christ, the chick was fast. He caught the edge of her frayed coat just as she burst through the front door of the downstairs unit that was closest to them, but it was too late. She'd already seen the damage that had been done to the living room. A sofa, tables, bookcase and TV had all been ripped and smashed into pieces, as if a wild animal had gone ballistic in the place.

And in the far corner, beside the shredded remains of a small chair, were the mangled remnants of their tiny Christmas tree, every ornament smashed, the flickering lights looking somehow ominous as they lay tangled against the backdrop of such pointless, malicious violence.

"Vivian!" she screamed, her hands in her hair and a terrified expression on her pale face as she spun in a circle in the midst of the destroyed room.

"She isn't here," Max bit out, looking like he wanted to tear something apart with his bare hands as he came in behind them. He locked his glittering blue gaze on Elliot, and gave a frustrated shake of his head. "When we split ways at the diner, I came straight here. But after an hour or so, I headed over to the club where she works and found her there. One of the other girls said Vivian had been asked to work a little later tonight." Max shot a quick glance at Skye, who was staring at all the broken pieces of furniture like she was in the middle of a nightmare. He worked his jaw a few times, then shoved his hands back through his hair again as he muttered, "So I sat at a table and waited for the right time to talk to her."

"What did you say to her?" Skye demanded, suddenly going still and giving his partner a panicked look of accusation.

"She ran before I got the chance to say a goddamn thing," he growled, and Elliot shot him a hard glare, silently warning him not to snap at her. Max gave him a dark look that was full of suspicion, then rolled his shoulder and muttered, "The girl I talked to must have told her I was asking about her, because after that she never looked in my direction again. Then she left the floor, and I figured she was taking a break or something. But after a while, I got a bad feeling, so I got up to see what was going on. When I found the girl I'd talked to, she told me that Vivian had bailed on her shift."

Aw, shit. Having an idea where this was headed, Elliot asked, "Then what happened?"

"Then I got in my truck and raced back here as quickly as I could," Max said, forcing the words through his clenched teeth. "But she was already gone by the time I got here."

Elliot drew in a deep breath, trying to glean something from Max's scent that would tell him what was going on with the guy. Yeah, it would be natural for Max to be upset about screwing up a protection job. But this…this was different. Maybe guilt for not realizing she would run? Or had something happened at the club that Max didn't want him to know about?

Before he could ask another question, Max jerked his chin toward the door. "I'll be outside. I've been trying to pick up a trail that I can follow, but the snow isn't helping."

He knew Max meant a scent trail, but had been careful not to say anything suspicious in front of Skye.

"Watch your back," he muttered, worried that the assholes they were dealing with might still be close. And still not even sure *what* they were dealing with. Yeah, the apartment had that same musky odor that the other abduction sites had had. But did that mean that the bastards had already taken Vivian? Or was she on the run for her life, after managing to evade them? From what Max had told him, and the way his partner was acting, he knew that Vivian was in trouble. He just didn't know exactly how bad that trouble was.

"Just don't let her back in the roommate's bedroom," Max added in a low voice as he passed by him, obviously trying to make sure that Skye didn't overhear the quiet words.

Elliot tensed in response to the look on Max's face. "Why?"

His partner just shook his head again, a muscle pulsing in the hard edge of his jaw. "You'll know when you fucking see it, man."

"I don't trust him," Skye said in a hoarse rush, as soon as Max had shut the front door behind him.

Walking over to her, he murmured, "He's good people, Skye. I promise. Max is just pissed that Vivian gave him the slip."

"She's...cautious," she whispered, blinking at the moisture gathering in her eyes. "It would have freaked her out to know he was asking questions about her, instead of just talking to her."

"Yeah, I get that."

She suddenly started kicking at the debris on the floor, like she was trying to uncover something, then dropped down on her knees, rummaging through the books and broken bits of furniture with a desperation that had him coming a little closer and crouching down beside her. "What are you doing, honey?"

"Our phone! I need to find our phone so I can call her."

Elliot helped her look, and quickly found the cordless unit under what looked like the torn material of a sofa cushion. She gave him a grateful look as she took the phone from his hand, then quickly punched in the number. Her hand shook as she held the phone to her ear, her big eyes glistening with tears she was barely holding back. "Damn it," she croaked, shooting him a tortured look. "I don't think her phone is turned on."

"We'll keep trying," he said as gently as he could, taking the phone from her and helping her back to her feet. "But we can't stay here, Skye. I need you to go back to your room with me, and then you need to pack a bag. Okay?"

But she was in her own little world at the moment, and he didn't even think she'd heard him.

"Why would s-someone do this?" she asked, her voice cracking at the end from the tears that had finally started pouring down her face.

"I don't know." Looking around, it broke his goddamn heart to see how hard the two girls had worked to make this place as pretty as they could. Yeah, the outside might have been shit, but they'd put a lot of time and effort, if not money, into making the inside as nice as possible. The walls had been painted a pale gray, and it definitely had that shabby-chic look to it that his friend Sayre seemed to love so much. Cheap tables had been painted with chalkboard paint, and had had what looked like quotes written in a beautiful script across them. He wished that they had the time for him to fix the pieces, fitting them together like a puzzle, so that he could read their messages, curious about what his girl found important enough to make a permanent part of her home.

But they'd already spent far more time there than was safe.

"Come on," he said, reaching out and taking her cold hand. He kept his movements easy and smooth as he led her from the room, not wanting to spook her. "Let's get that bag packed."

Though there were three closed doors in the hallway, it was easy to tell which one was Skye's by simply searching out her scent. He quickened his pace, opening her door and dragging her into the untouched bedroom, grateful that she couldn't detect the scent of blood coming from her friend's room the way he could.

Elliot hoped like hell that Vivian Jackson was okay—but it was becoming harder to hold on to that hope with each second that ticked by.

"I'll just be a minute," Skye whispered, drawing his gaze as she opened her closet door and pulled down a big backpack from the top shelf. She set the bag on top of a weathered white dresser, then started rummaging through the drawers, throwing in what looked like an assortment of jeans, T-shirts and sweaters.

Bracing himself against the wall behind him, Elliot kept up a constant lecture in his head. One that basically went along the lines of how he needed to keep his shit together and that even though he was in her bedroom, surrounded by her so-perfect-it-killed-him scent, he needed to suck it up and stay strong. What he couldn't do was let his hunger get the upper hand on him. Or keep stealing heated glances at the double bed she had pushed into the far corner of the room, imagining what she would look like spread out over the pale gray sheets, her beautiful body completely bare to his burning, greedy stare, while her heavy gaze begged him to touch her...to *claim* her.

Time and place, man. Time and place. And this is neither!

"That's all for in here," she said, clutching the bag to

her chest as she turned to face him. "I just need to grab a few things from the bathroom, and I'll be done."

Holding her wide-eyed, fear-filled gaze, Elliot pushed off from the wall and slowly crossed the room to her. She blinked up at him as he took the bag from her trembling hands, hooking one of the straps over his shoulder. Then he leaned down, a hitching breath surging past her lips as he pressed a soft kiss to her forehead. "I'm so sorry," he whispered, keeping his lips against her smooth, silky skin. "I wish like hell that this wasn't happening to you."

She hiccupped as she reached up and grabbed two fistfuls of his Henley, and he could feel how hard she was trying to be brave. "You're so strong, Skye, and I know you can handle this. I just want you to know that you don't have to do it alone."

She clutched at him tighter, the sound of her soft voice as she whispered his name making his throat and chest burn with emotion. Knowing he needed to stay sharp and get her out of there, he forced himself to stand straight and reach for one of her small hands again, holding it tight in his. Then he headed for the door, pulling her along behind him, and out into the hallway, relieved that they were almost on their way. But then she suddenly pulled her hand from his grip and lunged for Vivian's door.

"Skye, don't!" he shouted, as she quickly twisted the doorknob. "You don't want to go in there."

"I have to, Elliot." She turned her head to the side, a shattered but determined expression on her face as she glanced up at him. "Please don't try to stop me."

He cursed under his breath, but damn it, this was *her* apartment. As badly as he wanted to protect her, he didn't have any right to tell her what to do. Not when it wasn't a life-or-death situation. And going into the room wasn't something that could kill her. It was just going to cause her a shitload of pain, and he hated it.

Then she opened Vivian's door, and the most unholy scream he'd ever heard a woman make came tearing out of her.

There was blood. A lot of it. Spattered over the floor and one wall, and as he drew in a deep breath, his stomach clenched with knots.

It was human blood. Vivian's blood. And the assholes had left a message written for them with it on the wall.

Too late Runners. This bitch is ours.

Chapter 5

It wasn't until Elliot's strong arms wrapped around her from behind in a warm, comforting embrace that Skye realized the high-pitched wail echoing in her ears was her own.

"Shh," he whispered in her ear. "It's going to be okay. I promise. It's okay, sweetheart. Just calm down for me."

With her back still to his front, he lifted her off her feet and quickly pulled her from the room, reaching back with one arm to yank the door shut before carrying her into the living room. Since there was nowhere to sit down, he set her back on her feet, but kept his powerful arms wrapped around her, and she trembled as she felt him place his cheek against the top of her head.

"Come on," he crooned, surrounding her in his warmth as she tried to stop making the god-awful sounds that were being pulled up from deep inside her. *Oh,*

God... Vivian! She silently screamed that phrase over and over inside her head, feeling like she'd slipped into some kind of macabre, demented nightmare. What the hell had happened to her best friend? Was she hurt? Was she...gone? And why? Why was this happening?

Squeezing her eyes shut, she tried to block out the sinister images of Viv's room that kept flashing through her mind. But it was impossible. Who could do such a thing? Who *would*? And why?

"Skye, listen to me." He'd lowered his head, speaking the urgent words against her ear, and she could feel the warmth and smoothness of his lips against her sensitive skin. "I need you to take a deep breath for me, okay? Come on, honey. I know you can do it."

Somehow, Elliot's deep voice managed to reach in and capture her attention from the painful chaos of her thoughts, the husky timbre grounding her when everything around her seemed to be spinning so violently out of control. She gasped, trying to do as he said, but it seemed to take long, endless moments before her lungs could finally work. She coughed and wheezed between sniffs and hiccups, her muscles twitching as she let him hold her up, her limbs as weak as a rag doll's. If he'd let her go, she would have simply fallen into a heap of broken sobs and fear on the floor. One more broken thing there to add to all the others.

But he didn't let her go. He held her like he would stand there and hold her forever, if that's what it took, and as the seconds ticked by, she could feel his strength seeping into her, until she was able to blink her vision clear and pull in a slow, deep, shuddering breath. At that moment, Skye honestly didn't know what she would have done without him. She didn't even want to think about it. And, yeah, she was going to have about a million and one questions once she'd managed to calm down. Just… not now. Right now, she needed to keep feeling his strong arms holding her close, his chest rising and falling at her back as he matched the rhythm of his breathing to hers.

"That's it," he murmured, giving her a gentle squeeze. "Just one deep breath after another, nice and slow."

She gave a hard swallow and sniffed, needing to make her throat work so that she could at least thank him. But as she turned her head, wanting to look up into his rugged, gorgeous face, she caught the flash of something on the floor from the corner of her eye. Her stomach clenched when she realized it was the flashing red light on the answering machine that Viv had found for them at her favorite thrift store, and she tried to lunge for it, but Elliot's arms were still wrapped around her, holding her tight.

"Let me go!" she cried, pulling at his arms. "I need to check the answering machine. Someone's left a message and it might be Vivian!"

Lowering his arms so that she could cross the room, he asked, "Why wouldn't she just call your cell?"

"My battery's completely broken, remember?" She flicked him a quick look as she crouched down to hit the play button. "Look, I know it sounds weird, but you can check this thing remotely by calling the number and punching in a code. So this is how we sometimes leave messages for each other, because my cell phone is pretty much a piece of crap. Something always seems to be going wrong with it."

He muttered something under his breath about her needing a new phone, then turned and quickly made his way over to the front door, yanked it open and shouted, "Max, get in here!"

His partner came rushing through the open door just as the message began to play.

"Skye, it's me. I hope you're calling and listening to this from someplace safe. But if you are *in the apartment, please, please get the hell out of there and go to the shelter. Something's... I don't... Something weird is going on, but I don't know what. It...it might have to do with the club, and I'm so sorry I didn't listen to you about that place. I should have, and now...now I think I'm in trouble, so I'm getting out of town. It's the only thing I can think of right now to keep these assholes away from you. I know your stupid phone isn't working, so I just called the diner. That bitch Robin said that there had been some kind of robbery, but that you were okay and might have had to go and give a statement or something. Just...please don't stay at the apartment, in case someone comes there looking for me. I'm on my way there now, to quickly pick up some clothes and that stuff of my mom's, and then I'm heading out. I'll call you as soon as I can. Love you, girl. Stay safe!"*

As a heavy, leaden silence settled over the room, Elliot glanced at Max, and he thought the guy looked like he was going to be ill, his face too pale and his breaths coming sharp and fast.

With his hard gaze focused in tight on the answering machine, Max quietly muttered something that sounded like *Christ, I'd hoped they were just fucking with me.*

"I don't understand," Skye whispered, drawing Elliot's attention back to her. "Wh-what assholes? How did she know she was in trouble if she hadn't even gotten here yet?"

"Something must have happened at the club. Or when she snuck away," he offered, catching Max's gaze, hoping he might have an explanation. But his partner looked just as confused as he was.

"I don't think she was even trying to get away from Max," Skye murmured, swiping at the tears on her cheeks with her fingertips, while the machine continued to play a soft static sound, even though Vivian had ended the call. "She was probably running from whoever's hurt her."

Elliot rubbed his palm over his whiskered jaw and nodded. "You could be right, Skye."

Shifting her gaze to his partner, she blurted, "I'm sorry I snapped at you earlier. I get that you were only trying to help her."

Max blinked, clearly caught off guard by the apology. Then he managed to jerk his chin up in acknowledgment, before scraping out a low "Don't worry about it. It's good that she's got someone like you looking out for her."

Skye's bottom lip quivered, and Elliot was worried she might start to break down again—but then she surprised him by sucking in a quick breath and moving back to her feet. She started to step away from the machine when the first message finally ended, and it beeped to signal that a second message was about to play.

"What the fuck?" Max croaked, just as Vivian's hoarse, terrified voice filled the room.

"Shit, Skye... My stupid battery is dying, but I don't think I should keep my phone on anyway. Remember that show we watched where the stalker traced the girl's cell signal? I know I sound paranoid...but, God, Skye,

you didn't see these guys. They showed up at our apartment while I was there, and it...it was freaking crazy and I—" She broke off, hissing as if she was in pain, before muttering a sharp curse, and then going on in a tight, breathless voice. *"They tried to follow me when I got away, but I managed to ditch them on the road. Now I just... I need to disappear for a while. I tried to call the diner again, just in case Robin was wrong and you were still there, and this time I got Cheryl. She said you weren't with the police, but that she thought you'd left with some...some badass hottie. She said he stopped the robbery and saved you. God, I hope you're with him and not coming home tonight. Just please...please be careful! I promise to call as soon as I ca—"*

The machine beeped, and Skye looked like she wanted to kick it for cutting off her friend, even though it was Vivian's phone going dead that had ended the call. "I hate freaking technology!" she muttered, fisting her hands at her sides as she turned her head, locking her raw gaze with his. "Her phone charger for her car is broken, so who knows when she'll be able to call back."

Elliot opened his mouth, but before he could say anything, Max made a deep, guttural sound that drew their attention.

"Holy shit," the guy growled, looking like he might collapse in relief. "She must have been leaving that message just as I got here." He slumped back against the wall that was behind him, his chest jerking with each of his ragged breaths. Then he lifted his hands, scrubbing them down his face, and Elliot had the feeling that Max was trying to keep them both from seeing whatever expression he was wearing at that exact moment.

"Ohmygod, why am I even freaking out about her

phone? She got away!" Skye's hoarse words came out in a breathless rush as she brought her stunned gaze back to his. "They don't have her, right?"

"Yeah. That message they left in her room—it's bullshit."

Her slender brows pulled together with worry. "But where did the blood come from? Could it…could it be from an animal or something?"

"Maybe," he lied, flicking his tongue over his lower lip. He knew damn well that it wasn't from an animal, because he'd already been able to tell from the scent of the blood that it was Vivian's. "Or she might've gotten hurt fighting them off—but hopefully not too badly. As much as it sucks that she's run, she's actually being smart by getting away from here. And I think she really does believe she's keeping the bad guys away from you. Which means she's one hell of a friend."

"This is…this is *crazy*." She shook her head, looking like she was caught in some painful, confusing place between shock and terror and relief. "My head is spinning."

Wanting to hold her again so badly he could taste it, he told her, "Just take another deep breath." Then he tacked on what was starting to sound like his goddamn mantra for the night: "It's gonna be okay."

Her beautiful green eyes, still red from crying, went wide. "How the hell is it going to be okay?" she asked with a bitter, scratchy laugh. "None of this is okay, and I'm so pissed off about all of it. And that stupid sentimental crap of her mom's! She got hurt because she came back for it."

Elliot took a step toward her, wondering what she was talking about. "What exactly was she keeping for her?"

Voice tight with frustration, she said, "Viv's dad was

a complete bastard who abandoned them years ago, but her mom, Marcia, is still completely hung up on him. And her taste in men never improved. Marcia didn't want the loser she's getting ready to dump to trash the few things she has left that were Viv's dad's out of spite, so the last time Viv saw her, Marcia asked her to hold on to them for a few weeks. They're the only keepsakes that she has from their marriage, and Viv knows how badly her mom would freak if anything happened to them."

Cursing under his breath, he understood exactly why Skye was so frustrated. If not for the mementos, her friend probably wouldn't have come back to the apartment at all that night. "In that first message," he rasped, recalling something that Vivian had said, "what did she mean about the shelter?"

She winced as her gaze skittered away from his. "That's, um, where we met. Viv lived there with her mom and her little brothers."

Already knowing he wasn't going to like how this story went, he asked, "How old were you?"

Her mouth twisted, almost like she had tasted something bad, and then she slowly brought her gaze back to his. "Sixteen."

His jaw tightened, and he could feel the muscle pulsing there, just like Max's had done when he'd been warning him about Vivian's bedroom. The idea of his life-mate living in a women's shelter at the age of sixteen made him burn with a raw, desperate feeling of rage. Christ, there were so many questions running through his head, jamming into each other, he couldn't even think where to begin.

And Max… Oh yeah, Max was onto him. Big-time. He could feel the weight of his partner's questioning stare burning against the side of his face, and knew that Max had picked up on the fact that there was more going on between him and Skye than Elliot merely doing his job.

But this wasn't the time for him to start explaining that she was *his*. If he did, Max would push him to tell her everything, and that wasn't something he was ready for. Hell, he hadn't had time to even figure out *how* he was going to do it. Wasn't like he could just blurt out that he was a fucking werewolf, and then tack on an *Oh, and by the way, we're also meant to spend the rest of our lives together.* She'd probably think he was insane and run so fast it'd make his friggin' head spin.

No, right now his main objective needed to be her safety. Then, once that was settled, he could start the terrifying prospect of trying to figure out how to lay it all out on the line for her, while still holding his most painful secrets close to his chest. Max would tell him he was stupid, and that he was making a massive mistake by not telling her *everything*, but Max wasn't the one walking around with that kind of shit staining his soul.

So, yeah, Skye knowing the truth about him, and about the things he'd done, was the last damn thing that Elliot wanted.

And yet, how the hell was he meant to claim her, binding them together body, heart and soul, without ever being completely honest with her? He didn't know, and this really wasn't the time to figure it out.

Breaking the awkward silence that had settled over the room, Skye murmured that she needed to get her things from the bathroom. Elliot stayed where he was as she hurried past him, but kept a careful eye on her, while doing his best to ignore Max's questioning stare. Jesus, he could feel the pressure of that look battering against his skull like a hammer, until it started to make his head hurt.

"Are you going to tell me—?"

"Let it go," he grunted, cutting the guy off just as Skye came back into the room with a small pink bag in her hand. Sliding her backpack off his shoulder, he held it open for her as she added the smaller bag to the inside, setting it on top of her clothes.

"Don't close it yet, please," she said, turning and heading toward the small kitchenette. "There's one more thing I need to pack."

Curious, Elliot followed Skye into the small room, watching as she opened one of the painted cupboards and pulled down a colorful box of cereal. She opened the top, reached into the box, and instead of pulling out a handful of Cheerios, she was clutching a rolled-up wad of cash being held together by rubber bands.

"Do you really think it's safe to hide money in this place?" Max asked, coming to stand beside him.

"It's not like it's a lot," she murmured, sounding embarrassed.

Max tilted his head as he watched her add the money to the backpack Elliot was still holding. "You got something against banks?"

"No, I don't have anything against banks—I just don't have time to go to mine every day. So I usually hold on to my cash tips during the week, and then make a deposit every Monday morning."

With her explanation made, she zipped the backpack closed, then tried to take it from Elliot, but he just pulled it back up onto his shoulder. She frowned, but didn't argue with him about it, her gaze cutting back to Max as she added, "And not that it's any of your business, but I put almost every penny I make into a business savings account. And Viv is trying to save up enough to go to dance school. So it's not like we're backward idiots who don't understand how the banking system works."

Jesus, at least this explained why they lived in such a shithole. These girls had been working their asses off without enjoying any of the rewards, hiding away every penny they could spare in order to better their futures. As much as it frustrated him that they hadn't been taking better care of themselves, he knew it spoke volumes about what kind of women they were.

Clearing his throat to get her attention, he held her troubled gaze as he said, "We need to get going. You have everything you need?"

He watched her pink tongue swipe across that juicy lower lip, and nearly growled from the blistering surge of untimely lust that tore through him, damn near burning him alive. But then it was like a cold bucket of water had just been tossed in his face, because she shook her head, and Elliot already knew what was coming. "I have everything, but I'm not… I'm not leaving here with you. I really appreciate everything you've done for me tonight, but I'm driving myself to the shelter."

Frustration crawled up his spine like an animal, clawing at his skin, making him want to gnash his teeth. "Why the fuck would you do that when I'm here?" His voice came out gruffer than he'd wanted, but there wasn't any way he could pull off something mellow and calm right now. "I'm here to help you by taking you someplace safe. Someplace where I can protect you."

"Elliot." She sighed, and he could see the arguments building in her head without her even having to say a single word.

"Max," he scraped out in a low, tightly controlled tone, "you mind waiting for us out front?"

"I'll be in my truck," his partner murmured, turning and making his way over to the door. But he stopped before he went outside, adding, "Don't make me wait too long. You know what I need."

"What did he mean by *that*?" she asked, as soon as Max had shut the door behind him. "What does he need?"

With one hand hooked around the back of his neck, and the other holding the strap of her backpack, Elliot answered her questions. "To know where to look for Vivian. He's going to need you to tell him where you think she might go."

Blinking, she took a step back, coming up hard against the edge of the counter. "I…I can't," she stammered. "Vivian left because she didn't want anyone to find her."

"After seeing her room, you really want her out there on her own?" he demanded, figuring that if he didn't start being a little tougher with her, they could end up standing there and arguing in the small-ass kitchen all goddamn night.

She blanched, and her eyes went glassy. "No."

"This is what Max and I do, Skye. Let him do his job, and let me do mine. I swear I won't let these assholes get anywhere close to you."

"*But who are they?* Everyone keeps talking about these mystery b-bastards, but won't tell me anything. I just… I need to understand what the hell is going on."

"I get that. I do. But there's a lot that I can't explain right now, because—" he paused and licked his lips "—because we don't have the time. What I *can* tell you is that Max and I were asked by a friend in the FBI to

look into a strange case the Feds are investigating. Seven
women have recently gone missing on the East Coast,
most from different towns, and the circumstances are
all similar. We think they're being collected by a group
of males who are being paid to bring the women back
to *one* man. We just don't know who he is, or what he's
doing to the victims once he gets them."

"And you think…me and Viv?" she asked awkwardly,
her eyes so wide the irises were surrounded by white.
"You think he wants these guys to kidnap *us*?"

"We got some vital intel that marked you both by
name as the next targets, so yeah, that's definitely what
I think." Lowering his hand, he stepped closer, narrow-
ing his gaze on her upturned face as she tilted her head
back. "I also think that if you're not smart, there's a good
chance you're going to find yourself in a situation that
could end up getting you killed. And I don't think it'd
be a quick death. I think this psychotic son of a bitch
would probably make you suffer a hell of a lot before he
ever got around to taking your life."

She immediately started crying again, her beautiful
face crumpling with misery. Feeling like a complete
jackass for goading her, Elliot drew the sobbing girl into
his arms. He expected her to fight his touch, at least a
little, but she was obviously desperate for the comfort,
because her arms immediately wrapped around his waist
as she buried her face against his chest.

"Christ, I'm sorry for sounding like such a jerk," he
rasped, holding her as tightly as he could as he rested
his chin on top of her head. He wished he could just take
this all away from her. The entire night, and all the shit
that was sure to follow.

"If this is what's really happening, then he m-must

have seen Viv at the club." Her voice was kind of muffled, since her face was still pressed against his chest,
her tears soaking into his Henley, but he could still make
out the husky words. "Men tend to go a little crazy when
they see her. But…why me? What have I done to draw
his attention?"

"You haven't done anything. These bastards working
for him are kidnapping beautiful women, and you're a
beautiful woman."

"Oh, God. Just…don't." She pressed her hands against
his chest and pushed, forcing him to either be an ass or
let her go, so he lowered his arms. Moving back until she
was pressed up against the counter again, she gave him
a dark look that made him think she was considering if
she should kick him or just hit him. "You don't need to
lie to me, Elliot. I'm…heavy. I'm not like Vivian. Not at
all. I'm…fat, and I—"

"Whoa," he cut in, holding his hand up. "Just wait
and shut up for a second."

It almost killed him to see that lush mouth pressed
into a hard, flat line. "What?"

"Just don't, okay? Don't *ever* let me hear you call
yourself *that* word again," he growled. "I don't know
where you got a ridiculous idea like that in your head,
but you *are* an incredibly beautiful woman, Skye. Every
inch of you. Goddamn gorgeous."

She bit her lip, face so flushed she looked like she'd
been standing too long beneath a sweltering summer
sun. Then she suddenly went into motion and started
pacing the small kitchen, one hand pressed to her
forehead, shoving back her hair, while the other arm
wrapped around her middle. "I'm trying to figure out the
right thing to do here, but I can't even get my thoughts

straight." She flicked him a searching look, then lowered her gaze and kept right on pacing, her nervous energy so sharp he could feel it in the air. "I have no freaking idea if I should even believe what you're telling me, and I'm sick with worry over Viv, and I… I know I should call the police, but I… I don't… I mean, I wouldn't even know what to say to them."

Pushing his hands deep in his pockets, so he couldn't get himself into trouble by grabbing her and hauling her right back into his arms, he said, "You don't trust the cops because of Derek, right?"

A crease formed between her brows as she frowned. "Yeah. And Viv, she wouldn't want that. She hates cops. I mean freaking *hates* them."

"I can help you, Skye. I *want* to help you. We'll figure this out and help Viv, too. All you need to do is trust me."

"And, God, that right there. It's so…so crazy! What is it with you?" Her head shot up, her big eyes bright with emotion, and he figured she was finally losing her patience with everyone and everything. Or maybe it was her temper, because she even stamped her foot against the floor. "Why are you being so damn nice to me? You're scaring the hell out of me!"

Well…shit. "I'm sorry if I'm making you nervous. I just want to take care of you. Make sure you're okay— that you have everything you need."

Looking completely baffled, she started to scowl. "You want to take care of someone you're not even interested in? That doesn't make any sense."

"Wait. *What?*"

Crossing her arms over her chest, she pulled in a deep breath, and then blurted what sounded like the biggest load of bullshit Elliot had ever heard. "What you're offering, it isn't like a paid bodyguard or PI doing his job. You're acting like you're actually worried about what happens to me on some kind of personal level. But when a man is determined to take care of a woman like that, and that woman isn't family or a woman who's involved with a friend—you know, like part of his inner circle— then it usually means that he *wants* her. Or that he at least wants something *from* her. And I know that's not the case here. Guys like you don't waste your time with girls like me."

Jesus, what the hell was she thinking? Shaking his head a little, he tried to wrap his brain around it, but it was impossible. "Okay, there's actually a lot about all that I could argue with, but I'm too hung up on the other thing you said. How can you think I don't want you?" he demanded, his voice so rough he was nearly growling at her again. "That I don't want *inside* you?"

Her mouth popped open—snapped shut—and then popped open again. "I, uh, I know you don't."

"I just stood here and told you you're beautiful, right? I didn't imagine that, did I?"

"No," she mumbled. "But that…that was probably just to make me feel better, because I've already figured out that you're a nice guy."

"I'm not *that* nice," he muttered, hating that freaking word as much as every other guy in the world.

She went on like she hadn't even heard him. "So what exactly is your deal? Because my head is going in way too many directions tonight to figure it out."

Biting back a guttural, explosive curse, Elliot had a good idea of what was making her so edgy. She was picking up on the primal, animalistic, damn-near-magnetic connection between them, and that intense awareness was making his restraint all the more glaring. And for a girl who clearly didn't have as much confidence as she should, the situation was throwing up all kinds of red flags and signals, when he needed her to just let go of the fear and trust him.

Christ, he was already screwing this up and he hadn't even known her more than a couple of hours!

Gripping the back of his neck, he struggled to find the right thing to say, wishing he had someone there to help him, like Mason. Then again, Mason's way of handling the situation when he'd found his life-mate had been to trip her in the middle of a crowded café, so maybe he wasn't the best choice for advice on women.

You think? his wolf drawled, and Elliot could've sworn he heard the smart-ass animal snickering.

Yeah, he was just going to have to stumble through this on his own, and hopefully not fuck it up so badly she ended up thinking he was an idiot.

Bringing his hooded gaze back to hers, he willed her to believe in him with everything that he had. "You're wrong, Skye. I want you so goddamn bad I can barely see straight. I just…can't ask you for anything like that right now."

This time, she was the one who just stared, her expression full of confusion and curiosity.

Feeling the weight of every lie he'd already told—and every secret he kept—pressing down on him, Elliot had to lean back against the counter for support. "There are things you don't…know. Things I need to explain before I… Before we…"

"Jesus." Her soft voice was breathless with shock, a dazed look on her face as she finally started to believe him. "You're serious, aren't you?"

"About wanting you?" he asked in a husky rumble, catching his lower lip in his teeth. "Woman, you have no idea."

She took a deep breath, closed her eyes, then slowly opened them as she shook her head in a helpless, frustrated gesture. "Elliot, even if I wanted to, I can't just leave with you. That…that would be like the ultimate play in the *How to Do Something Stupid If You're a Woman* handbook. I don't even know you."

"You know I've protected you." He licked his lower lip again, his gaze sliding away as he said, "And that I'm a PI."

"I would need more than some license to make me leave with you. That thing could be fake for all I know."

"Shit," he cursed under his breath, rubbing the hard line of his jaw with his palm. "We don't have time for this."

"I know," she said quietly, the look in her big eyes imploring him to understand when he finally glanced her way. "I swear I'm not trying to be a bitch, and I'm not ungrateful for what you've done. But…I can't just run off with you because I'm scared. That would make me stupid. And stupid girls end up dead."

He paced across the floor, taking a moment to think. Though his wolf pretty much thought tossing her over his shoulder and telling her how it was going to be seemed like a sound plan, Elliot figured he needed something a bit less caveman if he wanted to win her over. He rapidly went through about ten different scenarios, before he finally landed on one that might have a chance at working. "Okay," he muttered, pulling his phone from his back pocket. "Just give me a few seconds. I need to make a call."

She nodded, her gaze filling with questions as he put the phone to his ear and waited for Monroe to answer. Three rings later, the Fed's deep voice said, "Elliot, what's up? You guys make it to Charity?"

He kept his attention focused completely on Skye as he replied. "Yeah, we're here. Where are you?"

"FBI headquarters in DC."

"Great. The camera's bigger on your laptop, so use it to contact me over Skype. Right now, if you can."

"You want to talk over Skype?" Monroe sounded as worried as he did confused. "What's going on?"

"We've hit a…snag. Vivian Jackson got into some trouble and ran before Max could talk to her. But I'm with Skye Hewitt at their apartment. The guys coming after them have trashed it, and I need to get her up to the safe house. But she won't leave with me." Since he was still looking at Skye, he caught the embarrassed wince that she tried to hide, and knew she was feeling torn about whether she was doing the right thing or not. "She, uh, thinks there's a chance my PI license might be fake, so I need you to vouch for me."

"Got it," Monroe murmured, sounding like he was already on the move. "Give me five to grab my laptop and get down to the lobby, and I'll call you back."

Elliot told him thanks, and just as he ended the call, Skye asked, "Who was that?"

"Jared Monroe. He's the FBI agent who asked Max and me to help him out on this case."

"Oh." She chewed on her lower lip for a moment, her worried gaze focused on the cheap kitchen linoleum. Then she took a quick breath, like she was reaching deep for her courage, and looked right at him. "Why does it say 'Runners'? You know, on the message in Viv's room?"

He licked his lips. "That's the, um, name of our company."

"Hmm." If she thought it was a strange name, she didn't remark on it. Instead, she shifted her attention to the phone he was still holding in his hand, waiting for it to ring. Thankfully, Monroe didn't make them wait long, and less than a minute later Elliot was answering the Fed's video call. As soon as the guy's face filled the screen, Elliot held his phone out so that Skye could not only see the agent, but what was being captured in the camera shot, as well.

Though Monroe was barely forty, he looked tired, and Elliot knew the guy's job was taking its toll on him. That, and the bitter divorce he was currently going through. For a while, he'd thought the Fed might end up with someone in the pack, the way his sister had. Then he'd gone and married a woman who worked as an analyst for the Bureau, and from what the Runners could tell, the marriage had been a rocky one.

"Before I say anything, I want to show you where I am." Monroe twisted the computer around, so that Skye could see where the Fed was standing. With a twitch of his lips, Elliot realized that Monroe was showing her the main entrance of the FBI building. Armed guards manned the security checkpoint, the President's photo hung on the wall, along with the Ten Most Wanted list, and then Monroe tilted the computer down, letting the camera pick up the official government seal that was located in the middle of the floor.

When he brought the camera back to his face, he said, "I assure you, Miss Hewitt, I'm the real deal, and Elliot and Max are two of the best at…what they do." A gentle smile curved his lips. "I know this is frightening, but you don't have to do it alone. Let Elliot help you."

Sounding a little in awe, she said, "Thank you for taking the time to do this."

"We all just want to make sure you stay safe. And have Elliot put my number in your phone. If you ever need anything, you call me."

"I will," she murmured, giving the guy one of her brief, but beautiful smiles. "And that's… I, um, I really appreciate it. Thank you."

Monroe murmured, "Anytime," and Elliot didn't miss the appreciative gleam lingering in the Fed's eyes as he shifted his attention back his way. Not that he could blame the guy, seeing as how Skye was fucking gorgeous, even when she'd been through an emotional wringer.

"So what exactly happened with Vivian Jackson?" Monroe asked, his brow creasing with concern.

"I'm not really sure. But I'll have Max call you in five."

"I'll be waiting." Looking at Skye again, Monroe said, "Try not to worry. We're going to find these people, and when we do, they're going to be put away for a long, long time."

Not if I find them first, Elliot thought. No way in hell was he letting the son of a bitch responsible for this nightmare, and the ones working for him, live.

He said goodbye to Monroe, then ended the call and slipped the phone back into his pocket.

"I like him," Skye murmured. "He…he seems really nice."

"Yeah, Monroe's a good guy."

She tilted her head a bit to the side, and he had the feeling there were a million thoughts going on behind her beautiful eyes at that exact moment. "He thinks a lot of you. I mean, that was pretty obvious."

"We've, uh, been through a lot together." Worried he might do something to spook her, Elliot was keeping his responses as neutral as possible. "I've known him for a long time. Since I was seventeen."

When she pulled that juicy lower lip through her teeth, and gave him a shy smile, his damn knees nearly buckled with relief. "I'm sorry for being such a pain, but if the offer still stands, I would… I would like to go with you."

Inside his head, he was running victory laps like a fucking gold medalist, fist pumping in the air. But to Skye, he simply curled his hand behind her neck, her hair like silk against his skin, and pulled her close enough he could press a quick kiss to her forehead.

It's about fucking time, he thought, desperate to get her out of there. "You won't regret this. I promise," he told her, as he took a step back.

She gave him another brief, tentative smile. "Everything else I need is already in my purse in my car, so I'm ready when you are."

Grabbing her hand, Elliot pulled her along behind him as he headed for the door. "Before we go," he murmured, sliding her a careful look, "I need you to talk to Max."

Her shoulders tensed, but she didn't argue. "I know."

They found Max sitting in his truck with the window down, a cigarette stuck between his lips as he rested a hand on top of the steering wheel. There were dark shadows in his partner's eyes, and Elliot knew Max was blaming himself for all the shit that had happened. He needed to talk to the guy and get the whole story, but knew better than to ask in front of Skye. He just hoped Max wasn't being too hard on himself.

Stepping up to the driver-side door, Skye curled her fingers over the bottom of the window frame. "Vivian drives a gray, older-model Ford Silverado, and her mom and brothers live in Ohio now. I don't know the exact address, but the name of the apartment complex is River Shores and it's on a road called Prospect in Dayton. Her mom's name is Marcia Jackson. Her maternal grandmother, Cecilia Jackson, lives just a few towns over, in a place called Perryton."

"Thanks," Max rasped, stubbing the cigarette out in the ashtray as he reached for his phone. She gave him Vivian's cell phone number, and Max was still typing everything Skye had just told him into his notes app, when she cleared her throat to get his attention.

"I...I don't know that she'd go to her family. I mean, I know how she thinks, and she'll be worried that she might bring trouble to their doorsteps, which she wouldn't want."

Max's dark brows knitted with a frown. "If not her family, then where?"

"I'm not sure," Skye told him, her quiet voice husky with emotion. "She might just want to be close to her family, without putting them in danger. I know she has an old boyfriend who also lives in Dayton, so she might try to crash with him. His name's David Hanson and he works at Hanson's Automotive Repair, but I don't know his address."

Max nodded, and gave her a gruff "Thanks." As she stepped back from the door, Max passed Elliot's duffel bag to him through the window. Then he asked, "What the hell was Vivian talking about in those messages when she mentioned a robbery?"

"I'll tell you about it later," Elliot muttered, at the same time Skye said, "Your friend saved my life."

Max looked between the two of them, then shook his head as his lips twitched. "Okay, I'm outta here. But I look forward to hearing that story."

"We'll be at the safe house," Elliot said, as Max cranked the truck's engine. "As soon as you've got her, you go straight there. And whatever the hell you do, be careful. And call Monroe right now. He's waiting to hear from you."

His partner jerked his chin in agreement, then reversed out of the space and drove away, the truck's red taillights gleaming in the darkness.

Sensing Skye's tension as she stood beside him and watched Max drive off, he said, "Max is one of the best trackers I've ever known. If anyone can find her, it's him."

"I hope so," she whispered, the quiet words nearly lost in the wintry wind as it whipped around them, pulling at her long hair.

"You did the right thing." With his bag in one hand and her backpack on his shoulder, he steered her toward her car with his free hand against her lower back. "Giving him that information, it could be the thing that saves Vivian's life."

She turned her head up to him as they walked, her green eyes glistening like jewels. "I hope you're right about that, too."

"Trust me, Skye. Everything's going to work out," he told her, feeling like he was making a sacred vow. "There *will* be an end to this nightmare. I give you my word that I will do whatever it takes to make that happen."

And it was true—he would do anything for this woman. *Anything.*

Elliot just hoped that when it was over, and the dust had cleared, she was still standing by his side.

Chapter 6

It was difficult for Elliot to think he was with Skye simply because he'd had the luck of a coin toss. A random turn of fate that could have so easily gone in Max's favor, instead of his.

Though most Lycans subscribed to the belief that life-mates were predestined, he knew there were some more progressive-thinking shifters who believed that the connections were made when two souls came into contact with one another and shared a spark. A moment of recognition that they were a perfect match, in all the ways that mattered. Ways they wouldn't completely understand at first, but would come with time…and the seeds of deeper emotion.

It was a concept that had troubled Elliot more than once over the years. At times, he'd found it impossible to believe that he would ever be able to find a woman whose soul reached out to his and thought *Yes, him. He's perfect for me. He's mine...*

Now that it'd happened, he was... Christ, it was difficult to explain. So damn happy he could barely process it, and yet so terrified it was ripping him to shreds inside. Because having something meant you had something to lose, and that... Yeah, that scared the ever-loving hell out of him.

They'd only spoken in bits and pieces since they'd set out in her beleaguered little car. She'd asked Elliot if he would drive, and he was more than willing, sensing she needed some downtime. She was drawn with worry, quiet in a way that he guessed wasn't natural for her, but he didn't push her to engage. At the moment, as they sped down the dark highway that climbed steadily toward the mountains, he was too busy focusing on their surroundings, ensuring they weren't being followed by anyone who might have been watching the apartment, to navigate his way through a tricky conversation.

And until he'd told her at least part of the truth about what was going on, every damn conversation they had was a tricky one.

Before they'd left Charity, he'd found an electronics store that was open late, and was able to grab a new battery for the older-model cell phone Skye had in her purse. As soon as they were back in the car and on the road, she'd put the new battery in and had sent Viv a short message that simply said: Phone working. Saw the apartment. Men were trying to kidnap you! Please call me! X

Then she'd bitten her lower lip and set the phone in her lap, staring down at it like it was suddenly going to give her direction. "I feel like I should call Viv's mom," she'd said in a quiet voice, "but I…I wouldn't know what to say."

Fiddling with the heater, since he hadn't wanted her to be cold, he'd said, "It's probably best to just hold off on that for the moment."

"Yeah?"

Elliot had nodded. "As soon as we have some solid news, you could call her then. But right now, you'd just end up scaring the shit out of her."

She'd sighed as she leaned back in her seat. "You're right."

That'd been almost an hour ago, and as they came up on one of the last towns they would pass through before changing onto a more rural road that would lead up to the safe house, he asked her if she was hungry. She said she could probably eat something, and so they grabbed some burgers and fries from a drive-through. Elliot ate as he drove, desperate for the food, since his body burned through twice as many calories as a human male. But Skye only picked at hers, her thoughts clearly still on her friend as she said, "Couldn't Monroe do like an APB on Vivian's truck? Wouldn't that help Max find her?"

With one hand on the wheel and the other holding his burger, he said, "He could, but that might just lead them to her even faster. These guys are too good at what they do to not be monitoring the police systems."

His skin sizzled with awareness as she looked over at him. "They were expecting you and Max to be at our apartment tonight. Do you think they know you're working on the case? That you're trying to catch them?"

He shook his head as he swallowed the last bite of his burger. "I'm not sure they knew about us before we showed up in Charity. But after that message on her wall, you're right. They definitely know about us now."

When her phone suddenly buzzed, signaling a text alert, she nearly jumped out of her seat. "Ohmygod," she gasped, scrambling for the phone and quickly reading the message. "It's from Vivian. She says that she was able to charge her phone for a few minutes at a rest stop, and wants to know if I'm okay." Her fingers started flying over the keypad. "I'm telling her that a lot has happened, but I'm fine, I have help and I'm going somewhere safe."

"Ask her how badly she was hurt, where she is and where she's going."

"Okay." She typed some more, and a moment later, her phone buzzed again. "She says she got a bad cut, but that it's stopped bleeding and that she's still on the move. That she just needed to know I was safe. But that's…that's all."

Elliot glanced over at her, and his stomach tightened when he saw the shattered look on her face. Voice hoarse with emotion, she said, "I don't think she wants me to know where she's going. But that doesn't make any sense. Why wouldn't she tell me?"

"I don't know, Skye. She's probably not thinking very clearly right now, so try not to read too much into it."

He had to shift his attention back to the road, but he could see her still chewing on her lip from the corner of his eye. "Yeah, I guess."

"Do me a favor and tell her that there's a guy named Max who's trying to find her and is probably trying to call her. Tell her he's a PI who wants to help her. That he'll be able to explain what's going on and that she can trust him."

"Good idea," she murmured, quickly typing in the

message. They waited, but when a response didn't come through, she said, "Damn it. I think she must have turned her phone off again."

"She'll check it eventually." He wished there was something more comforting he could tell her, but he honestly didn't know what the fuck was going through Vivian Jackson's head at the moment. He just hoped she stayed smart, and listened to Max when he finally caught up to her.

Skye held the phone tightly in her hand for the next half hour, but when it stayed silent, she finally set it down on her lap again, leaned her head back and closed her eyes. Elliot kept trying to think of something to say to make her feel better, but couldn't come up with a single goddamn thing. He didn't want to spew another lie, and so he bit down on the useless platitudes that lingered in his mouth and kept silent.

Hoping it would help her to relax, he turned the radio on low, and she eventually dozed off. Despite the heavy snowfall they'd recently seen in that area, the roads were relatively clear, and he made good time, the directions he'd been given to the remote cabin easier to follow than he'd thought they would be. Less than an hour later, they were there, and he parked the Beetle on the side of the cabin, then gently nudged Skye awake with his hand on her knee.

"Skye, honey, wake up. We're here."

She looked around for a moment, disoriented, then sat up and pushed her hair back from her face. "I'm so sorry I fell asleep. I'm hopeless in the car when I'm not driving."

"No need to apologize. You needed it after the night you've had. Come on. Let's check this place out."

"You've never been here?" she asked, giving him a curious look over the roof of the car after she'd climbed out.

Elliot grinned. "Nope."

He grabbed their bags from the backseat, shut his door, and they met at the back of the car, the two of them walking together as they made their way to the front of the cabin. Six steps led up to the wide, wraparound porch, the exterior stained a deep gray that was so dark it looked black in the moonlight. It wasn't as nice as the cabins he and the other Runners had in the Alley, but it was still a beautiful place, and Skye obviously thought so, too.

"Wow," she murmured, shooting him a wide-eyed look of surprise. "Who owns this place?"

The truth? The cabin was part of an interregional pack alliance that Mason had been working on, its purpose to establish safe locations for Runners to stay at while on assignment outside of their area. But that wasn't exactly an explanation Elliot could give Skye, so he licked his bottom lip, and said, "It's a cabin that some of my PI friends own. A good place to use as a safe house when one of us needs to lie low."

"It's beautiful."

"Yeah," he grated, unable to look away from her as she tilted her face up to the moonlight, the silvery beams making her look like a fairy creature. Making her so breathtaking he had to rip his gaze away before he did something stupid, like grab her and cover that pink, delicious-looking mouth with his own.

Unfortunately, that was the *last* friggin' thing he needed to be thinking about, unless he wanted to scare the hell out of her. He might not know all that much about women, but he *did* understand that after bringing her up to a cabin in the middle of freaking nowhere, the fastest way he could put her at ease was by keeping his hands to himself. Christ, he'd gone without for nearly his entire life. Not like waiting until she was ready for more was going to kill him.

Though with her so close, and looking so goddamn beautiful, while that mouthwatering scent kept screwing with his head, he figured there was a good chance he might go a bit mad.

"Whoa, what was that?" she gasped, gripping on to his arm when an owl suddenly swooped down just off to their right.

"Just an owl heading out to get his dinner."

"Oh." She breathed out a huge sigh of relief, and let go of his arm.

Sensing her fear at being in the woods, he couldn't help but ask, "Haven't you ever been camping before?"

With a wry twist of her lips, she shook her head. "My family didn't do the vacation thing, and Viv and I…" A quiet, hollow laugh slipped past her lips. "I don't think camping would really be our thing."

Elliot lifted his brows. "You don't like the forest?"

"Oh, I like it just fine. I'm just not entirely sure that *it* likes me."

"Naw, I think you'll find it likes you just fine," he said in a low voice, giving her words right back to her. The wildness and freedom of the forest was such a part of his animal-side, he couldn't help but believe that the connection between him and Skye would eventually help her to feel as at home there as he did.

Of course, that meant that the same should work in the reverse, and he would eventually feel more at ease whenever he had to venture into a big, bustling human city, and he wasn't sure how he felt about that. Then it hit him—how much of a jerk he was being—and he gave himself a mental kick in the ass as he finally started up the porch steps, Skye right at his side.

Instead of needing a key to unlock the door, he punched the code Mason had given him into the keypad just above the handle. A second later, there was a distinct click, and the door opened with a little popping sound.

"Cool door," she murmured, following him in.

Looking around, Elliot immediately felt some of the tension ease from his shoulders. He'd been worried the place would be a bit on the barren side, but it was actually clean and well furnished, with colorful rugs covering the hardwood floors, comfortable-looking sofas and what looked like a high-tech kitchen off to their left.

Together, they took a quick tour, neither of them commenting when the only functional bedroom sported a massive king-size bed, the second room set up with weights and a desk. He figured one of the sofas probably turned into a bed, but didn't like the idea of not having her in the same room with him.

Thinking it was probably best to get the issue out in the open as soon as possible, he set their bags down on top of the dresser and turned toward her as he shoved his hands in his front pockets, hoping it made him look a little less threatening. "You okay with me sleeping in here with you if I use the cot in the closet? It'd make me feel better to know I'm close in case we have any trouble."

She slipped her coat off, laying it on the foot of the bed before sliding him a worried look. "Do you think we will? Have any trouble, I mean?"

"We shouldn't. But that doesn't mean we let our guard down. Especially when there's so much about this group that we don't know." *Not to mention the asshole they're working for.*

"That makes sense." She angled her head a bit to the side and frowned as she looked him over, from his short hair down to the heavy black boots on his big feet, every single one of his muscles hardening beneath her attention. "But let me take the cot. I don't think you'd fit on it."

"I'll be fine," he assured her, the fact that she wasn't freaked out at the thought of sleeping in the same room as him making him want to smile like a damn idiot. Needing to distract himself, and quick, he jerked his chin toward the door. "Let's finish checking out the place."

They took a quick look around the kitchen, examining the contents of the cupboards and the fridge, and he was relieved to find that there were enough provisions to get them through for at least a couple of days before they would need to head back down to a store. Mason must have had someone come up and stock the place with supplies, when he'd learned that they might need to use the cabin.

The last time Elliot had talked to the Runner, he'd told him that he and Max planned to bring Skye Hewitt and Vivian Jackson up there, giving them a safe place to stay while they went after the assholes coming after the women. But learning that Skye was his life-mate had definitely changed the game. No way in hell was Elliot leaving her side, which meant he and Max would need to come up with a new plan as soon as his partner showed up with Vivian.

"I want you to know that I appreciate what you're doing for me," Skye said, as he shut the door to the fridge. "And I...I didn't mean to be a pain earlier. It's just…it's scary to rely on people. To trust them. And I'm… I'm not very good at it."

He turned around, resting his back against the stainless-steel front of the fridge, little more than a few feet between them as she stood by the breakfast bar and stools that separated the kitchen from the rest of the open floor plan at the front of the cabin. "How about the next time I need to rely on someone, it can be you? Then we'll be even."

"That sounds like a plan," she said with one of those shy smiles that made him feel a little dizzy, they were so adorable, and he was sure that he'd surprised her.

It was after eleven, but Elliot was nowhere near ready for bed yet, and he knew she had to be hungry. "Let me make a fire for you before I get started on the food," he said, straightening away from the fridge. "It's pretty cold in here."

"You're hungry again?" She shook her head as she laughed, and he was glad to hear the sound was a little less hollow this time. "How is that even possible?"

He walked past her, heading toward the fireplace, but shot her a playful wink over his shoulder. "I'm a growing boy."

Elliot could tell she was trying to sound casual as she asked, "You're what…twenty-eight? Twenty-nine?"

"Twenty-seven," he told her, glad she was trying to learn more about him. Looking back at her again as he went down on his knees in front of the hearth, he said, "And you hardly touched that burger and fries we picked up. You need to at least have a go at something before you call it a night."

There was something incredibly soft in her eyes as she

held his gaze, her voice a little huskier when she asked, "Are you really offering to cook for me?"

He couldn't help but grin, thinking that he would happily cook for this girl for the rest of his life, if she'd let him. "I'm not much of a gourmet, but I can make a killer omelet."

She smiled, but turned quiet again while he got the fire going. He watched from the corner of his eye as she looked out one of the front windows, so hungry for the sight of her that he almost singed his hand as he got the kindling going. Then he went back into the kitchen and began putting everything together for their omelets.

"I've never had a guy cook for me before," she admitted with a note of embarrassment, after he'd finished chopping the peppers and had started cracking the eggs into a mixing bowl. The fire was heating the room, and it'd soothed his protective instincts when the color had come back to her cheeks, her smooth skin no longer covered in chill bumps.

Surprised by what she'd said, he lifted his brows as he looked over to where she was perched on one of the stools, her crossed arms resting on the tiled surface of the breakfast bar. "Seriously?"

She nodded, biting her lip, her creamy complexion turning pinker as she blushed. "That sounds crazy, doesn't it? I mean, you've probably cooked for hundreds of girls, and now you think I'm a dork."

Taking a deep breath, Elliot set the eggs down, washed his hands, then locked his hooded gaze with her curious one as he slowly made his way over to where she sat.

"I've only cooked for friends," he said quietly, unable to stop himself from turning her toward him and settling his hands on her waist. He leaned down and pressed his lips to her temple, then trailed them down the side of her face, before letting himself steal a quick kiss against the corner of her soft, quivering mouth. "I've never cooked for a girl that I wanted," he added, his lips brushing against her cheek. *And I've never wanted anyone like I want you. Not even close.*

She shivered, and he nearly died when she turned her head and pressed those supple, velvety lips against the side of his throat. He swallowed so hard that it hurt, and knew he needed to step back. He allowed himself one brief moment to run his hands from her waist, down over the feminine swell of her hips, damn near drooling over the lush curves of her body, his grip tightening for no more than a second. Then he forced himself to let her go, careful to shield his eyes with his lashes as he headed back to his task, knowing his normally dark irises were glowing in a way that was so much more Lycan than human.

"Elliot?" she whispered, sounding...unsure.

He took another deep breath, shoving the lust down so hard it made both him and the animal flinch, and then he looked at her, smiling just a little. "Sorry. I was about two seconds away from kissing the hell out of you, and I wasn't sure you were ready for it."

Her eyes went wide, and she slowly blinked. *"Oh."*

"Yeah," he said unsteadily, focusing on the eggs that needed to be whipped. He desperately tried to come up with a new topic, because God only knew he needed the distraction—and then one finally managed to claw its way through the lust and into his brain. "So, uh, I'm taking it you grew up a city girl. Is that where you lived with your family?"

"Yeah, but...I don't really like to talk about them."

"All right." He fought to keep his thoughts from showing on his face, those protective instincts she sent into overdrive not liking the things that lay beyond those halting words.

"What…what about yours?" she asked, and he felt a bit of the tension in his shoulders ease. Finally, a question he could answer without having to fudge the truth for her.

Getting the omelets cooking on the stove, he said, "I haven't seen my family in years. But when I was seventeen, I was kinda adopted by another one, and now they're more my family than my birth parents ever were."

"Wow. You're…lucky."

"Trust me, I know," he murmured, flashing her a quick grin.

"Do you enjoy your job?"

Well, shit. He licked his lips, feeling that invisible noose tightening around his throat all over again. Choosing his words with care, he focused on the pan as he said, "Yeah. It's…the best thing that could have ever happened to me." *Until now. Until you.*

"And it must feel good to be doing something meaningful. I mean, look at me. You're not much older than I am, and I'm just a waitress in a crappy diner. I've done nothing my entire life except scrape by."

Elliot's natural instinct was to argue that she had that all wrong, but one look at her face, and he could tell that this wasn't the time. Instead, he said, "You mentioned a business savings account. What's that about?"

"Oh, um, nothing really." She seemed flustered that he'd remembered her even mentioning it. "Just some dream I have of owning my own business one day."

"Yeah? What kind?"

She tilted her head a bit to the side again, studying him in a way that made him think she was trying to decide if he was genuinely interested or just being nice. Since he figured there was no hiding the fact that everything about her interested the hell out of him, he wasn't all that surprised when she seemed to realize he wasn't just being polite. "Well, I still need to take some online classes to learn about small business management. But I would love to have my own gift shop one day. Someplace where I could sell things like scented candles, unique pieces of jewelry, and these painted shelves and tables that I love to make."

"Like the ones you had in your apartment?"

She blinked, looking a little shell-shocked that he'd noticed, considering the pieces had been, well, literally *in pieces*. "Yeah, like those."

"That would be awesome. I know my friend Sayre would go crazy for that stuff. Torry, too." When he suddenly realized he'd started talking about other women without explaining who they were, he awkwardly added, "They're both like family to me. And I, uh, work with their husbands."

Thankfully, the food saved him from saying anything more on the topic. Dishing up the two veggie-and-cheese omelets that he'd made, he carried the plates over to the round dining table that sat in a little nook, and Skye grabbed them two bottles of water from the fridge.

"Ohmygod," she moaned, after taking her first bite. "This is really good."

"You didn't think I'd offer to make you an omelet if I sucked at it, did you?" he asked with a smirk.

She snuffled a soft laugh under her breath, shaking her head no, and Elliot couldn't keep the stupid grin off his face, relieved that he'd gotten at least one fucking thing right that night. They kept the conversation light while they ate, and when his plate was empty, he wiped his mouth with one of the paper napkins that sat in a basket in the center of the table and leaned back in his chair. His gaze slid toward the bay window that surrounded the table on three sides, and he caught sight of the moon hanging just above the tops of the trees that edged the property, thick forest spreading out beyond. It was only a quarter moon, but the silvery crescent still called to the most primal, instinctive parts of him. He felt like he could pull its power in through his eyes and nose and mouth, breathing the moonbeams into his lungs like a surge of adrenaline.

It made him feel almost *whole* in a way that it never had before.

Then again, that was far more likely the beautiful woman studying him from the other side of the table.

"I get the feeling you enjoy being in the woods," she murmured, no doubt picking up on the ease he felt at no longer being surrounded by so many people. Like most of the Runners, towns and cities were something he endured, but never enjoyed.

"Hell, yeah," he rumbled, bringing his gaze back to hers. "I love it. It's where I'm from."

She looked intrigued, chin resting on her palm, elbow braced on the table. "You're from the woods?"

"In a way. Max and I both live in the mountains down in Maryland."

"Well, no wonder you seem so comfortable up here," she murmured, sliding her gaze toward the window. "I'm kinda jealous."

Voice pitched low, he told her, "You know, there's nothing to be afraid of."

Her lips twitched, and she rolled her eyes. "Only wild animals that can hunt and kill you, making you their dinner."

Elliot knew it might rattle her, but he couldn't stop himself from saying, "They'd have to get through me first. Like hell am I letting anyone touch you, much less hurt you."

She blushed like she could sense the deeper meaning behind those husky words, her head turning until she was practically hidden by the fall of all that long, wavy hair. And he could've sworn she was biting that fucking beautiful lip again. He wanted to violate it just as desperately as he wanted to worship it. Lick it. Claim it. Nip it with his teeth. He wanted to bend her back over his arm and kiss her so hard she'd feel the pressure of his lips for days, the taste and shape of his tongue imprinted on her senses so deeply she couldn't cut him out.

Not the time, idiot. Not the time...or you're going to lose it.

Lifting his arms, he let them fall back as he stretched, his muscles still cramped from the long drive, not to mention the strain from walking around in a constant state of mounting hunger, and when he snuck another look at Skye from under his lashes, he caught her staring at his abdomen. His shirt had lifted enough to show a tanned strip of skin, his muscles hardening to stone beneath the searing heat of her gaze. There was lust there in those gorgeous green eyes, as well as need, and as he pulled in a sharp breath, the heady scent of her arousal had him choking back a deep, guttural groan.

God, he wanted her. So fucking bad it was killing

him. So bad he knew he needed to give himself some relief, and soon, or there was a good chance he'd go out of his goddamn mind.

Pushing back from the table, Elliot grabbed his plate, then reached for hers. "You sleepy?"

"Not just yet."

He flicked her a careful look, hoping she couldn't read the raging, primitive need on his face. "Then make yourself at home and see if you can find a good movie on or something. The place has satellite TV, so we should get some decent channels. I'm just gonna grab a quick shower."

If she seemed startled by his abrupt departure, she was good at hiding it. He left her washing up the dishes, since she all but pushed him out of the kitchen when he said he'd handle them, and he pulled his phone from his pocket to check his email as he made his way back to the bathroom. He swore under his breath when he saw that Mason had contacted him, wanting to know why he and Max hadn't checked in. Even though they were both adults, the others worried about them like they were two of their kids. It would have irritated the hell out of Elliot, if the fact that they cared about him enough to worry didn't mean so damn much to him.

He took a moment to call Mason and bring him up to speed on everything that had happened, with the exception of the part about Skye being his life-mate. That wasn't something he wanted to get into over the phone, and he knew Mase would pretty much give him the same advice he would have heard from Max: *Tell her. All of it. Now!*

Choking back another guttural groan, Elliot left the phone on the countertop by the sink, in case Max tried to get in touch with him, turned the shower on hot, stripped and climbed in. He stood under the stinging spray, welcoming the burn, and then he reached for the soap.

With one hand braced against the tiled shower wall, he lowered his head, closed his eyes and wrapped his other hand around his granite-hard shaft, wishing it were Skye's soft hand that was holding him…squeezing him… stroking him. That it was her sweet scent filling his head, making him dizzy. Her warm blood coating his tongue, slipping down his throat like the sweetest sin he'd ever tasted as he marked her.

Claimed her.

And made her his own.

Chapter 7

When Skye had first gotten up from the comfy sofa—she'd curled up there to wait for Elliot after finishing with the dishes—and gone into the hallway, it'd been because she'd thought she heard him call out. But after nearly a minute of waiting for the sound of his voice, she realized that was no longer what she was listening for.

No, now she was listening for the sound of the water hitting his gorgeous body. Straining for it, actually. For anything that could help her visualize what he looked like at that moment. With her breaths shallow in her chest, and her cheeks flushed with heat, she felt like the biggest perv on the planet, but she couldn't stop herself. Couldn't even find the strength to walk away, and it made her wonder what was wrong with her. Her best friend was on the run from some psycho group of kidnappers, their apartment had been completely trashed and she'd been involved in an attempted robbery, all in one night—and there she was stalking the poor guy's shower time, getting turned on by the thought of his naked body beneath the warm spray of water, when she should have been having a category five breakdown.

Seriously, what was she doing? Because this...this *way* she was feeling, this wasn't her. She didn't get flustered and twisted up over guys. Didn't really ever give them much thought at all, because they were never all that important to her, compared to the other things going on in her narrow existence. Things like simply surviving, and trying so hard to make plans for her future. Any romantic notions of some happily-ever-after that would change any of that had been pretty much doused with gasoline and set on fire after the whole Derek debacle. Not because she'd been desperately in love with him or anything, but more that she'd felt like such a naive fool for putting her trust in a guy who was so completely playing her.

And yet, given all that, she was honestly crushing on Elliot Connors so hard it had her feeling almost electric, like she'd been plugged into a circuit, her heart pumping and her senses tingling, when she should have been dragging with exhaustion. All she could think about as she stood there in the hallway, softly panting and flushed with need, was the way he'd gripped her waist and pressed his lips to the corner of her mouth during that charged moment when he'd been cooking. She'd completely shocked herself when she'd turned her head and pressed her sensitive lips against his strong, tanned throat. But even more surprising was the fact that she'd been a nanosecond away from flicking her tongue against his hot flesh, before he'd quickly pulled back from her.

Skye couldn't even imagine how embarrassing that would have been, if she'd actually done it, because she honestly didn't know how he would have reacted. The guy had her freaking head spinning, casting hot-as-sin looks at her one moment, like he wanted to devour her, and then deliberately backing off the next, as if he'd been caught doing something wrong. Did he honestly want her? Or was he just a hopeless flirt with *all* the women who ended up under his protection?

God, she wished she knew. Wished she had a Magic 8 Ball to give her some answers here, because she was only getting in deeper with this beautiful, rugged, heroic stranger with every second that went by. She'd never thought someone like Elliot Connors would even look twice at a girl like her—and now that he had, there didn't seem to be any way to slow herself down.

I'm losing it, she thought, snuffling a soft laugh under her breath. *And what's really crazy is that I'm not even sure that I care.*

Realizing it was probably far past time to take her crazy, obviously traumatized ass to bed, before she started fantasizing a bunch of X-rated, breathtakingly erotic scenarios that probably never had a chance in hell of happening, she forced herself to walk past the closed bathroom door and headed straight into the bedroom. With her gaze focused on the gleaming hardwood floor, she was trying to recall what she'd packed to sleep in, hoping it wasn't too skimpy to wear in front of him without getting embarrassed, when she looked up and suddenly found herself standing no more than a yard away from his damn-near-naked, mouthwatering, I-think-I-just-saw-Jesus body.

"Ohmygod!" she gasped, pressing her hands to her hot cheeks, her shocked-wide eyes practically eating up the sight of him. She'd been so lost in her spiraling thoughts out in the hallway, she hadn't even noticed that the shower had stopped. "I'm so freaking sorry! I didn't realize the rooms were connected. I thought you were still in the bathroom."

He didn't say anything in response—just stood there like he was frozen in place by the side of the bed, the small towel barely managing to cover his junk, leaving nearly every inch of him on display. And, God, what a freaking amazing display it was.

His body was just…magnificent. From head to toe, he was pure perfection, and not in one of those pretty-boy ways, though he was definitely beautiful. But he was also one hundred percent male, battle-hardened and rugged, the silvery scars that marked certain parts of his golden skin only adding to his beauty. Broad-shouldered and tall, he was covered in lean, ripped muscles, from his upper body to his abs, and that crazily sexy V of muscle just above his groin. Then there were those long, athletic legs. All night long, she'd noticed the way the denim of his jeans had hugged the powerful muscles in his thighs, hinting at what lay beneath. But she was still unprepared for how those muscular legs looked in the flesh.

Unable to help herself, Skye drank in the sight of him like someone dying of thirst. It took everything she had to fight the instinctive urge to cross the space between them, until she was close enough to feel his heat, and then lean in even closer, until she could touch her mouth to that gleaming, hair-dusted skin and taste him with her tongue. Until she could sink her nails into those broad, muscular shoulders and hold him to her, begging with the silent demands of her body for him to *want her*, even if it was only a fraction of how badly she wanted him.

And then it suddenly dawned on her that she was still just standing there, hands on her hot cheeks, eating the poor guy up with her eyes!

"S-sorry," she choked out, and in her panic, she grabbed her backpack off the top of the dresser and ran into the bathroom, slamming the door behind her. She set the bag on the counter by the sink, trying to avoid her reflection in the mirror as she ripped it open and started searching for something to sleep in.

"I'm such a pathetic dolt," she muttered under her breath, knowing she'd just acted like an idiot. An idiot who, judging by what she'd found so far in the backpack, was going to be stuck going back out there dressed in nothing more than a skimpy tank-and-shorts set. One that was going to showcase her huge boobs and hips and backside. Ugh! She was tempted to just throw on one of the T-shirts and pairs of jeans that she'd packed, but if she came out wearing something like that to sleep in, she was going to look like an even bigger idiot than she already did. Especially if he'd noticed her packing the pajamas when they'd been in her bedroom at the apartment.

Biting her bottom lip, she kept searching through her clothes, and nearly cried with relief when she found the robe Viv had given her for her last birthday at the bottom of the bag. Soft and silky, it was by far one of the prettiest things she owned, and would at least give her a bit of cover as she made her way from the bathroom to the bed.

By the time she was finished changing and finally

opened the door, stepping back into the bedroom, Elliot had the cot set up on the far side of the room, by the window, and was already lying down on it under a light blanket, his big feet nearly hanging off the end. He'd left the light on in the hallway, the door cracked open just enough that she could easily make her way to the bed. But she didn't move.

No, she was still just standing there like a statue, with her bag and work clothes clutched against her chest—her heart getting all warm and fuzzy as she wondered if he'd kept the light on so she wouldn't be scared—when he turned his head on the pillow to look at her, their gazes locking so hard it gave her a physical jolt. A slow, barely there smile touched his wide mouth, and then he curved one of those powerful arms behind him, resting his head in his open palm. He had big hands, like the rest of him, and she couldn't keep from imagining what it would be like to feel them on her body, gripping with enough strength that she could actually *feel* how badly he needed to touch her.

Then he lowered that dark, hooded gaze, taking in what he could see of the light gray robe behind everything she was holding, down to her dimpled knees that peeked beneath the hem, before slowly making his way back up to her eyes. "I've locked up for the night and set the alarm," he said in a hushed, deliciously husky tone, "so we shouldn't get any surprises."

"Thanks," she murmured, unable to look directly at him for too long, since she was afraid she might start to drool or something. Forcing herself into motion, she quickly set her dirty work uniform in a neat pile on the floor beside the dresser, glad to not be wearing the damn thing anymore, even if it had covered more skin than

her jammies and robe. With her long hair falling like
a shield around her flushed face, she quickly spun toward the bed, her breath quickening as she felt the heat
and weight of his attention stay on her the entire time
as she crossed the room. With trembling hands, she set
her phone on the bedside table, in case Vivian tried to
call her in the night, then pulled the robe off so quickly
she was surprised it didn't rip, before climbing under the
covers, the cold sheets making her gasp.

"You okay?" he asked, his deep voice rough with
concern.

"Yeah…just…the bed's cold."

"Ah…that, um, sucks."

Thinking that it was kind of adorable, how awkward
he'd just sounded, she had a little grin on her lips as she
lifted up onto her elbow and reached for her phone, wanting to send Vivian a quick message before she went to
sleep. Her fingers were still a bit shaky, but she finally
managed to type in:

Please call me when you can. So worried about you!
And please let Max help. I met him & trust him. X

With that done, she set the phone back down and
snuggled under the covers, the pillow beneath her head
so soft she felt like she was lying on a cloud. She should
have been so exhausted she could barely keep her eyes
open, but her thoughts kept spinning, while scenes from
the night played out in her mind.

"Elliot?" she murmured a few moments later, keeping her voice soft in case he'd already fallen asleep. But
he hadn't.

When he said "Hmm?" Skye rolled onto her side to

face him, disappointed when she realized he'd rolled onto his side as well, but was facing away from her.

Staring at the shadowed view of his broad, beautiful back and the short, caramel-colored hair that looked like it might curl if he let it get long enough, she asked, "How do you think the guy responsible for all this craziness found me and Viv? Do you think it was through the club where she works? I keep thinking that has to be it. That maybe…maybe he came in to watch the strippers, and got hung up on how gorgeous Viv is instead."

The questions had him rolling onto his back again, and it looked like he was staring up at the ceiling. "I don't know, Skye. That might have been how it happened. Or, hell, it might have been something as easy as just coming across one of you online."

"But that wouldn't even make any sense. We're both really private people, so we haven't ever bothered with any social media accounts. No Facebook or Twitter or Instagram."

"Whatever his means," he grunted, popping his jaw, "this asshole has definitely set eyes on both of you."

A frown wove its way between her brows, while her stomach twisted into knots. "That's so creepy. I mean, I could have served him at the diner and never even realized he was some sicko creep."

He cursed something gritty under his breath, and she wanted to tell him not to hold back on her account. Then it suddenly occurred to her that she wouldn't be going into work for… *Oh, God.* She didn't have any idea how long this nightmare might last. A few days? A week? Would she even still have a job when it was finally over?

Unable to deal with all those uncertainties just then,

she forced herself to take a deep breath, and simply said, "I need to let the diner know I won't be in...for a while."

"Let me have Monroe contact them for you," he said in that rough, rumbly way of his that made her think of sex, no matter what he was talking about. "I'll shoot him a message first thing in the morning. We don't know if they've tapped into the phone lines at the diner, and I don't want them listening in on anything you might say."

"I didn't even think about that," she admitted in a slightly panicked tone, thinking of the text she'd just sent. "Should I have my phone turned off? Could they track it to our location?"

"Shit," he muttered, turning his head toward her. "I should have told you not to worry about that. My phone has a scrambler in it that will affect the signal on yours, as well. So long as we're within a three-hundred-foot radius of each other, it'll be okay."

Her brows lifted with surprise. "Wow, that's pretty high-tech."

"Yeah," he agreed, the shadows making it difficult to read his expression. "But I still think you should limit your phone use to Viv and no one else. I don't want to take any chances."

"Not a problem," she told him, realizing he really had no clue just how isolated she kept herself, aside from Viv and the people she interacted with at the diner. "There's no one else I would want to contact."

He let those quiet words linger in the air for a moment, and she swore she could hear the rasp of his beard scruff as he rubbed his fingers along the rugged edge of his jaw. Then he jerked his chin toward her, and said, "It's been one hell of a night for you, Skye. You should try to get some sleep."

"You, too," she murmured, rolling onto her back. "Good night."

"Night," he echoed, and though she was no longer looking at him, she could tell he was turning onto his side again by the way the cot creaked.

Squeezing her eyes shut, she tried to find a way to relax, but she was too keenly aware of every sound in the quiet room, the fact that Elliot was so close making it impossible for her heart to do anything but pound like a drum. She heard the lightweight blanket he'd covered up with rustle once, then again a few seconds later. His breathing sounded a bit deeper than it'd been when they were talking, and she swore she could feel the heat and tension blasting off his long body, despite the distance between them. She pressed her thighs tightly together, trying to ease the ache that was building there, and realized that her movements had caused that same kind of rustling in the sheets. And that...that was bad, because her imagination immediately took off, heading straight down Dirty Lane and taking a quick right onto Do Me Avenue.

Oh, God, just...just stay calm, she whispered in her head, but it was already too late. Before she could find the strength or common sense to stop herself, she turned onto her side and said his name again. "Elliot?"

"Yeah?" he grunted almost at once, making it clear that he'd still been as wide-awake as she was.

With a hard swallow, she cleared the husky note of lust from her throat. And then the question burning through her mind tumbled from her lips in a hoarse, breathless rush: "Are you touching yourself?"

He groaned as he rolled onto his back, then muttered one low, gritty word: *"Fuck."*

"It's okay," she whispered, wondering where in God's name she'd found the courage to actually ask *that* question out loud. But now that the damage was done, she found herself needing to follow through with it. "I mean…if you are, p-please don't be embarrassed."

Voice tight, he said, "I'm not."

Disappointment spread heavily through her veins. "Oh…okay."

There was just enough light for her to see that he'd turned his head toward her, his dark gaze burning with a molten, blistering gleam that almost didn't seem human, it was *that* intense. "I mean that I'm not embarrassed."

"Oh," she murmured, while inside she was thinking *Ohmygod…ohmygod…ohmygod!* "So, then, you…um, you *were* touching yourself?"

He cursed under his breath again, stabbing his fingers back through his hair, and his sudden response was so harsh it made her jump. "Whether I was or I wasn't isn't important. What do you want, Skye?"

"Oh…um, n-nothing," she stammered, so mortified she could have died. "Sorry for bothering you. Night!"

"Don't be sorry," he bit out, and it was impossible to tell if he was pissed…or just really, *really* turned on. Then his head went back, his nostrils flaring as he pulled in a slow, deep breath, like he was scenting the air, a raw sound immediately rumbling up from his chest. "And don't *lie*."

"I'm not," she lied again, wondering why she hadn't just kept her freaking mouth shut. What in the hell was wrong with her? She quickly twisted onto her back, choking off a husky moan as her tight, cotton-covered nipples dragged against the sheet. Her sex felt so hot and wet and painfully sensitive she couldn't help but rub her thighs together to try to ease the ache there.

For one heavy, weighted moment, there was nothing but a sharp, piercing silence that made her feel like she couldn't draw any air into her lungs. And then a deep, serrated groan slipped past his lips, and her eyes shot wide as she turned her head just in time to see him suddenly sit up, swing his long legs over the side of the cot and move to his feet.

Is he leaving? she thought wildly, her eyes stinging with a sudden wash of tears. But instead of heading for the door, he started walking right toward her, his only clothing a tight black pair of cotton boxers that did nothing to hide the fact he was hard as hell. Not to mention... uh, massive. And so damn sexy she couldn't have looked away to save her life. Which was why she was still lying there on her back, staring up at him with wide, lust-glazed eyes, when he reached the side of the bed.

His powerful biceps bunched beneath his tight skin as he fisted and released his hands at his sides, his jaw working for a moment, before he spoke in a rough, almost guttural rasp. "Yeah, I was touching myself. And, yeah, you were in my head while I was doing it. I'm sorry if that was way out of line, but being this close to you is making me so fucking hard. I jerked off in the shower like I was gonna die if I didn't relieve some of the pressure, but it didn't work, because here I am, *still* so goddamn ramped up it's all I can do to keep myself from begging you to let me touch you."

"Elliot." She couldn't get out anything more than his name, her own hands grabbing fistfuls of the bedding as she desperately tried to anchor herself in this crazy, raging storm of lust that surrounded her, but it wasn't

any use. She was lost in it, her body so hungry for him she felt like she'd been starving for this moment her entire life.

"Hell, Skye. I know you've had the most screwed-up night in the history of nights," he growled, his chest lifting with another hard, shuddering breath. "And I know that we've only just met. But I can't stop thinking about you lying there, under those covers, and wondering what you'd do if I got under there with you."

"I want you to," she gasped, unable to hold the confession inside. But then some ingrained sense of self-preservation immediately had her saying, "Only…girls like me shouldn't reach."

She couldn't see his expression all that clearly, since the light from the hallway was directly behind him, but she could almost *feel* his frown, and so she rushed to explain. "I reached once. And it…it didn't go well."

He shocked her by sitting down on the side of the bed, his weight making the mattress dip so that she rolled toward him. Leaning over her, he braced his upper body by placing one of those big hands beside her head on the pillow, while the fingers of his other hand curled under her chin. "Are you talking about that damn cop?" he asked, bringing her face up to his.

"Um, yes."

He slowly shook his head from side to side. "You didn't reach for something good, Skye. All you did with that jackass was reach down into the gutter, and that's not where you belong."

She blinked up at him as she caught her lower lip in her teeth, feeling a little in awe, and a whole lot in…lust. "I…I get what you're saying, but it didn't seem that way at the time. It seemed like a fairy tale. He was the boy all the girls wanted." *And you're even better. You're so freaking amazing, I can't even think straight around you.*

"If all the girls wanted him," he drawled with a wry grin, "then all the girls were stupid. Because that guy is a complete douche."

Her lips twitched, and she found herself shaking with a soft, warm rush of laughter. "You have an answer for everything, don't you?"

"Not everything," he murmured, staring at her mouth for a heated, provocative moment, before looking her right in the eye. "Just you."

With that husky, yet tender admission giving her the burst of courage she needed to see this through, Skye kicked at the covers that lay between them, until they were bunched up down by her feet. He drew back just far enough that he could run that smoldering, heavy-lidded gaze over her body, lingering on every swell and curve, and for the first time in her life, she actually felt beautiful. Like she was worthy of desire and want and need, and *Oh, God*, it was…it was freaking incredible.

Then he brought that hooded, glittering gaze back to hers, and asked her the same exact question he'd asked her only moments before, each word punctuated by a harsh breath. "What. Do. You. Want. Skye?"

Sweet, blissful emotion washed over her at the guttural sound of his voice, almost as if his hunger were as brutal and demanding as hers. And yet, she knew he'd get up and leave if she wanted him to, and it was that surprising feeling of safety that gave her the courage to finally say, "I want you beside me. On top of me. I want to feel you everywhere, Elliot. I don't want to feel anything *but* you."

His gorgeous face went hard with need, but his reply was soft. "You sure, sweetheart?"

"Yes." And then, with a flash of concern knitting her brow, she said, "It's just that… I mean, you don't have a girlfriend, do you?"

Shaking his head, he told her, "No. There's no one I'm seeing. Not even casually. You?"

"No. No one." No longer able to hold back, she reached up and placed her greedy hands against his wide shoulders, his firm skin deliciously hot beneath her palms, like he was burning with fever. Nearly dazed with excitement, she dug her fingers into the dense muscle there, keeping her gaze locked tight with his as she added, "I wouldn't… I wouldn't be here if there was someone else. I would have gone to him."

"But you're here with *me*," he scraped out, sounding almost like he couldn't believe it was true.

"Yes," she whispered, and she could have sworn the possessive gleam in his dark eyes was saying *I'm keeping you. You're mine.* And then he was there, on the bed with her, her legs instinctively parting to make room for him as he came down over her, so tall and broad that he nearly blocked out the light streaming in from the hallway.

His face tightened as his lean hips settled against hers, his cotton-covered cock a thick, breathtaking ridge against the sensitive seam of her sex, her panties and shorts already damp with arousal. "God, I hope you don't regret this," he growled, those dark eyes wild with need as he rolled his hips, surging against her.

"I wouldn't. I *couldn't*," she gasped, the heavy, liquid ache inside her making her want all of him, everything, *now*. Lifting her hands, she threaded them through the warm, thick strands of his hair, and hoped he could see the truth of what she was about to tell him shining in her wide eyes as she stared up at him. "I know… I know this sounds bizarre. I mean, I *just* met you. But it doesn't feel like we just met. It feels like we've shoved months' worth of getting to know each other into one night. That we've compressed weeks into hours." She searched his gleaming gaze, and wet her trembling lips with her tongue. "Does that…does that make any sense?"

"It makes sense," Elliot rasped, her words causing a scorching wave of heat to crawl up his chest, searing beneath his skin. Unable to stop himself, he curled an unsteady hand around the back of her neck, holding her still for him as he lowered his head and touched his greedy mouth to hers in the barest whisper of a kiss, his heart hammering so hard he was surprised it didn't burst from his chest. She was fucking addictive, and he was already undone by the pillow-like softness of her lips, their cushiony give and silken texture making him *throb* with raw, visceral hunger.

Unable to wait, he sank his tongue between those velvety lips, stroking the tender insides of her mouth, and her warm, exquisite taste drove him straight into desperation. Quiet, guttural sounds vibrated deep in his throat, his tongue thrusting and licking, claiming her mouth like it was what he'd been born for. For *this*, right here. This one perfect, primal, mind-shattering moment.

And all the while, she was kissing him back just as hungrily, her soft hands clutching at the flexing muscles in his back like she wanted to bring him closer, until there were no frustrating layers of cloth between them and he was pressed against the very heart of her.

"You're so fucking sweet," he groaned against her lips, unable to believe this was happening. "So goddamn delicious."

"You're hot," she panted, rubbing her hands down his back, to the top of his ass, and then back up again. "Feels so incredible."

Every muscle in his body coiled with craving; his cock painfully hard and blood-thick inside the confines of his boxers, swollen to the point that the veins bulged against his tight skin. The pressure was so intense he felt he might burst, and every time he stroked himself against the drenched seam of her shorts, he had to fight back the violent need to rip the cotton from her body and drive himself inside her, the mouthwatering scent of her desire making him raw with lust and the animal-need to stake his claim.

He could feel his wolf prowling beneath his surface, driven by dark, primitive hunger, its instinctive need to protect its mate the only thing that kept him from retreating in fear. He knew the beast wouldn't hurt her. Bite the hell out of her, yeah. But it wanted to feel her coming so hard she was screaming when he did it—in pleasure, not pain.

With his pulse roaring in his ears, Elliot tore his mouth from hers, his thoughts fracturing as he trailed his lips down her chin, and over the tender, vulnerable arch of her throat, her head flung back in a breathtaking act of surrender. Feeling the scalding pressure of his fangs in his gums, he kept his heavy-lidded gaze trained on her with piercing focus, studying her every reaction so that he would know what she liked—what made her *burn*—while his hips kept up a steady, stroking rhythm between her legs. He trailed his open mouth lower, licking and nipping his way over the top of her chest, until he reached the quivering rise of her full, heavy breasts. Bracing himself on one arm, he reached down for the hem of her shirt, only a second away from ripping it off and exposing her bare skin, when he suddenly froze with a chilling wave of panic.

"Shit, this is wrong, isn't it?" he grated, his lungs heaving as she dipped her chin and locked that beautiful, hazy gaze with his. "Touching you right now puts me in serious dickhead territory."

"Bullshit," she argued, fisting her hands in his hair and pulling his mouth back to hers. "I'm a grown woman, not a child. I know what I want, Elliot."

"Goddamnit," he breathed roughly against her lips, sounding as if he'd been running for miles and miles. "I *can't* resist you."

And it was true. Jesus, it was crazy, what this one little perfect human could do to him.

"Take them off," she panted, reaching down and tugging on the waistband of his boxers, and he had to bite back a wry, laughing curse. The fearless, addictive girl had no idea just how badly she was tempting him.

Reaching back, Elliot caught her slender wrist, pulling it up and pressing it into her pillow. Then he did the same with her other wrist, knowing the only way to keep his sanity was to keep her eager little hands *off* his body. "The boxers need to stay on tonight," he groaned, pressing his forehead against hers as he rocked against her. "I can't... My control isn't... *Christ, Skye.* You fucking wreck me."

"Good," she moaned, bending her knees so that she could push up against him, the surge of her hips nearly making his eyes roll back in his head. "I want you wrecked. I want you to give me *everything*."

He lifted his head, staring down at her like she was some kind of miracle, his heart turning over when she gave him one of her sweet, breathtaking smiles. "Come for me," he heard himself say, the husky words thick with emotion. "I want to feel you fall apart for me. I want to watch it happen."

"I want to watch you, too." Her luminous eyes were heavy with desire. "Please."

He started riding her harder, rubbing his rigid shaft over that sensitive bundle of nerves where she needed the most pressure. It was raw and achingly sweet, being this close to her—but he wanted to do so much more. Craved it, even though he knew he'd already tested the bounds of his control for one night. And this wasn't about doing what *he* wanted. This was about proving to his conscience, as well as to her, that he could rein himself in when he needed to. Because the day would most definitely come when she would *need* that proof.

"When you look at me like that," she told him, licking her lush, kiss-swollen lips, "it makes me feel like you're already inside me."

He growled deep in his throat, so damn close to losing it, because he could *see* it in her eyes, the fact that if he wanted her, he could have her. Could press himself against her silky entrance and make her *his*. Claim her with his body, if not with his fangs, the way his instinct was driving him to.

But he couldn't do it. Not...not like this, when there were still so many secrets and lies between them. Because if he did, she was going to feel the sharp sting of betrayal when she learned at least some of those truths.

And she *would* learn them. Once he could convince her to come back to the Alley with him, and live with him there, she would have to be told the truth about what he was. That he was so much more than just a man. That living inside him was a creature capable of extreme violence, but also unwavering loyalty. An animal that would fight to protect her with its dying breath.

That would worship her for all its days, if only she would let it.

Want her. Need her. Now! his wolf roared, and Elliot shook his head in sympathy for the poor devil, understanding *exactly* how he felt.

"Oh… Oh, God!" she suddenly cried, her chest and throat flushing with a rosy burst of color, and he knew she was coming. Lowering his head, he covered her trembling mouth with his, his tongue thrusting past her parted lips, eating at the delicious sounds that she made, unable to get enough. They were like drops of honey on his tongue, warm and succulent, making him ravenous. And in that moment, it was almost impossible to ignore that darker spill of hunger spreading through him—the one that was biting and sharp, demanding he sink his fangs into her tight flesh and lock on to her—but he somehow managed to hold himself in check.

Clawing on to his control with every ounce of strength he possessed, determined not to screw this up, Elliot thought only of Skye. Of how much he wanted to please her. To be good for her. Not to mention how badly he wanted to press his open mouth against that drenched, softly cushioned mound he was thrusting against and fuck her with his tongue, licking her until she shuddered and begged and screamed for him.

And then he was following her over, his release slamming into him with a violent, jolting force that made him shout, the guttural sound echoing through the room. Their lips stayed in contact the entire time, her hot, tender mouth driving him mad, as the pleasure kept rolling through him in wet, blistering waves.

They stayed like that for several long minutes, sweaty and breathless, and it took everything Elliot had in him to finally find the strength to pull away from her. He pressed one more soft, grateful, my-head-is-still-spinning kiss against her lips, then moved to his feet. Feeling her curious gaze on him, he grabbed a clean pair of boxers from his bag and stumbled toward the bathroom, his legs like goddamn jelly.

"Be right back," he rasped over his shoulder, before closing the door, just needing a moment to get himself together. He turned toward the sink and washed up, then splashed some cold water on his face, trying to get his useless brain to kick into gear. But he felt... *Christ*, he felt like he'd just been caught in the eye of a storm. One that had completely changed him. Slipped into his DNA and shifted everything around, creating something... new. Something that was...unknown.

He felt like a man who had just been given a gift of blinding sunshine after years of endless night, and his eyes were still adjusting to the light. It was sappy as hell, but what man wouldn't be spouting off like this after getting the chance to lose himself with Skye?

When he came out of the bathroom, she was lying on her side, facing him, with that juicy lower lip caught in her teeth. Her big eyes were watching him with a cautious optimism, as if she hoped he would come back to her, while a tiny part worried he might brush her off. He forced a crooked smile onto his lips and went to her, climbing back onto the bed and reaching for her, pulling her close.

She fit so perfectly against him, he couldn't help but give her a possessive squeeze, his damn heart tumbling over when she pressed a soft kiss to the middle of his chest. And then she completely blindsided him as she said, "You're so different, Elliot."

He wanted to curse, knowing it would have been impossible for her to miss the way he stiffened beside her, his long body going hard with tension. And then he had to make it worse by choking out a gritty, defensive-sounding "What do you mean?"

"Just that you're not like other guys."

God, if she only knew.

Guilt sat heavily in his gut, making him feel like shit. "Skye, I…"

"No, don't say anything," she murmured, wrapping her arm around him as she snuggled closer. "Just…just hold me, and let's sleep."

Elliot knew a reprieve when he heard one, and he was desperate enough to grab it, holding on to it—*to Skye*—with everything that he had. And then…then a miracle happened. For the first time in years, he didn't toss and turn, jerking awake from nightmares that were more horrific fragments of actual memory than anything conjured by his imagination.

Instead, he slept like the dead.

Or a man who had finally found exactly what he needed.

Chapter 8

There was definitely something to be said for sleeping in the arms of a gorgeous, rugged, warm-skinned male who held you like you were the best thing he'd ever found. Especially when that male was Elliot Connors. With everything going on in her life, Skye had expected to have a restless, frustrating night, when in actuality her sleep had been deep and peaceful.

She'd literally loved every single perfect moment of it—of being in Elliot's arms—and yet, the only thing that saved her from a world of embarrassment over how forward she'd been was the fact that when she opened her eyes that morning, she was alone.

It probably made her sound like a wimp, but she honestly didn't know what she would have done if she'd had to face him first thing. As she sat up in the middle of the bed, she couldn't even see her robe—and it was going to be a cold day in hell before she pranced around in front of the guy wearing nothing more than a tank top and tiny shorts. Elliot didn't have an ounce of fat on his ripped, mouthwatering body, and despite how much he'd seemed to enjoy touching her, she didn't see how she could ever feel confident about her shape in front of him.

It kind of made her pissed at herself for feeling that way, but damn it, she didn't know how to change it.

Climbing out of bed, she spotted her robe folded up neatly on top of the dresser, a small smile on her lips as she grabbed her backpack and headed into the bathroom. She took a long shower, taking the time to wash her hair and shave her legs, grateful for the scalding temperature of the water as it ran over her head. Then she brushed her teeth, dressed in a pair of jeans, black tank, and her favorite gray sweater that was so slouchy it hung off one shoulder. She couldn't find a blow dryer in the bathroom, so she towel-dried her hair and then scrunched her fingers through it, knowing it would dry in loose waves. When she was younger, she'd hated her wavy hair as much as she'd hated the curves that had started to develop on her long before the other girls she went to school with. But as an adult, she appreciated how easy it made her hair to maintain and style.

Padding down the hallway on her bare feet, she didn't think it was possible that Elliot could have heard her coming. But he was leaning back against the kitchen counter when she stepped around the corner, a sexy, almost boyish grin kicking up the side of his mouth as he held a steaming cup of coffee in his hands, looking for all the world like he'd been expecting her.

"Good morning, sleepyhead," he said in a deep voice

that was a bit rougher around the edges than it'd been the day before.

"Sorry I slept so late," she managed to scrape out, completely dazzled by him in his jeans, boots and tight black T-shirt, as he stood in a stream of wintry sunshine pouring in through the kitchen window. Holy mother of God, but he looked good in the morning. She loved the dark scruff on his cheeks and the way his thick hair was still all tousled. Loved the way his eyes crinkled at the corners when he grinned at her.

"Don't be," he murmured, after taking a sip of his coffee. "You needed it."

She thought she might have mumbled something in response, but wasn't sure, too caught up in staring at his mouth. Every scorching, erotic detail from the night before was playing through her head, and even as the telling heat started in her chest, rising steadily higher, she couldn't look away. The guy kissed like it was his most favorite thing in the world. Like he could live off it, each brush of his lips and swipe of his tongue like a sweet that'd been left to melt in the tender recesses of her mouth. She'd never been kissed like that in her entire life, the experience so intense it'd probably destroyed a few of her brain cells. So deep and drugging and scalding with pleasure, she couldn't help but crave more.

And that was before she even thought about the wicked, wonderful things he'd done to her body. The way he'd moved over her…against her…his deep voice rough and low as he'd told her how sweet she tasted. How *delicious*.

"You're such a blusher," he said with a teasing, husky rumble of laughter that pulled her back to the moment, his dark eyes gleaming beneath his thick lashes. Pushing off from the counter, he caught her around the waist and pulled her closer to him, before leaning down and placing a gentle kiss against her...forehead.

Uh... What the what? My forehead?

Skye tried not to frown as he stepped back and asked her if she wanted coffee or tea. She murmured something about loving a cup of coffee, sick with disappointment. *Oh, God.* Had...had she only *imagined* that he'd enjoyed what they'd done as much as she had? Had he simply been humoring her? Passing time? Trying not to hurt her feelings?

She started to grimace as he turned to the coffeemaker, ready to run and hide under the covers, when he angled his head to the side, sliding her a quick glance from the corner of his eye, and she could have sworn he looked like he wanted a hell of a lot more than that innocent touch of his lips to her forehead. He looked like he wanted to bend her back over his arm and kiss her until she was melting for him. The surge of relief that rushed through her was so sharp she had to reach out and brace a hand against the counter, trying to force a neutral expression onto her face as he turned back to her.

Handing her the cup of coffee he'd just poured, he murmured, "I got another fire started for you."

She smiled a little at him from behind her mug, her voice a bit thick as she said, "Thanks."

With a sigh, he leaned back against the counter again, a wry smile tugging at his lips. "I hate that you're feeling weird about what happened."

"I'm not," she said in a rush, squeezing her hands around the warm mug as she forced herself to hold his gaze. "I just don't want you to have any regrets."

His brows shot up. "Are you kidding me?"

She exhaled a shaky breath. "No."

"Skye, the only thing I could regret is if you didn't let me touch you again." He set his mug down and closed the distance between them, until she had to tilt her head back to see his handsome face. Reaching up, he pushed her hair back from her brow, and pressed another one of those sweet kisses to her forehead. But this time, instead of stopping there, he made his way lower, kissing the upper curve of her cheek, then the corner of her mouth. "I'm just trying to be good this morning. I don't want to scare you off."

She blinked up at him as he took a step back from her, straightening to his full height, and all she could get out was a dazed-sounding *"Oh."*

"Yeah," he breathed, then shook his head a little, an almost shy laugh slipping past his lips. "So, uh, let's get some breakfast."

They ate thick slices of toast and honey at the breakfast bar, chatting about little things, like their favorite movies and bands, and she was surprised by how easy it was just to be with him. When they'd finished the dishes, he said he needed to use the laptop in the office to send a few emails, one of which would be to Monroe, asking the guy to sort things out at the diner for her. Rolling her eyes at herself after she gave him a dorky little wave goodbye, Skye settled into a corner of one of the sofas, took her phone from her pocket and sent another short message to Viv that basically said the same thing as the one she'd sent the night before.

It was driving her mad, not knowing what her best friend was doing. Was she okay? Was she still running? Had she found a safe place to stay? Had she seen any sign of the assholes who were likely chasing her? And if they'd found her, had she been hurt?

The questions just kept looping through her head, over and over, until she was ready to slip on her sneakers, go out into the woods and take it out on one of the innocent, unsuspecting trees with the toe of her shoe. But that wouldn't solve any of her problems, and Elliot would probably end up thinking she was crazy. Or a flagrant tree abuser, which didn't seem any better.

Less than a half hour later, he came and joined her on the sofa. He sat on the other end, leaving plenty of space between them, and she could tell he was doing his best to keep her comfortable around him. She was trying to figure out how to tell him that it wasn't necessary, that he didn't *have* to keep his distance, without sounding like she was dying to jump his bones, when a text came through on his phone. He frowned as he read the message, telling her it was from Max.

"What's it say?" she asked, fighting the urge to grab the phone out of his hands so she could read the message for herself.

"He says that Vivian's phone has been broken, but that she's with him and she's okay."

"Ohmygod! That's awesome!"

Dark eyes still focused on the illuminated screen, his brows started to pull together as he went on. "But he's going silent for a few days. Says that he'll explain later, but for us not to worry. That he'll contact us again as soon as he can, and for us to watch our backs. That the assholes coming after you and Viv are everywhere."

"I...uh... Wait. I don't understand."

He typed something into the phone, then sighed as he shoved it back in his pocket. "They're going off the grid," he explained in a low voice, turning his head toward her, his shadowed gaze impossible to read.

"Yeah, I get that." She licked her lower lip, trying to get her thoughts straight. "But…why?"

"I honestly don't know," he replied, and she could tell there was a bit of frustration at the edges of his calm tone. "But I trust Max to do right by her, Skye. I swear I wouldn't let this go if I thought she wasn't in good hands with him. He won't let her get hurt."

She searched his brown eyes for several long, weighted moments, then leaned back against the sofa again. "Okay," she said softly, hoping he realized just how much trust she was putting in him. How desperately she needed him not to let her down.

He held her worried gaze for a few more moments, and it seemed there was a roomful of unspoken messages flying between them. Then he pulled in a deep breath, and as he slowly let it out, he nodded his head toward the TV that was mounted on the wall. "You, uh, want to watch a movie or something?"

"Sure, but…if there's something you need to be doing, I'll be fine. You don't need to babysit me."

Some of the tension around his eyes eased, and his wide mouth curved with one of those crooked grins that made her go all ridiculously gooey and warm. "Babysitting would imply some weird dynamic here, and I'm only a few years older than you."

Gripping one of the throw cushions to her chest, she shrugged her shoulders. "I just feel bad. You're going to be bored out of your mind up here in no time."

"Not likely," he said, stretching his powerful arms over his head, before laying them across the back of the sofa and motioning her closer. "It's cold outside, we have a roaring fire going and I get to relax back on this comfy couch and hold a beautiful girl in my arms while watching TV." With a wicked gleam in his dark eyes, he asked her, "What could be better than that?"

She gave a soft laugh to cover her nerves, but didn't shy away from him. Instead, she grabbed the remote off the low coffee table and settled against Elliot's side. With her legs drawn up on the sofa, and his booted feet propped up on the table, she turned the TV on, and ended up having fun, even if it did take a while to relax against him. She was keenly aware of his every breath, his warm scent and the way his incredible body felt pressed against hers, loving the way he'd casually lean over every now and then and press his nose into her hair, breathing her in. They watched the first Avengers movie, which was one of her favorites, and he teased her for pulling for Loki instead of the good guys.

"He's not bad. He's just misunderstood," she explained with a playful smirk, and she could have sworn Elliot spent the next ten minutes watching her mouth more than the TV screen, which had her heart pounding and her pulse rushing in her ears.

By the time the movie ended, she was restless and breathy, and she surged to her feet, her words all but tumbling over themselves as she headed toward the kitchen. "I'll just, um, make us some lunch."

Following after her, he said, "I was gonna do that."

"Let me, please?" she asked, looking over at him as he came up beside her. "I need something to do."

He took a moment to study her flushed face, then gave her a look that was almost heartbreakingly tender. "All right," he murmured, taking a seat on one of the stools at the breakfast bar. "But only if you let me sit here and keep you company."

She gave a quiet laugh, wondering for a moment how this could possibly be her normally boring, scraping-just-to-get-by-every-day life. Then she shook off her disbelief, and started looking through the cupboards for some chips and fresh bread.

"So," he said, watching her from his perch on the stool, his muscular arms crossed and braced on the tiled top of the bar. "Were you named after, you know, the sunny blue sky?"

Pulling what she needed for sandwiches out of the fridge, she snorted under her breath. "If only."

He angled his head a bit to the side as he studied her. "So then your mother isn't the nature-loving type?"

"She isn't anything," she murmured, pulling down two plates. "She's dead."

She saw him wince from the corner of her eye. "Oh, shit. I didn't know, Skye. I'm sorry."

"Don't be. It's actually for the best, as awful as that sounds."

He mulled that telling statement over while she finished up the sandwiches, and his voice was a bit rougher when he asked, "And your dad?"

"What is this, twenty questions?" She laughed a little to cover her nerves, and set his plate down in front of him.

"It could be." The corner of his mouth twitched with a shadow of a grin. "I'm not ashamed to say that I'm curious as hell about you."

Coming around the breakfast bar with her own plate, she climbed up onto the stool beside his. "Well, there's really not much to know."

"Hmm," he murmured, popping a chip in his mouth. "I'll get it out of you eventually."

She arched one of her brows at him. "You're welcome to try."

Shoulders shaking with a deep, husky laugh, he said, "Don't tempt me. I'm sitting here trying to be good."

"Instead of…?"

"Being bad." His laughter had trailed off, and she had the feeling that he purposefully wasn't looking at her as he quietly added, "Very, very bad."

Heart hammering in her chest, she took a deep breath, trying to keep her hands from shaking as she picked up her sandwich, those words playing on continual repeat in her head. From the edge of her vision, she watched as he took a bite of his own sandwich, his low moan of appreciation so sexy she could have moaned right along with him.

"God, Skye, this tastes amazing."

"Um, thanks," she murmured, "but it's just a sandwich."

She could feel the heat of his gaze against her profile as he said, "You're not comfortable taking compliments, are you?"

"Is anyone?" she asked, finally taking her first bite.

Swallowing another bite, he said, "I don't know, and I don't really care. You're the only one that interests me." He finished off the first half of his sandwich, and reached for the second one as he went on. "I'm not trying to freak you out. But I'm not gonna sit here and lie to you. I think you're incredible, both inside and out."

She turned her head and gave him a baffled look. "I'm just a waitress, Elliot. I don't even have a college degree."

"Baby, neither do I," he drawled, popping another chip in his mouth.

"At least you have an important career," she muttered, glancing away.

He went on like he hadn't even heard her. "Who gives a crap about a degree?" he asked, reaching over and curling his warm fingers under her chin so that he could get her to look at him. "It wouldn't make you any more incredible than you are now. And what the hell is wrong with being a waitress? You kick ass at it, and make killer tips from people I saw smile because of you, when I doubt they have much in life to smile about. That's something that's honest and real and worthy, Skye." He lowered his hand, but kept his gaze locked hard on hers as he added, "So don't you dare be ashamed of it. You should own that shit and be proud of it."

She shook her head a little as she pulled her lower lip through her teeth. "Seriously, Elliot. You are so not a normal guy."

Though the grin he flashed her was cocky, there seemed to be a shadow in his brown eyes that made her wonder what his own secrets were like…and if they were anywhere near as dark as her own. As they finished eating, another one of those heavy silences settled between them, and she couldn't help but feel awkward…restless. Moving to her feet, she grabbed his empty plate, along with hers, racking her brain for what they could do for the rest of the afternoon as she carried their dirty dishes to the sink. Without a doubt, getting him naked would have been right up at the top of her list, but he seemed to be dead set on keeping things platonic between them today. It was more than a little disappointing.

And then, as if he'd heard the explicit nature of her

thoughts, Skye suddenly felt him come up behind her, his big hands settling against the counter on either side of her as he leaned down and put his mouth close to her ear. "Tell me to walk away," he said huskily, "and I will, Skye. I will *always* respect what you want. But I'm really hoping that you won't."

She closed her eyes, trembling with excitement and breathless anticipation. "What *are* you h-hoping for?"

"This," he growled, pressing his warm lips to the side of her neck, just beneath her ear. "I've been trying to give you time, but it's fucking killing me. I just want the chance to touch you. Kiss you. Make you come for me again."

She moaned a low, shaky sound of surrender, and reached back, pushing her hand into his thick hair and holding him to her. She felt the press of his teeth against her sensitive skin…across the rush of her pulse, and then the carnal stroke of his tongue, slow and deliberate. "Wow," she gasped, her breath catching as he pressed his hands to her belly, pulling her back against his strong, heavily aroused body. "And to think I was gonna see if we could just find a b-board game to play."

His gruff, deliciously sexy bark of laughter gusted against her ear, and her lips curled with a satisfied smile. It might not be a big deal to most women, but Skye freaking loved that she could make him sound like that.

"You're smiling, aren't you?" he asked.

Before she could answer, he lifted his hand to her mouth, his rough fingertips stroking over her top lip, and then the bottom one. It was such an instinctively sensual act, and yet, there was a touch of innocence to it, the provocative combination making her tremble with emotion.

"Hurry, *please*," she panted, too desperate to worry

about the fact that she was *begging* him. With his mouth
open and warm against the side of her throat, he pressed
his hands to her sweater-covered ribs, then slid them up,
cupping her swollen breasts, a cry breaking from her
throat when he rubbed his thumbs over her tight nipples.
His hands were so big, and felt so good, it was a little
scary, in that *Ohmygod I only just met this guy, but I
feel like I was made for him...or he was made for me...
or maybe we were just made for each other* kind of way.
And *that* was the kind of craziness, if he ever found out
about it, that would probably send him running. Because
while she didn't know all that much about how guys
thought, she *did* know that they ran from clingy women
like they were escaping from a flesh-eating virus.

With one hand still molding and squeezing her breast,
he reached down with the other and unsnapped her jeans.
"Damn it, I *have* to touch you," he growled, watching
over her shoulder as he lowered the zipper, then slipped
his hand in under the elastic waistband of her favorite pink panties. "Ah, Christ. You're so wet, Skye." He
cupped her with his entire palm, then swept the tips of
two fingers between her slick, swollen folds, grazing her
clit. "I just want to keep touching you forever. Learning
you. Memorizing you."

As her opened jeans slid down her hips a bit, she
swallowed the knot of lust in her throat, searching for
her voice—but all that would come out was a breathy,
needy moan.

"Take your sweater off for me," he said in a low, raw
slide of words, slipping the tip of one finger inside the
tight clasp of her body and gently exploring.

Though her hands were shaking, she managed to re-
move her sweater and tank in one go, and simply let

them fall to the floor. He immediately pressed his open mouth to her bare shoulder, and her head flopped back, resting against his chest, the heat and desire building beneath her skin turning her bones to sun-warmed wax.

"You feel so fucking good," he groaned, running the damp heat of his mouth along her jaw, as he pulled down the cup of her bra and covered her naked breast with his big, hot hand. His other hand pressed deeper between her thighs, pushing that wicked finger farther inside her, where she was melting and slick, so slippery she could hear the wet sounds of his touch. "Can I give you another one?"

"Y-yeah," Skye replied shakily, gasping when he suddenly pulled his hand from between her legs and quickly turned her around. His dark eyes smoldered as he lifted his hand and rubbed the damp pads of his fingers across her lips, dipping inside to stroke her tongue. Then that big hand was back between her legs, two long fingers pushing up inside her with a hard thrust that had her making a sharp, thick sound of surprise. He grabbed her behind the neck, holding her still for the breathtaking storm of his kiss, the onslaught so deep and ravaging she was dizzy with sensation. She went under, lost, already hopelessly addicted to the way he touched her and kissed her. To the way his tongue sank into her mouth and claimed possession. Of her breath. Her taste. Her dreams. And every bit of desire she'd ever known. It was expanding like a never-ending universe, dark and endless with pulsing, searing points of light that burned behind her closed eyelids.

"You didn't touch me like this last n-night," she stammered, when she finally had to break the kiss for a desperate gulp of air.

With one hand still buried between her legs and the other holding her by the back of her neck, he kept his body curved over hers, his gorgeous face so close their noses were touching. His heavy gaze was burning and wild beneath thick, curling lashes, his breaths warm and rough and hard against her wet mouth, and as he did this mind-shattering thing with his thumb, he softly told her, "That's because I was still trying to be good."

Skye touched her tongue to her upper lip, completely mesmerized by the way he looked right then, as if it were taking every ounce of his strength to hold himself together. "Maybe...maybe I like you a little bad."

His dark eyes gleamed with a feral flash of surprise, a low growl rumbling on his lips as he quickly took her mouth again, and she could feel the powerful muscles in his arm flexing as he started pumping his fingers into her. She was a mess, her remaining clothes all twisted around her body, but it was the most perfect, erotic moment of her entire life. She cried out, unable to keep her hips from surging against him, her tongue rubbing against his with a desperate kind of hunger she'd never even realized she could feel. Had never even known she was capable of. But she was, and in the midst of that maddening craving, she was completely unraveling under his touch, like he'd found the string to the very source of her pleasure. The one that could simply take her apart, loop by loop, and damn it, she didn't want to unwind alone. She wanted him to fall apart *with her*, and as she panted against his open mouth, she reached between them, pressing her hand over the rigid shape of him inside his jeans.

"Fuck," he grunted, the guttural word punching from his lips as he pushed himself against her palm,

and she used both hands to quickly undo the top button on his jeans, her fingers shaking as she worked the zipper down. Then she slipped her hand under the waistband of his tight black boxers, her heart thundering so hard it hurt as she curled her fingers around as much of that hot, diamond-hard part of him as she could. Looking down, she couldn't help but lick her lips, stunned by how beautiful he was. He made the sexiest sound she'd ever heard in the back of his throat as she tightened her grip, his dark skin surprisingly soft to the touch.

She'd never been a fan of giving head, or hungered for the feel of a guy's cock in her mouth, but Elliot...he was different. She swiped her tongue over her lower lip again, the broad tip of his shaft so ripe and succulent looking she couldn't help but *want* to suck on him. Savor him.

Another thick, guttural sound tore from his chest, and he pulled his hand from between her legs as he suddenly grabbed her under her ass and lifted her up, setting her on the edge of the counter. With his hands holding tight to her hips and his heavy erection still trapped in her grip, he buried his face against the side of her throat, licking her skin like an animal tasting something sweet. And, um, yeah...she was definitely thinking about what that wicked tongue would feel like in *other* places on her body.

As if he'd read her mind, he stroked his rough palms over her thighs, pushing them as wide as he could with her jeans still on, and pressed closer as he put his mouth right against her ear. "I want to shove my face between your legs so bad," he growled, catching her earlobe between his teeth, then sucking it sweetly to ease the sting. "I want to put my tongue on that wet, pink part of you, and make you come so hard you scream. My name. Over and over."

She opened her mouth, ready to tell him she wanted the exact same thing, while she put her tongue on him too, when something from outside made her freeze.

"Elliot, what the hell was that?" she whispered, almost positive she'd heard what sounded like a gun firing.

"Oh, shit," he bit out, leaving her to slide down off the counter as he stalked over to one of the windows at the front of the cabin. He took a quick glance outside, then shot her a sharp look over his shoulder. "Get in the bedroom closet and lock the door, Skye. Whatever happens, you *do not* come out of that goddamn room, understood?"

"Uh…what?" She yanked her jeans up, then scooped up her sweater and tank and quickly pulled them over her head. "What are you talking about?"

"The closet door is reinforced and the locks are titanium." The words were low and clipped, his body somehow seeming to expand with a dark, visceral rage as he came toward her doing up his fly. "Nothing's going to get through unless you open it. So you keep that fucker locked until you hear from me. Okay?"

She blinked rapidly as she stared up at him, feeling like she'd just had cold water thrown in her face. "Are you serious? I'm not going to run and hide in the closet while you face off against God knows how many assholes out there! That's insane!"

Nostrils flaring, he pointed toward the hallway and growled, "I need you to stop arguing and just go. Now! Before you get someone killed."

Skye flinched as he said those harsh words, jerking back from him like he'd slapped her, and Elliot hated not being able to reach out and yank her back into his arms.

Shoulders stiff, she turned and walked away, leaving the room, and all he could think was *Son of a bitch!* He'd promised her they'd be safe there, and now it looked like that was just one more lie to add to all the others.

Turning his attention back to the front window, he spotted a flash of blue in the woods, near the far side of the cabin. It'd looked like a nylon jacket, and he did a quick visual scan of the area, but couldn't spot anyone else with so many trees surrounding the place. He didn't doubt they were there, though.

Needing to get this over with as quickly as possible, so that he could get back to her, Elliot headed across the room and down the hallway, stopping in the office to grab a handgun from the safe. As he stepped into the laundry room at the rear of the cabin, he slid the weapon into his waistband at his lower back. He didn't know why they were shooting at each other, but someone out there had a gun, which meant he needed to be prepared. He didn't imagine that bullets would be any deadlier to the assholes coming after Skye than they were to him— but they could certainly slow one of them down if he needed it done.

Slipping out the back door, he headed into the trees, determined to hunt down every goddamn one of them. The frozen patches of snow crackled beneath his booted feet as he lifted his nose, sniffing at the forest air, taking in their scent. They weren't Lycans, but they definitely weren't human, either. They smelled like wolves crossed with something else, like coyote. Maybe even some kind of cat. It was a strange, musky scent, and almost identical to the one that he and Max had picked up at the previous crime scenes.

Taking another deep breath, he could pick out possibly seven of them in all, the way their scent was getting stronger telling him they were closing in. It was still only late afternoon, which meant the moon was nowhere near high enough for him to fully shift into his Lycan form, but he could at least make a partial change. With his fingers shedding their human shape, transforming into lethal, razor-sharp weapons and his thick fangs bursting from his gums, Elliot faced off against the assholes as they reached him. At well over six foot, he was bigger than every male in the group, save for two. Not that it mattered. He was fighting to protect *his mate*. That alone would ensure he went at these guys ten times harder than they could come at him.

In almost perfect synchronization, they underwent changes of their own, releasing sinister-looking claws that were longer than his, but shorter fangs, their eyes turning completely black, like a shark's. The tallest of the group attacked first, and Elliot exchanged a flurry of blows with the asshole, their claws scraping together with a screeching sound that echoed through the forest. Drawing from the primal rage burning through his veins, he spun on his left foot, kicking out at the male's chest with so much force it cracked bones, the bastard's body slamming into a nearby tree so hard it nearly broke the trunk in two. The guy hit the ground face-first, and stayed down, which left at least six more.

As the next two came at him, Elliot struck with his claws again and again, tearing at flesh, the spray of their blood soaking him. They got in a few lucky shots, but nothing that his accelerated healing abilities wouldn't handle by morning. Flipping one of the heavy sons of bitches over his head, he sent him soaring through the air, then swiveled to miss the strike the other one was aiming at his throat, before countering with a blow that ripped into the guy's side until he hit bone.

Despite the brutal cold and biting wind, sweat dripped down the sides of Elliot's face as he fought the next one to engage. It took him no more than fifteen seconds to get his hands around the bastard's head from behind, and he twisted until he heard the satisfying snap of the guy's spinal column, then let his body drop to the ground. Pivoting, he flexed his blood-soaked claws at his sides, ready to face off against the remaining assailants, only to find them sliding worried looks toward the sky and drawing back into the trees.

"What the hell?" he muttered. Was something out there helping him? Something they were too scared of to stay and fight? Lifting his nose, he sniffed at the air, but couldn't scent anything beyond the musky odor of the males he'd been battling against.

Catching that familiar flash of blue from the corner of his eye, he went after the asshole, intent on getting some answers while he still could. The guy was fast, even in the snow, but Elliot was determined not to lose him. Allowing his right hand to retake its human shape, he reached back and pulled the gun from his waistband, aimed for one of the thug's legs and took him down with a perfect shot.

Falling to the ground, the idiot clutched at his thigh, the crimson blood gushing from between his fingers telling Elliot that he'd hit the femoral artery. "Raze, you bastard!" the male screamed, speaking the first words Elliot had heard from one of them since the fight began. "Help me!"

But no one came to his rescue as Elliot ripped the guy's belt off, used it to bind his claw-tipped hands and grabbed him by the foot of his injured leg, pulling him closer to the cabin, since he wanted to stay as near as possible to Skye. Crouching down beside the jackass in the snow, he retracted his fangs and glanced around. The forest was eerily quiet, and he looked back down at him, saying, "Looks like your Raze buddy has better things to do."

"Fuck you!" he spat, but Elliot could see the glaze of fear coating the pitch black of the male's eyes.

"Did you follow us here?" he asked, prepared to do whatever it took to get the answers he needed.

The idiot sneered up at him. "Didn't need to. This place was already on our radar."

Well shit, he thought. Mason wasn't going to be at all happy about that.

"How long have you been watching us?"

"Uh-uh," the guy said, shaking his head. "I'm not saying anything else. If I talk, Raze'll kill me, because if he doesn't, Chiswick will kill him."

"I'll ask again," Elliot said, pressing the barrel of the gun against the bastard's other thigh and pulling the trigger. "How long have you been watching us?"

Panting and looking ill from the pain, the guy snarled, "All right, all right. A group of us were here all night, waiting for the dark-haired Runner to arrive with the other woman. But then we had to move up our schedule."

"Why?" he grunted. "Who was shooting at you? Why did the others run?"

"Because they're covering their own asses! Fuck, why do you think?"

He didn't believe the asshole, but there were more important answers he needed. "Who are you working for?"

"I've already told you enough," the guy forced through

his gritted teeth, shaking from the draining combination of blood loss and pain.

Slipping the gun back into his waistband, Elliot let his claws slip free again, then reached down, digging his sharp-tipped thumb into the fresh bullet wound. As the male screamed, Elliot said, "You're going to fucking talk, or you're going to bleed out right here. It's as simple as that."

"Jesus, you just don't get it, do you?" he panted, his black eyes wide, wild with fear. "You have no idea what he's capable of. If he eats the bitches that displease him while they're still kicking and screaming, what the hell do you think he'll do to me if I betray him?"

"Nothing worse than what I'll do to you," Elliot promised, digging his thumb in a little deeper.

"Screw you!"

"Yeah?" he asked with a harsh laugh, leaning closer, letting the idiot see just how serious he was. "That's my mate that you're trying to get your hands on. You think I won't make you wish you'd never been born if you don't tell me what the hell is going on?" he seethed in a low, deadly voice.

The guy paled even more at Elliot's admission, which wasn't surprising. In their world, if there was one thing people knew, it was that you *did not* screw with a Lycan and his life-mate. Not if you wanted to live to tell about it.

"Look, m-man," he stammered, "you probably know about as much as I do."

"Where's he keeping the other women?"

"I don't know."

"Bullshit!"

"Seriously, I don't know! I've just heard stories about what he does to them!"

Gripping the front of the guy's bloodstained jacket, Elliot yanked him closer. "If you don't know, then how are the deliveries made?"

Shaking the sweat from his eyes, he said, "Chiswick specifies a location with coordinates. Usually some kind of forest or parkland. We leave the women tied to a tree, bound and gagged. Then we get the hell out."

Christ, Elliot thought, more than ready to make this bastard pay for his part in this evil. "And how does this Chiswick contact you with the details?" he asked, dropping the guy back to the ground before checking his pockets for identification.

"Burner phones," he wheezed. "New ones are always left at the drops."

"And Chiswick?" Elliot grunted, finding nothing on the asshole. "What is he? Lycan?"

A hollow laugh burst from the guy's chest. "Who the hell knows? No one I know has ever even seen him in person."

"And what exactly are you?"

This time, the asshole gave him a strained smile. "Why don't you ask those mercenaries I've heard the Silvercrest Runners are so friendly with? They'd be able to tell you."

What the...? The mercenaries were a group of four men that Eli Drake, one of Elliot's packmates, had worked with during his banishment from the pack. For the past eight years they'd had their own cabins at the far end of Bloodrunner Alley, the picturesque glade where Elliot and the others lived. And though the Runners and the mercs were close, there were still too many secrets that the mercs kept from their neighbors—the most important ones being where the hell they came from…and what exactly they were. Because even though they could take Lycan forms similar to the rest of them, it was clear that they were something a little bit *more*.

Needing to wrap this up so that he could get back to Skye, he asked his last question. "How many of you are there?"

The jackass smirked up at him. "More than you'd believe, Runner."

Pressing his claws to the male's throat, he said, "Try me."

"Look, man. You can kill me, but it won't make any difference. It won't stop them from finding her. For every one of us you take out, Chiswick will send five more. He has our kind by the balls." A slow, taunting smile curved the asshole's mouth, his black eyes narrowed with hatred. "No matter what you do, you can't save your little bitch—you can't save any of them—because he'll *always* win."

"Not this time," he said with soft menace, before sinking his claws deep into the guy's throat, and then ripping them to the side, damn near decapitating him.

With the bastard's blood dripping from his hand, Elliot had just moved back to his feet, stretching to his full height, when a strange, choked sound came from the direction of the cabin. As his stomach jolted up into his chest with an excruciating blast of fear, he turned his head…and found a pale-faced, wide-eyed Skye standing on the back porch, staring straight at him.

Oh…fuck. Just…fuck!

"Skye," he groaned, panic nearly bringing him to his knees on the blood-covered ground.

Jesus, she wasn't meant to learn like this! He'd planned on finding a way to ease her into it. To somehow make her feel safe when he turned her entire world on its head, and her perception of what was real and what was fiction became irrevocably altered. And now...now that chance was lost. She looked completely shattered. And terrified out of her goddamn mind.

"Elliot?" Her husky voice trembled, and she swayed on her feet as she rapidly blinked. "I was so worried about you, so I...I came outside. But I...I don't understand. What's happening?"

Feeling like someone had just reached into his chest and ripped out his heart, he quickly retracted his claws—but there wasn't anything he could do about the blood that covered almost every inch of him. Keeping his movements careful and slow, so that he didn't spook her, Elliot started toward her. "Just take a deep breath and try to stay calm. Everything's going to be okay. I promise you."

She didn't scream as he reached the top of the porch. She didn't have the chance—because she'd already fainted before another sound could leave her mouth.

"Shit," he grunted, lurching forward and catching her just before she would have cracked her head on the wooden planks. Clutching her close to his chest, Elliot carried her inside and laid her down on the bed so that he could quickly change his clothes, text both Max and Mason, and gather their things. With their bags slung over his shoulder, he picked her up again, and carried her out front, to her car. As gently as possible, he placed her in the passenger-side seat and reached for the seat belt, securing it across her chest.

Cupping the side of her face in his shaking hand, he

pressed a terrified kiss to her cold cheek, and quickly made his way around the front of the car, tossing the bags in the backseat before climbing in behind the wheel.

Then Elliot executed the only plan he had at the moment...

And got them the hell out of there.

Chapter 9

By the time Elliot reached the busy motel on the outskirts of a little town called Darner, nearly two hours had passed since he'd loaded Skye into her car and sped away from the safe house.

He'd spent every second of that time trying to stay calm, but it wasn't easy. He'd known the instant she came out of her faint—but she didn't try to talk to him. Hell, she didn't even *look* at him. So he'd held back everything he needed to say, waiting for the time when he could look her right in the eye and give her the explanations she deserved. God only knew what the poor girl had to be thinking. After everything she'd been through in the past twenty-four hours, she no doubt needed a timeout, so he'd done the mature thing and let her be, even though his friggin' nerves were twitching.

Amazingly, he no longer scented any fear on her, and

for that he was so damn grateful. It'd have killed him if she'd been terrified when she'd woken up and found herself alone in the car with him. He knew better than to think that meant their next conversation was going to be an easy one—but at least she wasn't going to be cowering in a corner of the room, waiting for him to take a goddamn bite out of her.

So, yeah, staying calm wasn't exactly a walk in the park at the moment. He was worried about Skye…and about what he would *say* to Skye. And then there was the issue of her safety, which had just gone from precarious to downright deadly. If the assholes working for this Chiswick guy knew about the safe house, then the only real safety he could give her was going to come from numbers. Which meant he needed to get her sweet ass up to the Alley as soon as possible—and to do that, he was going to need help.

He'd parked near the back of the crowded parking lot, so that the car wouldn't be easily spotted by anyone who might drive past looking for them. Not wanting Skye to get cold, he kept the engine running so that the heat would stay on. The temperature had dropped with the fall of darkness, and there'd been talk on the radio of a fresh snowstorm coming in. But he could see through the windows that the sky was still clear and dotted with stars, the moon hanging near the horizon like a glowing shard of silver.

Aware that Skye was listening to his every word, he pulled his phone out and called Max. Though he'd sent a brief text letting his partner know that the safe house had been compromised, he left a more detailed voice mail this time, explaining how things had gone down. Then he called Lev Slivkoff. He knew the mercs were wrapping up a job in western New York, not far from his and Skye's current location, which meant they could get to them quickly.

The conversation with Slivkoff was brief and to the point, and for once the merc didn't rib him about needing to get laid—a fact that Elliot appreciated, given the circumstances, and the woman huddled in the seat beside him, staring out the passenger-side window.

"Who were you talking to?" she asked, finally turning her head to look at him when he ended the call.

"A guy named Lev," he rasped, pressing the hands he'd done his best to clean back in the bathroom at the cabin against his thighs, so he wouldn't reach out and touch her. "He, uh, works with me and Max sometimes."

Her brows slowly lifted with a mixture of curiosity and confusion. "Is he…like you?"

Reaching for the handle on his door, he gave her a pleading look as he said, "I know we need to talk, Skye. But not out here. Will you come inside with me, after I get us a room?"

She pulled her lower lip through her teeth, studying his face for a moment, before she let out a slow breath of air and nodded. With relief piercing through him so sharply it hurt, Elliot hurried into the motel's office and secured them a room. Key in hand, he collected Skye from the car, along with their bags, and sent up a silent little prayer that the room wouldn't be a total disaster as they climbed the rickety metal stairs to the second floor.

"I know it isn't much," he murmured, flicking the light on as they walked in, "but we needed to get off the road for the night."

"It's fine," she said, glancing around the sparsely furnished, clearly dated, but surprisingly clean room.

Elliot shut the door, locked it and dropped their bags down on top of the dresser, before walking over to one of the bedside tables, where he took the gun from his waistband and set it down beside the lamp. When he turned to face Skye, she'd taken a seat in one of the chairs at the small table that was pushed up against the far wall, so he went and sat down across from her.

Rubbing his hand over his mouth as he leaned back against the spindly chair, he struggled to put the most important words he would ever say in his entire life into some kind of order that would make sense, and not just sound like a bunch of panicked rambling. "So, yeah," he murmured, keeping his worried gaze locked tight on hers. "I need to explain things to you, and the best way to do that, I think, is to just come out and say it. I'm a Lycan."

Her brows knitted with confusion. "Lycan?"

"A werewolf, Skye. A shape-shifter."

"Oh." She blinked, then slowly licked her lips, and he could tell she was thinking about a million different things at once. He held his breath, damn near sick with fear over what she might say. And then she shocked the hell out of him by leaning back in her chair as a soft, husky laugh fell from her lips. "I'm sitting here and I know I should be freaking out," she told him with a little shake of her head, "but after what I saw, I knew... I knew it had to be something like that." Green gaze warming with an unexpected flash of humor, she added, "It's actually kinda funny."

"Funny?" he croaked, and this time he was the one who must have looked confused.

"I've somehow missed the Lycan term before, but I've read a lot about werewolves," she explained, a pretty blush spreading across her face. "I actually have this thing about shifter romances."

"No shit?" he breathed, so shocked he couldn't do anything but sit there and gape at her like an idiot.

"Yeah." She caught her lower lip in her teeth for a moment, and when she let it go her mouth twitched with a wry grin. "I just never thought there was a chance they were really...you know. *Real*."

He frowned. "We're not exactly portrayed in a very good light by Hollywood."

"Yeah, well, those are horror movies. Romance books are completely different."

He heaved out a stunned, giant breath of relief, unable to take his eyes off her as he rubbed the heel of his hand over the middle of his chest. "Christ, Skye. I don't know what to say. I never in a million years thought you wouldn't be freaking out right now. My heart almost stopped when you passed out on me."

With a slow nod, she said, "I think I just needed some time to think—like my body needed a time-out, while my brain could be working it all out in my head. I mean, you have to remember where I live, Elliot. I've seen... I've seen some fairly scary stuff. And, yeah, I was pretty scared to see all that blood, and the claws... and his fangs." She paused and gave him a deep, searching look, before licking her lips and blurting, "I'm sure you have some, too, right? I mean, you must. But...that's not the point. The point is that I get it."

Thinking he must have misunderstood her, he tried his hardest to get a clear read on her. "You get what?"

"Why you killed him. I heard what he said. You were protecting me, so I can't really be grossed out by it, can I? Or judgmental. At that moment, I wanted to kill him, too. And he's hurt so many women. He could have even been the one who hurt Viv."

"Yeah, but I... I wasn't sure you would see it that way. I know the way we do things—the laws we have—are very different from humans," he heard himself say in a low voice, hoping like hell she hadn't overheard the part about her being his life-mate.

"I'm sure they are. And I... I'm not going to sit here accusing you of being a monster. The ones responsible for all this, they're the monsters." She closed her eyes for a moment as she drew in a deep breath, then blinked them open as she slowly exhaled, and his muscles tensed, because he knew what was coming. "You told Max in the message you left for him that you'd learned some sick stuff about someone named Chiswick," she said quietly, her green eyes burning with determination. "What did the guy you were questioning tell you?"

Shaking his head, he said, "Skye, you—"

"Don't," she whispered, cutting him off. "Just...please don't say something stupid about how I don't really want to know. This is *my life*, and *Viv's life*, that we're talking about. I deserve to know what you learned."

He frowned, but damn it, he knew she was right. Stabbing his fingers back through his hair, he cleared his throat, and forced himself to give her the truth. "He said no one knows what Chiswick is—but whatever his species, it sounds like he's a...cannibal," he scraped out, the hoarse words sitting like something sour on his tongue. Especially given his own twisted past. "The bastard said something about how Chiswick eats the ones who displease him while they're still kicking and screaming."

Hands suddenly cupped over her nose and mouth, her

green eyes wide with shock, she breathed out something that sounded like *Ohmygod. That's so freaking sick!*

Standing up, Elliot moved his chair closer to hers, then sat back down and reached for one of her cold hands, holding it pressed between his. "I swear we are gonna handle this, Skye. I am *not* going to let anything happen to you."

"But...you're not really a PI, right?" she asked, drawing her hand away and crossing her arms over her chest, her gaze troubled. "It was all a lie? Or a cover?"

He winced, hooking one hand behind his neck as he lowered his head and tried to think of the best way to explain. He hated that this was just one more lie he had to admit to.

"Elliot, just tell me."

Lifting his head, he hoped she could see that he felt like shit for what he was about to confess. "The license I showed you is a forgery."

"So that means that you got a federal agent to lie for you. *How?* I mean, why would he do that?"

Lowering his hand to the table, he gripped the edge, wishing beyond anything that he was holding on to her instead. "I, uh, don't think Monroe would see it that way—as outright lying. In his eyes, the work we do is similar in a lot of ways to that of a private investigator. We just don't get official recognition for it."

Curiosity filtered through her confusion. "He knows what you are?"

With a jerk of his chin, he said, "Yeah. His sister is actually married to one of the males in my pack. So Monroe has known about us for a long time now."

She looked intrigued. "When you say *we*, who are you talking about exactly? Your...pack?"

"No, it's more like my family," he explained, so incredibly grateful that he was able to say that. Because while he might not feel like he had a whole hell of a lot to offer someone as wonderful as Skye, his family was as kick-ass as they came. "Max and I, we're part of a small group called the Bloodrunners. Our job is to protect the secrecy of the Silvercrest Lycan pack, but first and foremost, we're hunters."

Her eyes went wide. "Wow. What do you hunt?"

Rubbing his hand across his jaw, he forced himself to give her another honest answer. "The bad guys, Skye. If one of our kind turns rogue and starts breaking the laws of our pack by feeding on humans, we hunt their asses down and take them out. We protect our territory, and look out for the human towns that fall under our jurisdiction."

A myriad expressions flashed across her face during his explanation, but she didn't freak out. She just pulled in another deep breath, then slowly let it out as she reached up and tucked her hair behind her ear. "And there are other packs? Like yours?"

"Yeah," he breathed.

"But you don't know what…what *species* Chiswick is, and I'm assuming that the women he's taken have all been human. So how did you get assigned to the case?"

"Monroe really did ask us for help."

He could tell by the way her lashes flickered that his answer had surprised her. "You and Max?"

"Yeah. We have a good relationship with him. And at the moment, we're the only single Runners. The others, they don't like to be away from their families, so we're the ones who take the cases like this nowadays. The ones that require traveling out of state."

"I'm…glad." She flushed, but still pulled her shoulders back as she looked him right in the eye and said, "That it's you, I mean."

Exhaling in a heavy rush, he collapsed back in the chair, his relief so potent he felt dizzy with it.

"What?" she asked, studying his expression.

He gave her a brief, crooked grin, and shook his head a little. "Honestly? I just… I didn't expect you to take this so well."

She gave a quiet laugh. "Did you think that once you explained everything, I'd start pulling at my hair and screaming like a crazy person?"

His lips twitched. "Something like that."

"Well, I won't lie and say there's not a part of me that wants to do exactly that," she murmured. "But…I know what I saw, and I know you did what you did because you wanted to protect me." Shoulders lifting with a deep breath, she went on, saying, "I know those things just as strongly as I know, in my gut, that you're a good man. So I'm going to pull up my big-girl panties and act like a rational adult. One who is probably going to think twice about ever going outside at night again," she added with a little laugh, "but that's all the crazy I'm going to allow myself. With everything that's going on, I just… I just have to suck it up and deal."

Carefully studying her with a narrowed gaze, he asked, "You're really not afraid of me?"

She tilted her head to the side a bit, the look in her beautiful eyes deep and breathtakingly tender as she quietly said, "Yeah, I'm really not afraid of you."

He had to curl his hands into fists in his lap to keep them from shaking, his throat so tight he could only swallow and nod.

"I'm sorry, by the way," she added with a slight wince.

His eyes shot wide, seeing as how that was one of the *last* things he'd expected her to say. "For what?"

With a rueful expression on her pretty face, she said, "Until they showed up at the cabin, I don't think I really believed that they wanted me, too. I should have listened to you."

"Nothing to be sorry for," he offered in a low voice, rubbing his palm against the hard, whiskery edge of his jaw. "I get how crazy this all sounded."

She looked as if he'd surprised her again. "It sounds crazy to you, too?"

"I've seen some insane shit over the years," he told her. "But...yeah, this isn't anything like our normal runs."

Leaning forward so that she could brace an elbow on the table, she rested her chin in her hand and gave him a wry smirk. "So be honest with me. Do you think I'll wake up tomorrow and completely freak out?"

Even though Elliot could tell she was teasing, it was his turn to wince. "Christ, I hope not."

"Me, too," she agreed with another soft laugh. And then, a bit more seriously, she said, "But I don't think I will. I mean... I knew you were different, in a special kind of way. I just didn't realize *how* different."

Figuring this was as good a time as any to tell her his plan, he started to speak, when she suddenly blurted, "What do you want?" And then, a bit more slowly, "I mean, what is it that you want to happen?"

He didn't even have to think about his answer. "I want you to be safe."

She searched his expression as she bit her lip, then softly said, "That's it?"

The air thickened between them, so heavy with anticipation Elliot could barely breathe it in, and he had to clear his throat a little before he could say, "I want you...*with me*, Skye. And that doesn't play into how safe I want you. I mean, I would protect you no matter what was between us. But I... I'd be lying if I said my interest in you didn't make the need to protect you more... *vital*." Leaning forward, he braced his elbows on his knees, and there was no mistaking the possessiveness in his low voice as he said, "I want to take you back to my mountains with me, and when we get there, I want you in my cabin. I want you *in my bed*."

Her cheeks flushed a beautiful shade of rose, and he could have sworn there was something even deeper than desire burning in her warm gaze as she asked, "Are you sure? Because we've only known each other for a few days, if that."

"You really think it makes that much of a difference?"

She kind of shook her head and nodded all at the same time. "Yes...no. I don't know."

"Some people know their lovers for years, and still don't really know them at all."

"That's true," she murmured. And then, with a slow blink, she asked, "You really want me to go home with you?"

Wondering if he'd slipped into some kind of fever dream, he said, "I just want you, period. You should know that by now. But, hell yes, I want to take you home with me."

He started to reach for her, intending to pull her onto his lap, when she suddenly sat back in her chair, moving out of his reach—and it was like a sharp slap of reality across his face, making him wonder if he'd been reading her as clearly as he'd thought he had.

Watching him carefully, she said, "And if I go to Maryland with you, you'll stay there with me?"

Of all the fucking questions she could have asked him, it had to be that one. "Um, yeah," he scraped out, licking his lips.

She narrowed her eyes, almost as if she could hear the lie in his words. But, damn it, it's not like he could tell her that he planned on leaving her in the safekeeping of his friends so that he could be free to track down the bastards trying to hurt her.

But after that—hell yeah, he would stay there with her. He'd spend the rest of his life doing everything he could to make her happy.

"I swear you'll like it there, Skye. I wouldn't take you someplace that you'd be uncomfortable. I promise."

"Then...okay," she murmured, giving him a brief smile. "I'll, um, go with you."

Satisfaction curled through him like a warm, lazy ray of sunshine. "Good," he rasped, hunger making his body hard and his eyes heavy. "Because there's another reason I want you there."

"There is?" Skye whispered, more than a little surprised by how quickly this guy could turn her on.

"Yeah," he said with a slow nod, his dark gaze hooded and hot as it moved over her face, lingering on her trembling lips, before lifting back to her own. "I want you to see with your own eyes that something between us could work. There are three other couples who are like us there, Skye. Lycan males and human females. And they're some of the happiest people you'll ever meet."

"You're serious about this, aren't you?" she asked in a soft, breathless rush of words.

The sin-tipped smile on his lips was so gorgeous, she felt a little dizzy just looking at it, the deep, rich timbre of his voice as he said, "You have no idea, baby. *None,*" making it impossible to ignore the fact that she was so aroused she was about to come out of her skin. And then there was the way he was looking at her, as if her agreement to go with him had actually meant something special to him, and it made her chest get this warm, gooey feeling that Viv would have said could get her into some serious trouble. But, then, Viv was the only girl in the world more wary of putting her trust in another person than Skye was.

"Enough with the damn distance," he muttered, suddenly reaching out and pulling her onto his lap. With his strong arms wrapped around her, he went for her mouth, but she turned her head at the last second, still struggling to believe this was actually happening—that it was *real*—and he ended up nuzzling the side of her throat instead.

"So many things I want to do to you," he said in a low, husky rumble, rubbing the words into her sensitive skin. "I thought I fantasized a lot about sex before I met you, but that was nothing compared to the things that fill my head now. I want to do *everything* to you, Skye. Want to touch you and taste you and get inside every beautiful part of you."

"Oh, God," she moaned, letting her head fall back so that he could press those breathtaking kisses to the front of her throat.

"And I want you to do the same to me," he growled, licking his tongue across her hammering pulse. "I want you lost in me. I want you as fucking hungry as you make me feel."

"Elliot."

Spreading his big hands across her back, he pulled her tighter against him, his warm mouth rubbing across the trembling line of her jaw. "And it doesn't have a damn thing to do with being in danger or fighting for our lives. I want you because you're the sweetest, sexiest fucking thing I've ever laid eyes on, and I'll do whatever it takes to have you. To make you want me again."

Wait...what? "Make me want you *again*? Are you freaking serious?"

He nipped her tender earlobe. "Deadly."

"Elliot," she huffed, gripping his hair and pulling until he was looking her in the eye. "I already want you," she said shakily, unable to believe he could have any doubt, since it seemed so freaking obvious.

"Then why the hell do you keep pulling away from me?" His tanned, corded throat worked as he swallowed, and his voice was softer than she'd ever heard it as he asked, "Are you sure you're not afraid of me?"

With her hands still buried in his hair, she said, "I'm sure."

His eyes narrowed, and he looked pale. "Jesus, Skye. Do you think I'd hurt you? Is that it?"

She shook her head, hating that he could even think that. "After everything you've done for me? No, of course not."

"Then *why*?" he demanded roughly, frustration bleeding into the raw edges of his voice.

Shoulders lifting in a helpless shrug, she said, "I'm not sure. I guess... I mean, I think it's because I'm... I'm just...*me*."

He looked confused. "Yeah? And?"

"That's it! I'm just Skye. Just…average. Boring."

A scowl wove its way between his dark brows. "What the hell are you talking about?"

"Elliot," she groaned, thinking he was adorably obtuse. "Just look at us. I already thought you were way out of my league before, and then I learn that you're like this amazing male who can turn into another creature. That's…that's pretty freaking incredible, and it puts you even *more* out of my league."

"First off," he muttered, looking at her like he thought she might be a little insane, "that's pure and utter bullshit. If anyone's reaching here, it's me."

Curving her hands over his broad shoulders, she said, "But I'm the one who's only a human."

His dark eyes flared with irritation. "You're not *only* anything. And I wouldn't change a goddamn thing about you."

"Elliot," she groaned for a second time in only a handful of seconds, wondering how she was going to get through to him.

"Yeah?" he rasped, giving her a look that said he still thought she was a little crazy, but that he also thought she was the most beautiful, endearingly frustrating woman in the entire world.

"I… You… We…" she spluttered, before finally giving up with a huff. "I'm trying to get you to see reason here, but it's impossible. You're *really* not easy to argue with."

With a sexy smirk on his even sexier mouth, he said, "In that case, good. I think we can both agree that you should just stop trying."

Bracing her hands against his firm chest, she locked

her troubled gaze with his, silently pleading with him to understand. "I just... I don't want to get hurt...emotionally. And I know that if I let myself get all crazy over you, it will completely wreck me when you finally see what I'm talking about."

Voice little more than a gentle, husky murmur, he said, "You could hurt me, too, Skye. More than you know."

"I don't want to hurt you," she whispered, his words doing something painful to her heart. "That's the last thing that I want."

His dark eyes went heavy with lust and need...and other breathtaking things that were far too primal for her human brain to read. "Then stop torturing me and give me that sweet mouth before I go out of my mind."

In the next instant, his lips were on hers, and she couldn't help but moan and open up to him. With her heart pounding and her pulse rushing in her ears, she lost herself in the hot silk of his mouth, thinking she could kiss this man or Lycan or whatever the hell he was for the rest of her life and die happy.

But despite all the incredible things that he'd said to her, Skye knew damn well that there was no promise of forever here. And if her past had taught her anything, it was that moments of peace and joy and pleasure were as fleeting as wisps of smoke. Which meant that she really needed to slap some sense into herself, and start devouring every moment with him that she could, before her luck ran out.

For some mind-boggling reason that she simply couldn't wrap her head around, Elliot Connors honestly seemed to be attracted to her, but who knew how long that would last? Those couples he'd talked about back in Maryland—they no doubt had a strong, powerful love working to keep them together, while she and Elliot had…lust? Budding friendship? Affection? Despite knowing him for such a short time, she already treasured those things, but she wasn't naive enough to think they would hold him to her. Not when he was the most amazingly awesome guy she'd ever met, and she was just shy, kind-of-chunky, so-normal-it-was-sad Skye Hewitt.

And, yeah, the irony of the situation wasn't lost on her. Here he'd spent all this time trying to reassure her that he was a good person—and not a monster—when she was the one with the stains of sin on her soul. Blots of darkness caused by stupid mistakes that hadn't saved people, like Elliot did, but had destroyed them instead.

With one last teasing stroke of his tongue against hers, he slowly drew back from the kiss, then set her on her feet as he stood from the chair. Taking her hand, he murmured, "Come on," and started pulling her along behind him. "I need to clean up, and I need you with me. So we're both going to take a shower."

Blinking at the tapered, masculine shape of his back under his tight T-shirt, she said, "Um, you mean in the bright light and everything?"

"Yep."

She groaned as he opened the bathroom door and flicked on the light, the damn thing even brighter than she'd feared. "I'm not completely comfortable with that," she mumbled, feeling whatever temporary confidence she'd managed to find in his attraction to her begin to shrivel like a grape left out too long in the sun.

"Stop worrying, Skye." He shot her a determined but somehow tender look over his broad shoulder as he reached into the shower and started the water. "In about five minutes, you'll be too busy coming to think about things like being comfortable."

Pulling her hand from his, she muttered, "Elliot, I'm being serious."

"So am I," he said, turning back to face her. "We had to break things off at the cabin before I could make you come. Then we had the what-could-have-been-heart-breaking talk about my non-humanness, that instead went so fucking well it's only made me want to make you come even harder." His dark eyes glittered with mischief. "So I'm gonna take care of that right now."

She couldn't help but grin at the goof, even when she was twisted up with self-consciousness. "At least turn the overhead light off. It's too bright."

"No way," he drawled, pulling his lower lip through his teeth as he reached down and yanked her sweater over her head, followed quickly by her tank top. Hooded gaze glued hungrily to her bra-covered breasts, he growled, "I want to watch every part of this. Every second."

"Elliot, I'm—" she started, moving to cover her chest with her arms, but he cut her off as he wrapped his big hands around her wrists, tugging them back down to her sides.

"If you're not about to say 'so fucking beautiful,'" he muttered, staring hotly at her body, "then don't."

Her lips mashed together, but her eyes must have given away exactly what she was thinking when he slowly brought that smoldering gaze back to hers.

With his hands working to open her jeans, he leaned down and pressed his open mouth to the side of her throat, his deep voice rough with lust as he vowed, "You're gonna believe me, Skye. You might not now, but I *will* make you see the truth."

She moaned, body flushed with heat and mind spinning as he set about stripping away every bit of material that covered her. His low voice filled her head, his sexy assurances only making her hotter as the steam from the shower filled the tiny room. Then she was naked and alone, her eyes blinking rapidly as he stepped back from her, looking her over. His chest rose and fell as he took his time, one hand lifting to hook around the back of his neck, firm lips parted for the quickening of his excited breaths. The only thing that kept her from diving for one of the thin white towels and jerking it around her was the way he was staring at her, with so much heat and possessiveness, as he raked every inch of her nude body with his gleaming, molten gaze.

Then she got completely distracted by the sight of him grabbing his T-shirt with the hand on the back of his neck, and pulling the shirt off, revealing a torso that was breathtakingly hard with powerful slabs and cords of muscle, sculpted to perfection. He had a few scratches and scrapes from the fight at the cabin, but they didn't do anything to detract from his beauty. When she saw him like this, so magnificently raw and tough and painfully gorgeous, it seemed so obvious that he wasn't just another average human. Like there should have been a big neon sign hanging over his head that read: *Open your eyes and see the truth! This perfect male is so much more!*

When he reached down and undid the top button on his jeans, Skye kind of forgot how to breathe altogether. He pulled the denim down his long, muscular legs, then kicked the jeans away, the thick, heavy length of his erection impossible to miss as he did the same with a tight black pair of boxers. She was desperate for the sight of him, but his hands were suddenly on her shoulders, spinning her around to face the wall, breath catching in her lungs as he dropped to his knees behind her.

What the what?

Bracing her trembling hands against the wall, she squeaked at the first touch of his lips at the top of her right butt cheek, and a deliciously low, utterly male laugh rumbled up from his chest.

"Jesus," he groaned, squeezing her hips between his hands, "your ass is so fucking sweet, Skye."

"My ass is b—" He nipped her with his teeth, making her choke off what she was saying with a gasp. "Hey, you bit me!"

"Naw," he drawled, rubbing those warm lips across her stinging skin. "I gave you a playful nip."

Breathless and so turned on she felt light-headed, she asked, "Um, why?"

"Because unless you were about to tell me that your ass is goddamn beautiful," he muttered, squeezing her round buttocks with his hands, "I don't want to hear it."

In the sexiest move she could have ever imagined, he licked and nipped his way up her spine, his big hands drawing up her sides, then reaching around, cupping her heavy breasts as he pressed his front against her back and touched his wicked mouth to her ear. "Come on," he whispered, and she could hear the sinful smile in his rough voice as he wrapped his arms around her middle and lifted her off her feet. "Time to get you wet."

She laughed as he carried her into the shower, amazed by his strength…his size…and the feverish heat of his skin. Then he set her down under the warm spray, turned her around to face him, and her breath caught at the desperate, almost violent look of need that was burning in his dark eyes. His lips parted, and he shook his head a little, looking as if he was dying to say something…to *do* something…but was as frozen in the moment as she was. Trapped by the power of it. By the crushing weight of need. The hands on her shoulders trembled, and as she took a reflexive step forward, she *had* to look down at the hard length of him pressing against her belly.

Heart pounding in her ears like a drum, Skye reached up and curled her fingers around him, loving the thick, gravelly sound that broke from deep in his throat. His head went back, eyes shut, tendons straining in his tanned throat as she ran her thumb over the broad, swollen crown, and her greedy stare pinged between that massive, magnificent part of him that she held in her hands and the mesmerizing look on his face as she touched him. He was so gorgeous it was unreal.

"Elliot," she groaned, every speck of her self-consciousness suddenly slamming back into her. "What are we doing? You're so freaking perfect, and I'm—"

"Don't!" He'd cut her off with the sharp command, and knew his eyes were about two seconds away from turning the golden color of his wolf. "I'm serious, Skye. If you say one more negative thing about your body, I'm putting you over my knee."

Her brows lifted with surprise, cheeks turning adorably pink again. And her eyes… *Oh yeah*, the look in her beautiful eyes was telling him all kinds of interesting things about how his little life-mate felt about having his hand on her bottom.

With a slow smile kicking up the corner of his mouth, Elliot shook his head. "God, baby, don't tempt me."

She gave a quiet laugh, the soft sound part embarrassment…and part arousal. "You're crazy."

About you, he thought, determined to show her just how desperate and aching she made him. But then she looked back down to where she was still stroking his cock, and he felt a fresh surge of blood rushing to the engorged shaft, his hand slamming against the tiled wall of the shower as his head began to spin.

"Damn it," he growled, popping his jaw. "The way you look at it, Skye. It's gonna make me come, and I'm not ready for that yet."

"Sorry, but I can't stop," she whispered, flicking a quick look up at him from under her lashes. "I love looking at you like this. And touching you. It's, like, the best thing in the world."

His chest lifted with a harsh breath, his voice so raw and thick it didn't even sound human. "Killing. Me. Skye."

He couldn't see her mouth with the way she'd lowered her head again—but he could have sworn she was smirking as she said, "If you don't want me drooling over it, then maybe you should put it somewhere."

"Yeah?" he croaked, sucking in a deep pull of her mouthwatering scent. "Got any ideas?"

Elliot almost swallowed his tongue when she suddenly knelt in front of him, her lush mouth hovering so close he could feel the heat of her breath. *"Oh, God,"* he groaned, unable to believe he was actually *there*. That this was actually *happening*.

A hot, slick pulse of moisture wet his tip, and she quickly licked it away with her soft, pink tongue, nearly bringing him to his knees.

"Oh!" she gasped, sounding surprised.

"Oh?" he repeated with a gritty laugh, lifting one of his brows as she glanced up at him.

Cheeks flushed and looking like a goddamn dream, with the shower spray falling down behind her like a watery veil, she murmured, "Never mind."

With one hand still braced against the wall, he shoved the other into her wet hair. "Uh-uh," he breathed. "You don't get to say 'oh' like that and not tell me why."

"You just, um, taste really good," she said softly, shooting him a shy smile before she opened her mouth and took him in.

Elliot tried to hold out and make it last, the way she licked and stroked and sucked on him driving him wild. And then there were the tiny, hungry moans she gave, the husky sounds vibrating around his throbbing flesh, her mouthwatering scent growing richer…sweeter…as if what she was doing was as much for *her* pleasure as it was for his. He wanted to enjoy every perfect moment of it, and make it last forever, but he couldn't hold back. He muttered some kind of warning that he was close, expecting her to pull back, but she only gripped his hips in her soft hands and gave an excited moan, and he lost it, coming so hard he nearly blacked out.

"Christ, Skye…so damn good," he rambled, slumping against the side of the shower as he rested his chin against his chest and struggled to catch his breath. She nuzzled her nose against his hip, then pressed a trail of delicious kisses up his torso, the feel of her beautiful mouth and feminine hands and the way her gorgeous breasts were pressed against him sending his blood rushing south again so quickly, his recovery time was a shock even to him. With a raw sound of need, he curled his hands around her upper arms and pulled her up onto her toes, his head already lowering so he could kiss her ripe, swollen lips. She opened for him with a sweet sigh of surrender, and he slipped his tongue between those soft lips, tasting himself there, the moment so blisteringly erotic he was surprised they hadn't burst into flames.

Feeding his throaty growl into her open mouth, Elliot reached between them and pushed two fingers inside her warm, slick sex, loving the way her back arched and she gasped, her long lashes lifting to reveal beautiful green eyes that were heavy with desire.

"Do these fingers feel good?" he rasped, nipping her succulent bottom lip with his teeth.

"Y-yes," she breathed. "So g-good."

"Good," he repeated, smiling against her quivering mouth before he licked the place where he'd nipped her. "Because my tongue is going to feel even better."

Her nails dug into his hard shoulders, every inch of her exquisite body shivering against him as she moaned, *"Oh... God."*

With a low, gritty rumble of laughter, Elliot picked her up in his arms and carried her out to the king-size bed. They were both dripping wet as he laid her down in the middle of the mattress, but he didn't care. All that mattered now was getting her under his hands and mouth and making her feel good. Making her feel fucking incredible.

Unable to wait a second more, he pushed her thighs wide and buried his face against her, slicking his tongue over her soft, sea-salty flesh, undone by how insanely perfect she tasted. He lashed her tight, thrumming little clit until she cried out, licked his way down to the tiny, tender opening nestled within the slippery folds, and thrust his tongue into her deliciously soft, snug core. And, God, it felt good.

It might have been his first time doing this to a woman, but Elliot didn't have time to worry or second-guess if he was doing it right. He was completely lost in the lush, intoxicating feel and taste of her. Already addicted to it. Already craving his next hit. Then she shocked the hell out of him by shoving at his shoulders and pushing him onto his side. She flashed one smoldering, searing look at his wet lips and chin, and then she crawled down the bed, pressing against him, and took his hard, thick flesh back into her mouth. He gasped, swelling hugely against her tongue, a deep, guttural sound tearing up from his chest as he shoved his face back between her thighs, tonguing her drenched sex like he was starved for her taste. And fuck if that wasn't true.

Their heat-glazed bodies slid against each other, limbs tangled as their hips pumped, mouths hungry and desperate as they feasted and gasped for breath, their lungs burning as the pressure built—and then they were both crashing over that violent, shattering edge together, the sounds they made so raw and visceral anyone listening would have thought they were in pain. But as he struggled for air and yanked her pliant body up into his arms, crushing her against his chest, Elliot knew that he'd never been closer to the sweetness of heaven.

Seconds ticked into minutes that slowly edged their way toward an hour, as he and Skye lay there in the tangled bedding, cuddling like lovers who'd only just discovered the rush of being intimate with someone they not only craved, but *needed*. And, Christ, he hoped she needed him, because he was in so deep with this beautiful girl, he knew he'd never find his way back out. He didn't even want to try.

He just…he just had to figure out how to keep from losing her. And not because of Chiswick or his asshole thugs.

But because of *him*.

His goddamn past and failures and mistakes.

And his own unforgivable sins.

Chapter 10

Elliot woke to the feel of Skye stirring in his arms, her soft breaths pelting his chest, one of her lush thighs nestled between his. The sun was only just rising in the sky, which meant they had hours to wait before the mercs showed around noon. On the one hand, he was frustrated it would take that long, since he wanted her in the Alley *now*, where he knew she'd be safe.

But on the other... Well, he'd have been lying if he'd said it wasn't sweet as hell, having this time for just the two of them, her womanly body warm in his arms. And she was there—nestled against him like she wanted to hold on to him forever—even *after* learning what he was. That meant the fucking world to him, even if there was so much she still didn't know.

So much he would need to make sure she never learned.

He'd held her so friggin' tightly through the night, as

if she could be ripped away from him at any moment. But he wouldn't let that happen. So long as he was still breathing, he would safeguard this woman with everything he had. Even his life, if that's what it took.

"Hey," she said softly, tilting her head back so that she could see his face. Her long, silky hair was draped across the pillow and his arm, more golden in the morning light than at night, her green eyes drowsy beneath the thick fringe of her lashes. And there was a small smile on those lips that were so perfect and pink, he couldn't think of a more delicious way to start his day than by kissing the hell out of her.

"Hey," he echoed, running his hand down the delicate slope of her spine. Her skin was so soft to the touch, it made him think of priceless satins and silks. Of sensuous, decadent things that were meant to be lingered over…savored…*worshipped.*

Things he damn well couldn't live without, now that he'd found them.

And yet, as badly as he wanted her, he couldn't be the one who brought up sex, because when all was said and done, he didn't deserve it. Not when he was the one holding back—still keeping secrets—being less than honest with her. And while he *did* plan to tell her about the life-mate connection, as soon as the time felt right, there wasn't a chance in hell he would ever tell her the others.

But did that mean he would be forced to go through life with this constant itching under his skin? A persistent sense of dread cloaking him like a shadow, as he waited for the hammer to fall, shattering everything they managed to build together in a single blow?

Dramatic much? his wolf muttered with disgust, chuffing at him.

Oh, without a doubt. But then, shit just didn't get more dramatic than this, so he didn't give a damn what he sounded like. He just wanted to figure out a way to make everything right, when he didn't have a clue how to do it.

The gentle touch of Skye's hand against the side of his face had him blinking back to the moment, and he found her staring deeply into his heavy-lidded gaze, asking him a silent question. His cock was so hot and swollen, wedged between them, there was no way in hell she'd missed it. *None.* And now she was wondering why he wasn't taking things to the next level. Why he wasn't pushing for it, after the wickedly sexual, intimate things they'd done before falling asleep together. Things that had crossed two firsts off his list, and in Elliot's mind, had been *more* than worth the wait.

"Are you hungry?" she murmured, misreading his restraint. "We never did have dinner last night. We should go and find somewhere to get breakfast."

"I'll order something in," he replied. "Or go and grab something. I don't want you leaving this room until my friends get here and we're on our way."

Concern marked her brow. "You really think the bad guys could find us here?"

"I think I don't want to underestimate anything they can do at this point. Not when your safety is on the line."

The tension in her face eased, and she pulled that succulent lower lip that he wanted to suck on between her teeth. Those lips… *Jesus*, those lips of hers were something else.

"What are you thinking about now?" he asked, curving his hand around her naked hip.

Her cheeks started to warm with color, but she only

shook her head a little, a soft "Nothing" on her lips as her gaze dropped to his chin.

Pushing her hair back from her face, he said, "Don't do that. Talk to me."

Her lashes flickered, and then that luminous green was locked back on him. "I just… I'm still getting used to how…protective you are."

Ah. And she no doubt meant possessive, as well.

"I'm nowhere near good enough for you," he started to explain, treading carefully through what he could—and what he couldn't—say. "Not by a long shot. And I don't deserve you. But something led me to you. Something twisted fate so that I could find you. And I'm not letting that go without doing everything in my power to fight for what I want. I haven't…" He paused, giving a hard swallow, before he went on. "I haven't allowed myself to want anything in a really long time, Skye, and now I'm done with that. Deserving or not, I *will* find a way to be what you need, and that means I'll do whatever it takes to keep you protected."

"Why wouldn't you be deserving?" she asked quietly.

His chest lifted with a gritty, bitter bark of laughter. "You think you're the only one with a past that's shit?"

"What?" He could see the panic bleeding into her expression as clearly as he could feel his own emotions. "What makes you think my past—?"

"Baby," he said, cutting her off, "you were living in a women's shelter at sixteen."

"Oh. Uh, that was…because…" Her voice trailed off, and she lowered her gaze, lip caught right back in the punishing grip of her teeth.

"I know there's a story there," he said, leaning forward and pressing a kiss between her slender brows.

"Obviously one you don't want to tell me. But I'm ready to listen the moment that changes."

She nodded, and he could see the relief in her incredible eyes just before her lashes swept down again, casting shadows on her cheeks. Lowering his head, he pressed another kiss to the tip of her nose, which made her give a small, shaky laugh that had his chest going hot. His lips veered right, sweeping over her freckled cheek, and he loved how her skin felt against his mouth. How warm and silky, the rising scent of her arousal filling his head with each hungry breath that he drew into his lungs.

She curled her hands around his biceps, the bite of her nails digging into his muscles pulling a rough growl from deep in his chest as he pushed her onto her back, bracing himself with one hand pressed flat against the bed. Her head went back, giving him easier access as he kissed his way down the vulnerable curve of her throat, a sexy gasp on her lips when he curled his free hand around a soft, heavy breast, her small nipple deliciously thick and tight beneath the pad of his thumb.

"You feel so amazing," he groaned, sliding one of his thighs over hers as he kissed his way over her collarbone, lips skimming across her upper chest.

"God, Elliot. You, too," she panted, curving her hot hands over his shoulders and squeezing, the tremor moving through her limbs telling him she was just as needy as he was.

Thank you, thank you, thank you, he groaned in silent gratitude to whoever the hell might be out there listening, unable to wait a second longer before he covered the candy-pink tip of her other breast with his eager mouth. She tasted so sweet he had to lick his way over to the one he held, his hand pushing the heavy mound up in offering as he sucked on it just as hungrily, while throaty little gasps of sound fell from her lips.

With one last swirling lick to her succulent nipple, Elliot braced his hands on either side of her shoulders, and lowered his face over hers. "I know we're in a shit-load of trouble," he murmured, "but I'd be lying if I said I wasn't really fucking happy right now."

A shy smile curved her mouth, pretty green eyes hazy with desire. "Me, too."

Lowering his head again, he touched his lips to a few of her adorable freckles, then the edge of her jaw, and finally those plush, velvety soft lips, his tongue sliding inside to rub against hers when she gave him a breathy sigh of pleasure. Desperate to feel her trapped beneath him, and no longer able to recall why he shouldn't take things too far, Elliot shifted his long body over hers… and kneed her legs apart. His breath hissed through his teeth as she spread her creamy thighs even wider for him, then reached down and yanked on his hips, bringing his erection flush against the hot, slippery folds of her sex.

"I want to *own* you, Skye. Every gorgeous, beautiful inch of you," he growled against her open mouth, stroking himself against her. "Want so deep inside you, you can't ever get me out."

She gripped him by the hair, pulling his head up until he was no longer kissing her, but looking her directly in the eye. "Then why?" she asked, searching his gaze.

Racking his brain for an answer, Elliot tried to figure out what she could be asking him, but he couldn't think through the thickening fog of hunger and lust that was clouding his head. "Why what?"

Pushing her fingers through his hair, she said, "If you

want me…like that, then why didn't you…take things further last night?"

His hips stilled, and a slow, wry smile started to kick up the edge of his mouth. "I wanted to. You have no idea how badly I wanted to get inside you," he admitted in a voice that had gone hoarse with need, then shook his head a little. "But I don't want to rush you, Skye. I don't want you to…"

His voice trailed off, but she wouldn't let it go. "You don't want me to what?"

Hating how goddamn vulnerable he felt, he forced out a gritty "To regret it. I don't want to do something that you can't go back and undo."

Her eyes went dark with determination. "If that's the only thing holding you back, then stop."

"Stop?" he croaked, pretty sure his heart had just clawed its way up into his throat.

"No, not this," she said, hooking her hands at the back of his neck as she lifted her hips in a sensual move that had the slick folds of her sex rubbing against him, and his heart dropped back down so quickly he almost flinched. "Stop holding back on me. Because the only thing I could regret about this is *not* having you. I've never…never wanted *anything* in my life like this, and I don't want to wait. I want you *now*."

Hoping like hell she wasn't saying any of that because she was worried she might not have all that much time left, he cupped the side of her face in his hand, his voice almost savage as he said, "You can trust me when I tell you I won't ever let anything happen to you. I swear that Chiswick asshole and the guys who work for him aren't getting anywhere near you."

"I do trust you. And I need you. So now it's your turn

to trust me. *Please,*" she begged, arching against him. "I know exactly what I'm asking you for. I swear this is what I want now, and it's what I'm going to want tomorrow. I'm not going to regret it. I could *never* regret it."

"Skye," he groaned, sliding down and pressing his open mouth to the hammering beat of her pulse at the base of her throat. It was like a little butterfly under his tongue, rapid and beautiful. Her life's blood pumping through her body, calling to the beast inside him until he was trembling with the need to release his fangs, bury them in the tender curve of her throat and mark her.

Using his shoulders for leverage, she did this wicked thing with her hips that suddenly had his crown pressing right against her small, delicate entrance, and he froze, shaking, throat so tight he could barely force out the words he needed to say in order to protect her. "I'm not…wearing a…fucking condom."

"It's okay," she breathed, threading those soft hands through his hair. "I'm on the Pill because of some problems I had with my cycle. So if we're both…healthy?"

His head jerked up so fast he nearly clipped her on the chin. "I am," he scraped out, sweating, unable to keep from pushing just the throbbing, heavy tip of him inside her. "Lycans…we can't carry those types of diseases."

"Then we're good," she encouraged him with a breathtaking smile, trailing her hands over the sides of his straining throat. "It's been…um, like forever for me."

His cock somehow shot even harder at those intimate words, veins pulsing beneath the tight stretch of his skin, and he could feel a muscle start to tic at the edge of his jaw. He was only seconds away from completely losing his shit, and as he shook the sweat out of his eyes, Elliot clawed on to every shred of control he could find.

"You better be sure you want this," he forced through his gritted teeth, his hooded gaze locked hard on hers. "Because there's no turning back once I'm in."

"I'm sure," she gasped, face rosy and flushed with heat, and the way she curled her calves around the backs of his thighs, trying to pull him deeper, nearly made his eyes roll back in his head. "I promise, Ell. I've never been more sure of anything."

Between the way she was touching him, and looking at him, and that sexy way she'd just shortened his name—yeah, he was done for. He couldn't keep himself off her now even if the Hounds of Hell themselves were on his back, determined to make a meal out of him.

Jaw clenched tight and nostrils flared like a stallion's, Elliot pushed in an inch...and then another, some kind of dark, primitive sound tearing up from his throat as he felt her drenched, pillow-soft flesh envelop him, taking him in. He pulled back, and his hips shot forward again, feeding his throbbing shaft deeper into that tight, plush opening, her husky cry of surprise ringing in his ears. It was a thick, hot slide, and he loved the way her body fought to hold him inside as he slowly withdrew, then shoved himself back in.

"I... *Oh, God,*" he rasped, his entire body shuddering from the primal, searing sensations, the muscles in his arms showing in stark relief beneath his dark skin as he fisted his hands in the sheets, dug his knees into the mattress, and gave it to her a little harder...a little deeper. She was impossibly snug, the lush, wet clasp of her body so good it was killing him not to just slam his way home and unload.

"Hey, are you okay?" she whispered breathlessly,

size," she added wryly, blushing so hard it suddenly made him want to grin right back at her.

"You sure you're okay?" he asked, studying her face for any signs of pain. But she just looked…happy, and the relief he felt was so piercing he could have collapsed with it.

Answering his question, she said, "Stop worrying, Elliot. I've never been better."

"You get any better," he rasped, leaning down and pressing a hard kiss against her mouth, "and it'll kill me."

She laughed as she pushed his hair back from his face again. "Death by sex?"

"Don't joke," he scraped out, shaking his head. "I'm serious."

Tilting her head a bit to the side, she slipped a fingertip under his top lip, rubbing it against the place on his gum where she would have seen one of his fangs, before he'd pulled them back. "Do you ever have trouble controlling them?" she asked, sounding more curious than afraid. "You know…biting something that you… shouldn't?"

He was pretty sure all the blood was draining out of his face, but he gave her an honest answer. "Not with you." *Never with you.*

Then he forced himself to move to his feet and headed into the bathroom. He came back less than a minute later with a warm washcloth, a husky laugh on his lips when he found her lying there with the sheet pulled up over her breasts and her legs demurely curled to the side. They engaged in a playful tussle, which he easily won by pushing those pretty legs apart and kneeling between them.

"You're such a spoiler," she whispered, as he carefully cleaned her up, and he thought it was completely adorable that she could still blush such a vivid shade of pink after the extremely intimate things they'd just done together.

"You deserve to be spoiled," he murmured, tossing the cloth aside, his heart beating with a hard, heavy thump as he watched his hand settle back against the soft, pale skin of her inner thigh, his thumb sweeping out to rub across her clit. The room was quiet but for their hushed, soughing breaths, and he kept up that slow, erotic stroking, until her sex was glistening and wet. Then he twisted his hand, keeping his thumb on her clit as he pushed two long fingers deep inside her.

"Sore?" he whispered, when she gasped.

Her shy reply was soft, breathless. "Only a little."

He flicked a look up at her from under his brows, the corner of his mouth twitching with anticipation at how hard he was about to make her blush. "You know, I really think I should kiss it and make it better."

"Ohmygod!" she said with an embarrassed laugh, covering her face with her hands.

"It's Elliot, baby. Just Elliot," he teased, making her laugh even harder. And with a wicked grin on his lips, he lowered his head, spread her open with his thumbs... and got lost all over again.

Chapter 11

In a perfect world, Skye had a strong feeling that she and Elliot would have stayed in that deliciously sex-thrashed bed the entire day, until the necessity for food finally forced them to leave it. The morning had been long and wickedly lovely, and she'd have been lying through her teeth if she'd said she didn't feel…different. Like something that had emerged from a cocoon, shaking off its old skin so that it could see what living in a new one was like.

God, she wished she had Viv there to talk to, because if there was ever a time that a girl needed her best friend to use as a sounding board, it was now. For the first time in her entire life, she was starting to feel that a guy like Elliot Connors—gorgeous, funny, protective, smart, successful and, yeah… Lycan—could actually be interested in a girl like her.

And it felt freaking incredible. Made her want to throw her arms around him and kiss him until she was drunk on the pleasure, but he'd already headed out to grab them some food, after slipping out of bed to throw on a gray Henley, jeans and his boots. Before he'd left, he'd read out a brief message from Max on his phone that simply said:

That was shit news about the cabin. Hope you destroyed the fuckers! Vivian still safe. Tell Skye not to worry. Talk soon.

She'd been thinking hard about Viv, sending up a silent prayer that she was safe and getting along okay with Max, when Elliot had leaned down, given her a quick kiss right on her sensitive lips and told her not to worry. Then he'd reminded her that he was only going to check out the food places that were right by the motel, and was out the door. So, left with a little time to herself, she'd burrowed back into the mound of pillows and let her mind wander over some of the scrumptious things they'd done together.

And while there was more than a little part of her that still felt guilty for getting so lost in Elliot, she figured Viv would understand. Especially seeing as how the sex had been…um, freaking insane. So incredible she was pretty sure she'd lost a few brain cells in the whole process of climaxing until she nearly passed out.

Smirking and shaking her head at herself—since she was clearly acting like a lovesick idiot—Skye finally forced herself to at least make a move toward the shower. She immediately winced as soon as she'd stood up at the side of the bed, a wry laugh on her lips as she realized just how sore she was.

Wrapping the sheet around herself, since her clothes were still in the bathroom, she started to turn around, when she spotted the gun sitting on the bedside table. And just like that, a jagged slice of reality cut into her rosy glow.

With a frown settling between her brows, she found herself thinking about Elliot's work, and wondering if his life was always this dangerous. Was that why he hadn't been intimate with a woman in so long? She'd been so freaking shocked when he'd told her that, but then, in a weird way, it'd made a lot of sense, since it helped explain why he was so determined to be careful with her. She'd expected at least a degree of that kind of care, seeing as how they weren't even the same species. In the shifter romances she loved so much, the hero would always rather do bodily harm to himself than hurt a female, the strong alpha types that they were, and she could so see Elliot feeling that same way. But…there seemed almost something deeper to how cautious he was with her during sex. Something even more…personal.

She couldn't say that it bothered her, because that would be stupid. What woman didn't want the man she was involved with to want to be good for her? But she trusted Elliot. For however long they had together, she didn't want him worrying when he was inside her. She wanted him lost to the moment, seeped in pleasure and acting purely on instinct. She wanted him wild. She wanted *him*—not some tightly controlled version he thought would make her feel safer.

And, yeah, it also wasn't lost on her that she'd thought the words *however long they had*. That, unfortunately, was reality, pure and simple. But she wasn't going to let it control her or get all weepy about it. And she…she wasn't going to just give up, either, and take whatever fate threw at her. For the first time in her life, Skye had found something worth fighting for—that she wanted, badly—and damn it, if the end came knocking on their door, she was going to give it one hell of a battle. Because they were good together, and something that good deserved a little blood and sweat and tears. Which meant she was going to do everything she could to hold on to Elliot Connors.

As if right on cue, the door opened, and the man— the Lycan himself—came stepping back into the room, a grin on his lips when he took in her very fashionable sheet. "There was no place I trusted not to poison you close enough that I could still get back to you quickly, if you needed me," he said, holding up the colorful paper menus in his hand. "So I grabbed some take-out menus from the front office. Figured we can just have something delivered."

"That sounds good. But do we have enough time before your friends get here?"

He tossed the menus on the nearby dresser, then headed right for her, his hair still all spiky, from her own hands instead of his, and she loved it. Loved how he'd seemed to crave her touch, growling with pleasure whenever she'd scraped her nails over his scalp, or skimmed her fingertips down his sleek, powerful back.

"We still have about an hour," he said, just before he reached her and pulled her into his arms. When he pressed his lips to hers, she swore she could still taste a salty hint of herself on them, and *ohmyfreakinggod*, that was hot.

"If you want to grab a shower," he said against her mouth, one hand stroking over the bare length of her back, "I'll get the order in."

"You're not joining me?" she asked, drawing her head back so that she could look him in the eye.

He bunched the sides of the sheet in his hands, looking like he very much wanted to rip it off her. "Trust me, I want to. But if I do, I'll never get you fed. And I need to keep my girl in top working order, when you take into account what I plan on doing to her when we reach my cabin."

"Hmm. She sounds like a lucky girl."

Voice husky and low, he said, "Oh, I definitely intend to make her feel lucky. You can believe that."

He lowered his head again, his mouth working over hers with delicious skill, rooting out her pleasure like he wanted it more than his own, until she was left in a dizzy, embarrassingly swoony state when he finally pulled away. She slumped against the side of the bed, flushed with desire, the cocky grin on his lips telling her he knew *exactly* what he'd been doing with that killer kiss.

Clearing her throat, she rasped, "I'm just…gonna… grab that shower…now."

"I already put your bag in there for you. But give me a shout if you need any help getting dressed!" he called after her, and there was a stupid smile on her lips as she shut the bathroom door behind her.

The hot water did wonders for her aching muscles, and she was feeling more refreshed than she had in days when she came out of the bathroom a half hour later, dressed in jeans and a slouchy pale green sweater that Viv always said did awesome things to her eyes. Their order must have only just been delivered, because Elliot was standing by the small table, unpacking what looked like cheeseburgers and fries from a paper bag.

"What's this?" she asked, when he held out one of the tall paper cups for her, the thick, spiral straw in the top making her suspicious.

"It's your chocolate milk shake," he replied with a smirk, taking a quick sip before holding it out for her again. "Mmm…a good one, too. I once had this gorgeous waitress recommend them to me. I got the feeling they were her favorite."

She took the cup from him, and couldn't help but smile. "So you got me one?"

"Hell, yeah. Just because we're in the middle of a shitstorm doesn't mean I can't be charming."

She laughed, thinking there were times when he was just too freaking perfect. "Thank you," she murmured, taking a long sip through the thick straw. It *was* delicious, and she couldn't resist taking another drink. "God," she moaned, clutching the shake to her chest. "My ass doesn't need it, but it's so freaking good."

Unwrapping his burger, he said, "Your ass is fucking perfect just the way it is."

She gave a delicate snort. "I wish."

He turned his head, giving her a sharp look. "Seriously, Skye. The first time I saw your ass in that tight uniform you were wearing at the diner, I nearly got down on my knees and thanked God."

"You are so full of it!"

"Just eat," he grunted, sounding a little frustrated with her, and they both sat down at the table without another word, digging into the greasy, but surprisingly good food. When they'd finished, she stuffed the wrappers back into the bag, and carried it over to the small trash can in the corner of the room, wishing she'd just accepted his earlier compliment and hadn't been such an idiot. Honestly! Why was she always trying to convince this guy that she was too heavy, when he seemed to enjoy her body exactly like it was?

She started to turn around and apologize, only to have her breath catch as she felt Elliot come up behind her, his chest pressing against her back, his big hands settling on her hips as he leaned down and spoke directly into her ear. "I meant what I said about your ass. I don't want you changing a single damn thing about your body for me. I'm addicted to it just the way it is."

"Sorry," she groaned, already turning her head so that she could find his mouth with hers. With a gravelly sound of hunger on his lips, he yanked her hips back against his thick erection and kissed her mouth just as wickedly as he'd kissed her between her legs, his tongue flicking and stroking, while he made the sexiest sounds deep in his throat.

When a loud knock suddenly shook the thin door in its frame, he cursed and pulled away from her. "Yeah?" he grunted, reaching down to rearrange his hard-on as he headed toward the door.

A deep, rough voice called out from the other side. "It's Lev, so open up. We're freezing our asses off out here."

Rolling his eyes, Elliot pulled the door open, and four intimidating-looking men came strolling into the motel room.

Skye lifted her hand, giving a lame little wave when their curious gazes swept over the room, then landed hard on her. *So these are the mercs he told me about,* she thought, finding them…um, yeah. They were something else. Like, literally. She didn't know *how* she knew, she just did. They weren't like her, but they weren't entirely like Elliot, either, and she made a mental note to ask him about it later, when they were alone.

The blond one who looked like something that had walked right off the screen of a blockbuster action flick came toward her, his smile charming and wide and more than a tad bit wicked. Elliot quickly moved back to her side, shooting the big, beautiful male a dark look of warning, and there was a guttural edge to his voice as he introduced the merc as Lev Slivkoff. He briefly explained to the group that she knew the truth about the Bloodrunners and the Silvercrest Lycans, and then the other males were introduced as James Bennett, Sam Harmon and Kyle Maddox. All dark, freaking-tall-as-hell giants like Elliot, and *almost* as handsome.

Lev looked between the two of them, noting how close Elliot was standing to her side, shot an interested look over at the still-wrecked bed, and then slowly smiled. "Now I get it," he said in a low, husky rumble as he settled his unusual blue-green gaze back on Elliot. "All these years I've been giving you a hard time about your monk-like lifestyle, when you were really just holding out for the good stuff."

"The good stuff?" Skye asked, thinking the guy couldn't possibly be talking about *her*. Though the sinful, appreciative look in his arresting gaze as it slid over her certainly made it seem that he was.

"Just ignore him," Elliot suggested under his breath. "Your life will be simpler if you do."

"Aw, don't do that," Lev drawled, giving her a mischievous wink. "I cry when pretty girls ignore me."

"Stop flirting with her, you ass," Elliot muttered, wrapping his arm around her waist and hauling her up against him. Lev's smile got even wider, while the other three just looked on with lopsided grins, as if they were used to this kind of thing.

Crossing his powerful arms over his chest, Lev propped his shoulder against the door and finally got serious. "Before we head out," he said, rubbing his hand over his jaw, "tell us about these bastards that attacked you at the safe house."

"They were big," Elliot started to explain, "though not quite as big as me, and they had a strange scent. Heavy on the musk, with almost a hint of coyote…or maybe cat. It was still daylight when I fought them, but they were able to release claws that were longer than mine, and their fangs were shorter. And their eyes, when they started to turn, went completely black."

Looking at the others, Lev said, "I told you guys they sounded like wargs."

"What the hell is a warg?" Elliot grunted, and Skye could feel the way he tightened his grip on her, his fingers digging into her hip.

The one named Kyle shoved his hand back through his dark hair and grimaced. "You don't wanna know, man."

"Kyle," Elliot muttered. "This isn't—"

"I'm serious," the merc said in a slow Southern accent, cutting him off as he pointed a long finger right at her. "Right now, we need to focus on getting the lovely Skye out of here."

She heard the low growl that vibrated in the back of Elliot's throat, and knew he was going to say something outrageously possessive before he even opened his mouth. "She's *my* lovely Skye. You can call her Miss Hewitt."

"Oh, God," the guy said with a hoarse laugh, shaking his head as he looked at the others. "It's happened to another one."

"What's happened?" she asked, hating the lost feeling she'd had ever since the conversation had started. And seeing as how they were talking about *her* again, she wanted some insight.

But Lev just gave her another wink, before pushing off from the door and checking the time on the thick black watch he wore on his wrist. Then he looked at Elliot, and asked, "What's the status at the safe house?"

"Mason was going to call in one of the local packs to get rid of the bodies. I'm hoping they might also find something that gives us a clue as to who the hell was shooting at the…wargs."

When the merc did nothing more than nod at the mention of gunshots and body disposal, Skye blinked, realizing that in their world, that probably wasn't as unusual an exchange as it was in hers. But it was one that she would no doubt hear about again, if this thing between her and Elliot managed to last. And *that* made her realize that there were actually a hell of a lot of questions she needed to ask him, if she wanted to start wrapping her head around this fascinating, clearly dangerous, sometimes terrifying world she'd been thrown into.

With the conversation wrapped up for the moment, Elliot grabbed their bags and slipped his gun into his waistband at his lower back, then the group headed out. There were two massive black trucks parked near her Beetle, and she knew without even having to be told that they belonged to the mercs. There was a brief discussion among the group about who would drive her sorry little car, and then James finally said he'd do the first shift, and someone could switch with him when they stopped for food. The others agreed, and then she and Elliot climbed into the backseat of one truck, while Lev and Sam got in the front, and Kyle climbed behind the wheel in the other one.

There'd been some light snowfall during the night, but nothing that made the roads dangerous. They made good time out of the dreary little town of Darner, before hitting one of the interstates that would take them south to Maryland. Since Lev and Sam were deep in discussion about some additions they wanted to make to their cabins once they were home, and there was Christmas music playing softly on the radio, Skye felt comfortable using the time to ask Elliot some of the questions she had. She was eager to learn as much as she could about his life and the people he lived with—in a place he called Bloodrunner Alley—before they arrived there later that day.

James hung back from the trucks on the road, since he was in her car and they knew that was the vehicle the wargs, as they called them, would be looking for. There was one scary moment when James called Lev's cell and said he thought he'd caught sight of someone tailing him. But it turned out to be a false alarm, and Lev distracted her by asking if Elliot had explained to her yet how the couples in the Alley were bonded as fated life-mates, which led to an entirely new set of questions that she could have sworn made Elliot more than a little uncomfortable. Reaching over and grabbing her hand, he basically mumbled his way through something about how "God, gods, or fate" could draw people together, but she couldn't get much more out of him than that.

As with some of the other things she'd asked him about, she could tell he was only giving her part of the story, glossing over a lot of it, almost as if he were walking a tightrope with what he wanted her to know…and what he didn't. Since there were things she was holding back on herself, Skye did her best not to press him too much, even as she acknowledged in the back of her mind that what they were doing wasn't healthy for a normal relationship. She tried to make herself feel better by arguing that nothing about their relationship so far had been what you could call normal, but it was clearly only a temporary fix. One that would no doubt blow up in her face.

Damn it, there really was so much she needed to share with him. So much that he deserved to know, before this thing between them went any further. They were heading into a serious relationship at warp speed, which was pure freaking madness, and she knew Vivian would be the first to tell her that she'd lost her ever-loving mind. That she could enjoy the sex, but needed to protect her heart. But she didn't care. She wouldn't change how fast or crazy it all was, even if she could, because this was what she needed. If they were in a "normal" situation, she'd have never found the confidence to keep seeing a guy like Elliot, writing him off because of her own issues before he even had the chance to prove himself.

It didn't make her proud to admit it, but that was the truth.

Eventually, they stopped for a break at an upscale rest station, giving everyone a chance to stretch their legs while grabbing coffees and some snacks, which Skye insisted on buying despite Elliot's cute, endearing protests. When they headed back out, Kyle switched vehicles with James, while she and Elliot continued to ride with Lev and Sam.

The guys had given up on the Christmas station, playing the Arctic Monkeys' latest CD instead. As the sultry notes of the music filled the cab, she reached over for Elliot's hand and drew it into her lap. She could feel the heat of his gaze against the side of her face as she turned his hand palm up, and then, using the tip of her finger, started to spell out a private message for him.

I.
Want.
You.
So.
Much.

She heard the catch of his breath, and knew she'd surprised him. With her lips curling up in a grin, she started to write another message, when he suddenly reversed the position of their hands, and wrote:

You're.
Playing.
With.
Fire.

Biting her lip, she turned his hand over, and replied:

Good.
I.
Hate.
To.
Be.
Cold.

A rough, deliciously sexy laugh slid lazily from his lips, and she thought she might melt right there into the leather seat, he made her so freaking hot. Curling his hand around the top of her thigh, he gave it a possessive squeeze as he lowered his mouth to her ear, whispering, "Should I just take you now, then?"

She turned his way a little, and slid him a hungry look from under her lashes. "Maybe *I'll* take *you*," she mouthed, loving the way his dark gaze warmed and his nostrils flared as he sucked in a sharp breath. Just when she was sure she could see his inner wolf there in his hooded, molten gaze, he grabbed her behind the neck, pulling her toward him, their mouths only a second away from crashing together, when Lev suddenly rolled down his window, saying, "Is it just me, or is it getting really friggin' hot in here?"

They both burst out laughing, and she couldn't even be that embarrassed, because Elliot looked so adorably happy. When she glanced toward the front seat, she caught Lev winking at her in the rearview mirror, and knew the gorgeous merc had been purposefully teasing them.

"We're almost there," Elliot said, taking her hand and linking their fingers together.

She wanted to smile at the excitement she could hear in his voice, but was simply too nervous. "That's…great," she said shakily, quickly realizing she hadn't asked him nearly enough questions to feel prepared for this.

"Hey, don't be nervous," he told her, the tender way he was looking at her almost managing to make her feel calm. "They're gonna love you. I promise."

She blinked, finding herself a bit dazzled by how gorgeous he was when their faces were that close together. And, geez, he really did have the thickest, longest eyelashes she'd ever seen.

"What?" he asked, giving her an inquisitive look when he realized how she was staring at him.

"Nothing," she whispered, licking her lower lip. "You're just incredibly pretty."

He snorted. "Guys aren't pretty, babe."

She grinned cheekily. "You are."

"Is that right?" he asked with a soft growl, leaning even closer to her.

"Yep."

"Do I need to prove my macho manliness to you right here?" he drawled with a slow smile, the look in his dark eyes so wicked she could feel her face flushing with heat. Then she lowered her gaze to his beautiful mouth, practically panting with desire, and knew he was playing with her as he ran his tongue over the edge of his teeth. *Oh...God.* It was such a freaking sexy move that she gasped, her mouth suddenly smashing against his so hard that it hurt, but she didn't care. She just wanted to kiss him until she forgot all about the Alley and how nervous she was- -but all too soon Lev's deep voice was saying, "Make out time's over, lovebirds."

"Fuck," Elliot growled against her lips, his hand on the side of her face as he pulled back. "We really are here."

She managed a little nod, then turned to look out the window as the truck pulled to a stop beside a beautiful, rustic-looking cabin that'd been decorated with white Christmas lights. And all she could think was *Wow. Just...wow.*

Elliot had described Bloodrunner Alley to her as a secluded, sloping glade surrounded by thick, lush forest. Originally, there had been ten cabins. But not long after Elliot and Max had become Runners, Lev and the guys had decided to make the Alley their permanent home base, and had built an additional five cabins at the far end of the glade, the fifth cabin belonging to Eli Drake, who had worked with the mercenaries for years.

Although they were basically in the middle of the woods, Elliot had assured her that it wouldn't feel anything like camping, which had caused the guys in the front seat to laugh. But she'd been relieved to hear that despite the natural setting, they had all the modern amenities there, from power to hot water and high-speed internet access. The same could be said for the Silvercrest pack's hometown, Shadow Peak, which was built farther up the mountain.

According to Elliot, Shadow Peak looked just like any other small mountain community—rather than the base for a thriving pack of werewolves. Only the inhabitants knew the truth about the town, and they seldom encountered visitors, since the roads that led this far up the mountain were all private. But as a precaution, there were scouts posted throughout the forest, ready to alert them to any humans who wandered onto the pack's land.

So yeah, she'd been given a lot of the basic information. But she hadn't been prepared for how truly beautiful the place was—or how many people would be there to greet them when they arrived. Because from what she could see, there were *a lot*. Enough that she was kind of freaking out on the inside, though she tried to keep a serene expression on her face as Elliot opened his door, climbed out, then reached in and simply pulled her across the seat, and out his door, as well.

"Come on," he said, grinning down at her as he set her on her feet and took her hand. "I told Mason earlier on the phone that I want to give you tonight to just settle in, so we're not going to have a meeting about Chiswick and all that shit until first thing in the morning. Right now, it's going to be really mellow and low-key. I just want to quickly introduce you to everyone who's here, and then we'll head over to my place by ourselves."

"Okay," she replied in a slightly breathless voice, walking with him toward the group that was gathered only about twenty feet away. As she looked over the faces of the men, women and children, she couldn't help but be a little awed by what a friendly, good-looking bunch they were, the men all as massive as Elliot, and the women just as beautiful as Viv. She expected them to notice the way Elliot was holding her hand, keeping her close to his side, and get perplexed looks on their faces, as if to say *What the hell is he doing with her?*

But that wasn't what happened. Not even close.

When a pretty woman with red hair and glasses came rushing up and gave Elliot a big hug, he introduced her as Torrance. Skye knew this was the human who loved to mother him, and whose children he considered to be like siblings. When Torrance's big green eyes took in the way Elliot was holding Skye's hand so possessively, she smiled like she'd just been told she'd won the lottery.

"How did you two meet?" she asked in an excited rush, as a big, handsome, dark-haired guy Skye knew must be Mason Dillinger came and threw his arm around the tiny redhead's shoulders. "I know Elliot was looking for you, because of the case. But how did you actually talk the first time? I hate to be so nosey, but I can't help it!"

Tucking her hair behind her ear, Skye grinned as she slanted Elliot a quick look, then said, "Well, he, um, came into the diner where I work and sat down in one of my booths. I noticed him, but it was busy and I hadn't been able to take his order yet. So he was sitting there, watching me, eating some of the peanuts that we set out on the tables. And when I walked by his table the first time, I couldn't stop myself from glancing over at him, wanting a closer look, and I realized he was choking."

Torrance's eyes went comically wide. "He was choking on the peanuts?"

Skye nodded as she laughed. "I know it's not funny, but you should have seen his face after I whacked him on the back as hard as I could. I've never seen anyone look so surprised."

It was pathetic, but Elliot knew he was blushing so hard his entire face must be red.

"This happened when you got close to him for the first time, is that what you said?" Mason asked Skye, though he was looking at Elliot as he spoke, giving him one hell of a knowing smirk.

"Yes." She grinned up at Elliot. "He was probably distracted by my ugly uniform. I look really hideous in it."

"Not true," he murmured, hating to hear her say anything negative about herself, even when he was kind of wishing the ground would just open up and swallow him whole. "You looked fucking hot as hell in that thing."

"Language," Torrance reminded him with a laugh. "Katie already has enough bad influences around here without you adding to the problem."

As if she'd just been waiting for the sound of her name, the little girl suddenly crashed into Elliot's legs, arms lifted high in the air, waiting for him to pick her up.

"You won't repeat any of the potty words you hear come out of Uncle Elliot's mouth, will you?" he asked her, loving the way she squealed when he tossed her up into the air, then perched her on his arm.

"Nope," she said, giving Skye a shy grin, before looking back at Elliot. "I promise!"

"That's 'cause my Katie Olivia is a good girl, right?"

"Yep," she agreed, before her dirty little face scrunched up, and she leaned in a little closer to whisper, "Only, I kinda kicked my brother this morning."

From the corner of his eye, Elliot could see Skye biting her lip to hold in her laughter. "What'd he do?" he asked, having to fight back his own chuckle.

"He told me I couldn't play with him and the other boys 'cause he said I'm a stupid girl."

Mason groaned, Torrance gasped and Elliot pressed a quick kiss to Katie's chubby little dirt-covered cheek. "Well, we both know that's not true. Girls are tons smarter than smelly boys, right?"

Katie's smile beamed. "That's what I told him!"

"Can we make you guys some dinner?" Torrance asked, reaching out and taking Katie into her arms.

"Thanks, Tor, but we'll be fine. I just want to give Skye a chance to get settled in tonight."

"Dinner now!" Katie argued, wiggling her way down to the ground from her mother's arms. "Please! Please! Please!"

Wrapping his arm around Skye's waist, Elliot looked down at Katie and said, "We'll eat dinner with you soon, munchkin. I promise."

Katie got that calculating gleam in her big eyes that Elliot recognized only too well. "Dinner *and* a movie?"

He looked to Skye, who was smiling her agreement, and told Katie, "I think we can probably swing that."

"Yay! And you *have* to bring Skye, 'cause she's pretty.

Me and Mommy will make your favorite cookies and she can eat them, too!"

He looked at Mason and grinned. "Your girl is starting to get some serious negotiating skills."

"Don't I know it," the Runner drawled, shaking his head.

"Come on, you little terror," Torrance said with a laugh, grabbing her daughter's hand. "It's bath time for you."

Katie reached up and ran her little fingers over her browner-than-usual cheek. "But Reece said the dirt makes it look like I'm tan like Daddy."

Elliot laughed. Reece was Jeremy and Jillian Burns's youngest son, and the little dude was already a handful.

"That might be so," Torrance muttered, "but it's made you smell like a *boy*."

Katie gasped with theatrical outrage, then started pulling on her mom's arm, obviously changing her mind about needing that bath.

"I'm looking forward to us having more of a chance to talk tomorrow," Torrance called out to Skye, and then a whole group of his friends—Jillian, Elise, Carla and Chelsea—were coming forward, introducing themselves to Skye and welcoming her to the Alley, while their kids ran around playing in the snow. He knew from talking to Mason on the phone that Brody Carter and his wife, Michaela, who was also Max's sister, were up in Shadow Peak, helping to care for Brody's ailing grandmother, which explained their absence. But Elliot didn't doubt he'd be getting a call from Brody soon, demanding to know what the hell was going on with Max.

As Elliot stepped to the side of the group, since Carla—the only female Runner—had pretty much shoved him away, Mason clapped him on the shoulder and laughed. "So I was done in by my feet, and you by some peanuts."

"Shut up," he muttered under his breath. He should have friggin' known the Runner would figure out what had happened, seeing as how he'd reacted just as crazily when he'd found his own mate.

"I'm just saying, it's pretty fucking funny," Mason drawled.

With a quiet snort, Elliot said, "At least I didn't trip anyone."

Mason just grinned. "Best damn decision I ever made in my life."

Torrance had had to run back to grab the scarf Katie had left in the snow, and since she'd been close enough to hear that last remark, she shot her husband a knowing look. "I thought that was marrying me."

"It's all connected, sweetheart," Mason playfully growled, suddenly lifting his wife into his arms. "If I hadn't stopped you, I might have lost you."

"Never gonna happen," she said with a warm smile, throwing her arms around her husband's neck as he told Elliot he'd see him at the meeting in the morning, before carrying her toward their cabin.

Thinking it was pretty awesome, how crazy in love those two still were, Elliot glanced over at Skye, and found her watching Mason carry his wife away with a dreamy expression on her face. He completely got how she felt, since it was hard not to be a little in awe of the connection that the couples in the Alley shared. They'd all lived and fought through hell together, to get to where they were today, and it'd made them stronger. Closer. And fucking unbreakable.

"Sayre wanted to be here," Cian Hennessey said as he stepped up beside him, "but she's taken Brannagh up to Shadow Peak to visit her mom."

"Still not the woman's biggest fan?" Elliot asked, knowing damn well that the Irishman's mother-in-law was a hard woman to take.

Cian gave him a wry smile. "We get along when we have to. But we sure as hell don't go out of our way to spend time together."

Elliot laughed. "I don't blame you."

"By the way, Sayre stocked up your kitchen with some fresh supplies."

"Yeah? That's awesome. Give her a kiss for me," he teased, but Cian just smirked at him. Dude was so friggin' blissed out and in love with one of Elliot and Max's closest friends, it was hard as hell to get a rise out of him these days.

Nodding his head toward Skye, who was chatting with an even bigger group of Elliot's friends now, Cian said, "Looks like you've finally got your own woman to kiss."

He shot Skye a possessive, heavy-lidded look. "That I most certainly do," he murmured, beginning to understand Cian and the others in a way he never really had before. If they felt even a fraction of the way Skye made him feel about their own women, then it was no wonder they were able to smile through even the toughest of times.

"And Sayre's got some news to tell you," Cian added, "so don't be surprised if she comes knocking on your door bright and early tomorrow morning, before the meeting at Mason's."

He lifted his brows as he brought his attention back to the Runner. "What news?"

The guy just gave him a crooked smile. "My girl will kill me if I steal her thunder."

Hmm. From the look of intense satisfaction burning deep in Cian's silver eyes, Elliot wouldn't be surprised to hear that they were adding a new little rug rat to their growing family, and he was happy as hell for them.

Making his way back to Skye's side, he told everyone they could talk to her more tomorrow, then took a leaf out of Mason's book and swooped her up into his arms, carrying her over to the cabin he'd been living in for about eight years now. It'd taken a while, but he'd finally come to think of the place as home. Especially after Torrance and the other women had helped him fix it up.

Once he had Skye inside, he kicked the door shut behind them, then slowly lowered her to her feet, enjoying the feel of her soft body sliding against his. He could not, for the life of him, get why this woman was so self-conscious about her figure. Sure, some men liked skin and bones, but Elliot wasn't one of them. He couldn't get enough of the way she felt under his greedy hands, or when he was covering her with his body.

And he sure as hell couldn't get enough of how impossibly good she tasted, from her warm, honey-flavored mouth down to her tender, juicy sex.

Unable to help himself, and not even wanting to, he pushed his hands into all that lustrous hair that fell over her shoulders, tilted her head back for him and leaned down, covering her lips with his. Then he kissed her like he'd wanted to kiss her back in the truck.

"Elliot?" she murmured, rubbing her cheek against his chest, when they both had to break away for air.

"Hmm?"

In a quiet voice, she said, "I love your cabin. And

the Alley…it's beautiful. I get it now, why you love it so much up here in these woods. But…there's something I need to ask you."

His lips curled in a smile against the top of her head. "What's that, baby?"

"It's kinda awkward, but you *are* house-trained, right? I mean, I won't have to worry about you cocking your leg up and peeing on any of the furniture, will I?"

He put his hands on her shoulders and stepped back so that he could see her face, hoping to God she wasn't serious—then burst out laughing when he caught the mischievous gleam in her eyes. "You little smart-ass," he growled, loving the way she shrieked with laughter when he started to tickle her. He was ruthless, going after her most sensitive places, until she was begging for mercy.

"Uncle, uncle!" she cried, desperately trying to catch her breath. "I was only teasing, I swear!"

"You better have been," he rasped, nipping her ear-lobe with his teeth, before reaching around and swatting her on the ass. "Now go grab that shower you said you wanted, and I'll see what I can scrounge up for dinner."

"I can cook," she said, green gaze still shining with humor as she rubbed her bottom and backed out of the room.

"I'd love you to cook for me," he said, unable to take his eyes off her. "But tonight it's going to be something quick, like sandwiches and chips, because I can't wait to get you in my bed. Been thinking about what you'll look like there from the moment I first saw you smile."

Suddenly, the look in her eyes wasn't so much teasing as it was hot. "In that case, just bring the sandwiches with you to bed. We can eat them there."

Elliot gave her a slow, wicked smile just before she

disappeared down the hallway. Then he rubbed his hand over his jaw as he turned and headed toward the kitchen, his voice little more than a guttural rumble of sound as he said, "I fucking love the way my girl thinks."

I fucking love the way my girl thinks. My girl. My girl. My.
Girl.

Pulling her brush through her hair, Skye shook her head at herself and laughed. God, she had it so bad when such an innocent little phrase she probably hadn't even been meant to overhear had her swooning like he'd proposed.

Lev or one of the other mercs must have brought their bags in for them, because she'd found her backpack and Elliot's duffel sitting on the foot of his bed before she'd taken her shower. Quickly throwing on a clean pair of jeans and a long-sleeved T-shirt, she padded on bare feet through the cabin, admiring the packed bookshelves that lined so many of the walls as she searched for him.

She found two plates loaded with sandwiches and chips sitting on the kitchen counter, but no Elliot. He wasn't in the living room, either, or out on the front porch, so she headed back into the hallway, figuring she'd find him somewhere in the back of the cabin. The master bedroom and bathroom were on her right, but there was a door farther down on her left, and then the back door at the end of the hallway. As she neared the door on the left, she caught the sound of Elliot's voice, but could tell by how low he was speaking that he didn't want to be overheard.

Crap. She knew the right thing to do would be to turn around and go back into the bedroom, giving him the privacy he'd obviously wanted for what had to be a phone call, since she heard him say Max's name. But... she couldn't. Something had her feet rooted to the floor, her lower lip caught tight in her teeth as she listened to him warning Max to be careful and to call his sister, because she was worried about him. Then he said something about wanting to send a few of the mercs to join him and Vivian, but from what she could hear, it sounded like Max wouldn't agree.

"Why the fuck are you being so stubborn?" Elliot asked with a harsh growl. "Just get your ass back here."

Max must have said something about Vivian, because Elliot's next words were: "Then convince her. Christ, her best friend is here. Skye is worried sick about her."

Thinking that she'd probably heard enough, since she really *was* feeling ill, she started to walk away, when his next words stopped her in her tracks.

"Look, before you go, there's something I need to tell you. Skye...she's *mine*, man."

What the what?

Max must have had a similar reaction, because Elliot muttered, "What do you think I mean? I knew the instant I caught her scent. She's *mine*."

Scent? Oh... *Ohmygod!* Was he talking about the life-mate connection—the thing he'd so awkwardly explained to her on their way up to the Alley, after Lev had put him on the spot? And now he was... *Jesus Christ!* Was he saying she was his *mate*? As in the one woman meant to be *his*?

Unable to process what she'd heard, Skye stumbled down the hall and through the back door, then down the porch steps. She didn't know why, but instead of being happy, she felt like something in her chest was being twisted and torn into pieces, and she put her hands on her head as she pulled in deep breaths of the cold mountain air, needing it to help clear her thoughts.

I mean, it's not like I don't want to be Elliot's mate, she thought, trying to make sense of her panic. *Any woman in the world would want that!*

No, it was something that lay beyond that that was wigging her out. Something else that was making her want to throw her head back and scream at the top of her lungs.

And then she had it. The reason. The thing that was breaking her heart.

All this time, she'd been thrilled that Elliot was attracted to her for who she was...just the way she was. That he genuinely desired *her*. Curvy and shy and awkward. Average. Human...

But that'd been a lie.

He didn't want her for herself. He only wanted the woman his instinct *told* him to want.

All the little things that made her the woman she was, they were... God, they were nothing. Heavy, skinny, short, tall. Funny, boring, quick, slow. None of it mattered. She could have been an ax-wielding psychopath and he probably would have felt the same. Seen her the same.

Elliot Connors only wanted her because of *what* she was. Because that animal part of him told him he *had* to feel that way.

And now she felt like the biggest fool alive.

Chapter 12

"Skye? What are you doing out here? It's freezing and you're barefoot!"

She flinched at the sound of Elliot's worried voice coming from the back porch, then slowly turned to face him. As she took in the way he stood there under the moon and stars, it was suddenly so easy to see that she'd been such a naive, crushed-out-on-him idiot. She should have freaking known!

Frowning as he studied her tight expression, he started down the porch steps. "Hey, what's wrong?" he asked, his deep voice rough with concern.

She swallowed so hard that it hurt, then somehow managed to scrape out, "I heard you."

"What?" Though he sounded calm, she could see the slight flare of panic in his dark eyes as he drew closer.

"On the phone, with Max," she said stiffly, finding

it difficult to get the words past her tingling lips, the frigid wind whipping at her hair. "I heard what you told him about *me*."

With only a couple of yards separating them, he froze like he'd just slammed into a brick wall. His big hands curled into fists at his sides, and his gaze narrowed as he muttered, "Shit."

Her voice was shaky, but sharp with accusation. "You've been lying to me, Elliot."

"Wait. What?" He drew in a deep breath, his brow furrowing with tension. "What do you mean *lying*?"

"You didn't tell me that you *have* to like me, which is as good as a lie." She could feel her anger rising, filling her up inside until she felt like she might explode with it. "That's kind of an important detail not to share. Especially between two people who are sleeping together!"

His worried expression started to bleed into a scowl. "Damn it, Skye. I don't know where your head is taking you, but just stop."

"Why?" she demanded hotly, fisting her own hands as she took another step toward him. "I haven't said anything that isn't true. If it weren't for my scent or whatever the hell is causing this, you would have never even looked twice at me!"

"That's bullshit!" he snarled, giving her a blistering glare.

Stomping one frozen foot against the snow-covered ground, she shouted, "The hell it is!"

He opened his mouth, then snapped it shut again, his nostrils flaring as he exhaled a harsh breath and did a quick visual sweep of the area. Then he brought that pissed-off, frustrated gaze back to hers, and stepped to the side. Lifting one long arm, he pointed his index finger toward the open back door. "You want to argue about what I feel for you," he growled, "then get inside the fucking cabin."

"Don't boss me around," she flung back at him, bristling and spoiling for a fight.

He worked his jaw a few times, seeming determined not to completely lose his temper. But he was clearly furious as he quietly seethed, "You can walk in there, or I'll toss your backward little ass over my shoulder and carry you in. Your choice."

"Backward?" she gasped, stalking toward him and shoving him in the chest. "What the hell?" she snapped, pissed that she hadn't even made him budge.

"Yeah, backward," he forced out through his gritted teeth. "You're coming at this thing so wrong it isn't even funny."

"I know it isn't funny!" She wrapped her arms around herself so tightly she could barely breathe, fighting back the stupid tears that wanted to fall. "Do I look like I'm laughing?"

With his brown eyes beginning to glow with a thin ring of gold, he leaned down and got right in her face. "I'm going to set you straight, Skye. One way or another. We can either do it out here, where I promise you everyone will hear us and you'll freeze from your stubbornness, or you can get inside, where it's warm, and we can sort this out in the privacy of our cabin."

"*Your* cabin," she huffed, giving him a wide berth as she decided he was right, and headed back inside. Her anger was only going to keep her from turning into an icicle for so long, and she really didn't want all of Elliot's neighbors hearing what she had to say.

"Go and sit on the sofa," he muttered behind her,

heading into his bedroom. He came into the living room a few moments later, tossing her a thick pair of socks for her feet and one of his sweatshirts to pull on, since she was shivering from the cold. She tightened her jaw, muttering an angry "Thanks" as she pulled the socks on, her feet instantly feeling better, even though her emotions were still bleeding and raw.

"I'm sorry I didn't tell you," he started in a harsh voice, rubbing the back of his neck with one hand as he began to pace the hardwood floor on the other side of the big ass coffee table that separated them.

"Good," she grumbled, pulling the sweatshirt over her head. "You should be."

Sliding her a frustrated look from the corner of his eye, he kept on pacing. "I know, okay? But…think about it, Skye. It's not like it's the easiest thing to explain to a woman who's only just met you. Who doesn't even know that Lycans are real." He rolled his broad shoulders, his tall body vibrating with a raw, visceral tension that seemed to fill the room, and she hated how what he was saying made sense. Turning his head, he locked his dark gaze with hers, and asked, "In all honesty, how the hell do you think that conversation would have gone?"

"And what about *after* I learned what you are?" she demanded hoarsely, her throat so tight she could barely get the words out. "You couldn't tell me then?"

He shoved his hand back through his hair with so much force she almost winced for his poor scalp. "I could have. You're right. But you were already dealing with the fact that werewolves exist. I didn't want to throw too much at you."

She had to swallow twice before she could manage to say, "And when…when we finally fucked?"

"Jesus, Skye. Are you serious?" His voice was low and clipped, and the look in his eyes as he stopped in the middle of the floor and just stared at her, hard, made her pulse race madly. "It was a hell of a lot more than fucking and you know it."

She lifted her chin and blinked furiously, refusing to let the tears building behind her eyes again fall in front of him. "What I know is that you only want me because you have to! It has nothing to do with *me* at all!"

"I told you before, that's bullshit!" The muscles in his arms bulged as he locked his hands behind his neck and dropped his head back, broad chest rising and falling like a bellows as he stared up at the beamed ceiling. He took five harsh, ragged breaths, before dropping his arms to his sides and looking right at her. "I...I might not have all the answers for how this mating shit works, but I don't really give a damn." And then, in a lower voice that shredded her, he said, "I'm just happy that it's you. Can't that be enough?"

Oh, God. She could have crumpled right then, but fear had her arguing, "You're just saying that because your instinct or whatever you call it is telling you to! Because you—"

"No!" he roared, the guttural shout shocking her into silence. A muscle pulsed in the hard edge of his jaw, while his dark gaze drilled into her...digging...searching for the truth. And then he slowly lifted his hand, and rubbed it over his mouth. "Oh...*hell*," he breathed, his hand curling into a fist as he dropped it back to his side. "Are you... Are you reacting this way because of that *Derek* asshole?"

"No," she whispered, even though she could feel the

angry flush of color leeching from her face. Talk about a direct hit. "It's, um, just that…"

"Just that what?" he barked, looking as if he'd like nothing better than to get his hands on Derek Carlton and wring his cheating neck.

Head spinning from the force of her past and present colliding, she grimaced as she heard herself slowly say, "He taught me a lot."

"What? To be blind? Is that what he taught you? Because it's bullshit, Skye. Fucking bullshit!" he growled, the dark of his eyes so golden now she felt like she was staring into that most primal, visceral part of him. And yet, there was so much tenderness there, in those beautiful eyes, it was breaking her heart. "I want you so badly I'm aching with it," he said low and rough, sounding completely shattered. "Going out of my goddamn mind."

She dug her fingers into the sofa cushions, trying to find her way through an argument that had shifted on her so quickly, she no longer knew quite where to go with it. Blinking with confusion, she looked up at him and blurted, "But you've already had me."

"Yeah, and it only made me want you more," he said huskily, taking a step toward her. "I'll never get enough, never get my fill. And I can't help that the pull is there between us, but this is *more* than that. I was drawn to you from the first."

She wet her lips with a nervous flick of her tongue. "I…I wish that was the truth."

Hooded gaze burning with determination, he stepped right up to the other side of the table, and said, "You want to hear some truths? Then you can damn well hear this one. Before I caught even the slightest whiff of your scent in my head, I had your face in my line of sight.

And it stole my breath. I stood outside the diner and watched you for over an hour that first night, studying you, growing completely obsessed. I watched you charm poor bastards down on their luck, making them smile. I saw you be kind to people for the simple reason that you *are* kind. And I couldn't wrap my head around how you could be so fucking sweet and so incredibly beautiful all at the same time.

"Right then, I started falling, hard and fast, before I ever even got up the nerve to walk inside and sit down at one of your tables. I was already gone for you before I even knew you were mine. And each day that goes by, I learn more about you, and I'm gone even *deeper*. That's not the connection. The connection makes me want to protect you, makes the lust I feel for you nearly impossible to control, but it doesn't control how I *feel* about you. That's all on you, Skye. Every ounce of it."

Her shivery voice was low, breathless. "And exactly how do you f-feel about me? I mean, now?"

There was an almost wry twitch to his lips as he stared back at her. "It's cute as hell that you can't see it," he muttered, shaking his head a little, "when my friends all knew the second they saw us together."

"Elliot, listen," she whispered, making a move to stand up—but he stopped her with nothing more than a look.

"No, *you* listen, Skye. Just shut up, sit there, and for once listen to what I'm saying." He shoved one trembling hand back through his hair again, his deep voice vibrating with emotion as he said, "I would choose you over and over and over again. Over any other woman in this pack or this state or the entire goddamn world, because you are *my* idea of perfection. I wouldn't change a single thing about you. You're what I want."

She bit her lip as she let those gravelly words linger in the air between them, soaking them in, wishing that she could find a way to have faith in them. Did she already believe him? Was it really that simple? Or was she just latching on to what she *wanted* to believe? Then she recalled what had started this whole argument off to begin with, and she shot him a sharp look of surprise. "How did you manage to get Max on the phone?"

If he was frustrated by the change in topic, he didn't let on. Coming around the coffee table, he sat down on its wooden surface right in front of her, his long legs on either side of hers as he leaned forward and braced his elbows on his knees. "I was calling him to leave another voice mail. Just wanted to let him know that we'd made it here. But he surprised me by answering his phone."

She searched his gaze, her stomach dropping when she read the worry there. "Did he tell you what's happened to them? Where they're at?"

There was a grim set to his jaw as he shook his head. "He wouldn't tell me anything. Just that Vivian is safe, but…"

"But what?" she pressed, when his quiet words trailed off.

Taking one of her cold hands in his, he said, "I don't think she's learned what he is. But even so, she refuses to come here with him."

Confusion creased her brow, and as the other parts of the conversation she'd overheard started to come back to her, her heart began to beat so hard she could feel each thump echoing through her body. "Even…even knowing that I'm here, she won't come?"

"I'm sorry, Skye. I don't know what's going on. I got lucky catching Max when I did, but I don't think he'll answer his phone again anytime soon. Something's going on between those two—but I don't know what. I just know that he'll do whatever it takes to protect her."

Her shoulders fell with disappointment and exhaustion. "At least there's that," she murmured, exhaling a shaky breath.

He gave her hand a comforting squeeze. "Yeah."

The silence stretched out, on the verge of becoming awkward, since she still didn't know what to say about all that other stuff. But then he used his grip on her hand to gently tug her to her feet, and said, "Come on. I know we still need to talk, but let's get you fed first."

They went together to the kitchen, grabbed the plates of sandwiches he'd made and two cans of Pepsi from the fridge, then sat down at the table. She picked at her food as she asked him a few questions about the people she'd met when they'd gotten there, but it was clear that they were both thinking about other things. When they'd loaded the plates into the dishwasher, she could no longer hold in the words that were burning in her throat. "Tell me, please," she said unsteadily, cutting him a curious sideways look from behind the fall of her hair.

"Tell you what, baby?" he asked, turning and crossing his arms over his chest as he leaned back against the counter.

She pulled in a deep breath for courage, then looked him right in the eye. "How…how *do* you feel about me?"

The briefest of smiles lifted the corner of his beautiful mouth. "I think I've made it pretty clear that I'm crazy about you."

She couldn't stop the answering smile that suddenly

twitched at the corner of her own mouth, while a fresh burst of tears burned at the backs of her eyes. "I'm... crazy about you, too. So much that you're all I can think about."

He managed to remain leaning against the counter for all of two seconds, the way he ran his tongue over the edge of his teeth as he returned her intense gaze so damn sexy it made her gasp—and then he exploded into action. Before she could draw her next breath, he was in front of her, one hand fisting aggressively...*possessively*...in her hair, pulling her head back so that he could claim her mouth with his, while the other gripped her hip and jerked her against him.

"We'll talk later," he muttered against her lips, before nipping her lower one with his teeth.

"Tell me what you want," she moaned, shoving her hands into his hair as he reached between them and started unbuttoning her jeans.

"I want to *have you* in every room in this cabin, Skye. On every surface," he said in a voice that was rough and raw with need, as he shoved his hand into the front of her panties. He found her warm and slick, the sexy growl that rumbled up from his chest an unmistakable sign of how much he liked it.

Rising up on her toes, she crashed her mouth against his, kissing him so hard and desperately she hadn't even realized he'd picked her up and started walking until he was tossing her into the middle of his massive king-size bed. She also hadn't realized she'd lost her jeans somewhere along the way, and she couldn't help but grin up at him, thinking *Damn, he's good*.

"Get the rest of your fucking clothes off," he growled, watching her with a sharp, predatory hunger from where he stood at the foot of the bed. As she followed the dominant, wildly erotic command, there was a part of her that probably should have been at least slightly terrified—but she was too in love with him to be afraid.

Too in love with him...?

Um, yeah...that crazy-ass thought had just come from her. She was too caught up in the way that Elliot was looking at her, though, to freak out about it. And, seriously, what woman wouldn't be head over heels for this man?

He'd already removed his shirt and his boots, and he took his jeans and underwear down in one move, kicking them away. Then he was crawling over her, all those powerful, mouthwatering muscles drawn tight under his golden skin, rippling and lean, and she made some kind of keening sound of need, desperate to touch him...to *feel* him. But he was already shoving her thighs wide, his open mouth covering her drenched sex a fraction of a second before he had his tongue pushed deep inside her. She cried out, arms flung wide, body trapped in a devastating maelstrom of pleasure as he started a delicious combination of ravenous, greedy licks and hungry, penetrating thrusts.

Needing to watch him go wild on her, Skye somehow found the strength to lift up onto her elbows, her breathing so rapid and fast she sounded like she was running a marathon. Then she was biting down hard on her lower lip, trying to choke back a deafening scream as she got caught in the power of a hard, explosive orgasm that tore itself all the way through to her soul. She gasped and moaned as she rode it out, unable to take her eyes away from how he looked lying there between her legs, his avid mouth moving against her slick, softly pulsing flesh, and as he lifted his hooded gaze over the shivering length of her body, his dark eyes *burned* as he watched her watching him. He didn't stop until the last tremor had eased its way through her, leaving her panting and flushed, and then he rose up and knelt there between her trembling thighs, his magnificent body hard and brutally aroused, making him look like a freaking god.

He wiped one of his big hands across his wet lips and chin, and with a primal growl in his throat, he came down over her, lapping and nipping at her flesh as he worked his way up to her mouth, his upper body braced on the hand he'd buried in the pillow by her head. Her breath caught as she felt him reach between them, and then the hot, thick head of his cock was pressing against her tight, tender entrance. He ran his tongue over her bottom lip, nipped it again with his teeth, then lifted his head just enough that he could watch her face. With one powerful thrust of his hips, he buried himself so hard and deep, she knew she'd taken nearly every inch of him.

"Skye," he said in a voice so raw and low she wasn't sure she heard it, so much as *felt* it. Felt the emotion behind it.

Her throat shook, melting, pleasure burning through every cell in her body as he started to move. Shoving her hands into his thick hair, she held him tight, drowning in the glittering depths of his beautiful, animal-colored eyes, and in a voice so husky it didn't even sound like hers, she said, "Tell me what you're thinking."

I love you...love you...love you. But I can't tell you. Not yet. Not until I... Until I've told you everything.

Those were Elliot's thoughts, but he couldn't utter a single one of them. Because he was afraid. Terrified out of his goddamn mind, actually, and feeling like the ground had just been ripped right out from under him.

Shit, he loved her. Was *in love* with her. And he wasn't prepared to deal with it. Not yet. He didn't know what the hell to tell her, when he couldn't tell her everything. It was all so screwed-up and wrong, when nothing should have felt more right.

Tell her the truth! All of it! his wolf snarled, and he flinched, knowing the bastard was right.

But instead of taking the beast's advice, all he heard himself say was, "I love how you hold me. How it feels to have this beautiful body beneath me, cradling me, so soft and warm. You've damn well ruined me for anyone else."

"Good."

He leaned down and pressed his lips to her tender ones. "Only you, Skye. I'll never want another woman for as long as I live. Only *you*," he breathed, keeping his eyes open and locked hard on hers, wanting her to see for herself that he meant every word. "So you have to trust me, baby. You have to trust in what I feel for you."

"I want to," she gasped, using her hold on his hair to crush his mouth against hers, her sweet tongue pushing between his parted lips.

Desperate to try yet another thing that he'd never done before, Elliot wrapped his arms around her, holding her close as he rolled onto his back. She gasped again as she suddenly found herself lying on top of him, her big eyes going wide with shock.

Voice little more than a guttural scrape of sound, he gripped her hips, and said, "Fuck me, Skye. Ride me."

Her lashes fluttered as she braced her hands against his chest and pushed up a bit, her long hair falling in wild, beautiful waves around her shoulders, heavy breasts swaying with her rapid breaths. "Elliot, I…I don't know about this."

"Am I hurting you?" he grunted, lifting her up and holding her there, about halfway up his shaft.

Her hair flew around her shoulders as she shook her head. "No. I mean…you're huge, but I can handle it."

He groaned, unable to keep his hips from punching up while he dug his fingers into her soft flesh and pulled her down, packing every inch of him deep inside her warm, wet heaven. "Then what's the problem?"

"It's…um…me. I feel too exposed. All the lights are still on, and…and I feel like you're going to—"

He cut her off with a rough, thick sound of frustration. "Unless you're about to say that you feel like I'm going to lose my friggin' mind because you're so damn sexy and beautiful, you need to just shut up."

Instead of arguing with him, she drew in a deep breath, and he could see the instant she finally decided to listen…and *try.* With that lush lower lip caught tight in her teeth, she gave herself a moment to simply stare down at him, those breathtaking eyes reading his face… every facet of his expression. He did his best to leave himself wide-open, wanting her to see it all, because in *this*—in his need and lust and desire for her—he had *nothing* to hide. Not a single goddamn thing.

See it, baby, he thought, stroking his hands over her soft skin, desperate for her faith in a way he'd never experienced. Not even when his parents had kicked him out at seventeen. Not in his entire life. *Believe it. Believe in me.*

He squeezed her hips between his big hands, then ran them down, over her creamy thighs, and his dick swelled inside her snug, slick sex. Somehow, he got even harder...thicker. She swayed above him...shivering...the tender tremors moving through her lush body, until they vibrated around his iron-hard shaft, the sensation so intense it nearly sent his eyes rolling back in his head. But he willed himself to keep his heavy-lidded gaze locked tight on her face, not wanting to miss the moment when she *finally* got it.

And God, it was worth it.

The tremors got harder, her eyes went wide again, and then those plump pink lips parted for the sweetest, softest gasp he'd ever heard. "You...you *really* mean it."

"Damn right I do." He curved his hands over the perfect swell of her hips, reaching around and squeezing the mouthwatering globes of her ass. "Your body is my heaven and holy ground and temple all rolled into one, and I just want to fucking worship it. I don't ever want to stop."

She leaned forward, bracing her hands on either side of his head, all that long, honey-blond hair falling around them like a veil as her soft lips found his. She teased him with fleeting butterfly sweeps of her lips, her tongue taking dainty licks that danced just inside his mouth, and he swore he could feel her smile when he gave a loud, impatient growl. And all the while, her tight, wet heat was squeezing that most sensitive part of him, making him throb.

"More," he scraped out, trailing one shaky hand up the sensuous line of her spine to fist in the back of her hair, close to her scalp, while the other curved back over her hip. *"Now,"* he demanded, pushing his tongue into that sweet little mouth at the same time he braced his feet against the bed and shoved himself deeper with a hard, driving thrust.

She moaned into his mouth, and he gave her a moment to get used to him being that far inside her. He was heavier and broader than he'd ever been, the shaft so swollen and tight he felt like he might burst.

"Christ," he gasped against her soft lips, when she started rolling her hips, moving on him...the feeling so intense he wanted to howl. "That's it, baby. Let go and fuck me back."

"Feels so good," she panted, her open mouth sweet and hot over his, the hard tips of her breasts rubbing across his chest as their sweat-slick bodies slid against each other, her thighs hugging his hips, her mouthwatering scent and taste all over him. It was so damn incredible—*too incredible*—and Elliot had to use his grip on her hair to pull her head back, his fangs suddenly dropping from his gums in a sharp, vicious burst of heat.

He started to turn his head away, terrified he would frighten her, when she shocked the hell out of him by laying her soft hand against the side of his face, silently telling him it was okay. Breathing so hard that it hurt, he flicked his tongue over the pointed tip of a fang, the way her eyes went hot making him bite out a hoarse curse. Jesus, this woman was killing him.

"Will you...will you claim me?" she whispered, still pulsing those gorgeous hips against him in a way that had him sweating and shaking, the pleasure so intense he felt like she could melt him down. "Will you bite me and bind us together, like the other couples here?"

He licked his lips, guttural voice more animal than man as he told her, "Only when you're ready."

"Are *you* ready?"

He gave her a sharp, wolfish smile. "From the first second I saw you." Then, a quieter "But...we'll wait."

"Will I like it?" she asked, the sensual smile touching her lips, as she pressed her hands against his chest and started riding him faster…harder, the most beautiful damn thing he'd ever seen.

"You'll love it," he growled, knowing he was about two seconds away from completely losing it. Reaching behind his head, Elliot fisted his hands around the metal bars of his headboard, his grip so hard there was no doubt he'd be leaving deep indentations behind. Fangs heavy in his mouth and eyes burning with what had to be a bright, molten gold, he told her, "Harder, Skye. Ride me harder. Show me just what that gorgeous body of yours can do."

She rose up and threw her head back, exposing the pale, vulnerable length of her throat, her beautiful breasts bouncing as she moved, and Elliot knew he wasn't going to last. With a thick, animalistic sound of hunger falling from his lips, he sat up and twisted, taking her down to the bed in a move that was too fast to have been done by any human. Her eyes went heavy with satisfaction, as if she loved seeing him so close to the edge of his control. And the way her nails dug into his hard shoulders, as she tried to drag him closer, made it clear that she wasn't afraid. Forcing his fangs to retract, he reached down and caught her behind her knees, shoving her legs up as he came down over her.

"You're mine," he growled against her mouth, grinding against her, determined to send her crashing over the edge. "Now come for me, baby. I want you to come all over me."

With those rough, raw-edged words echoing through her head, Skye cried out against his hot mouth, and gave him exactly what he'd asked for. Her orgasm was wet and tight and deliciously lush as he continued to pump his hips, prolonging her pleasure in a way that pulled another sharp cry from her lips. And then he was crashing over that dark, violent edge with her, coming so hard she could feel it. The wicked sensation shoved her into another screaming release, and he just kept thrusting so strong and powerfully, giving her all of him. Giving her everything.

God...just... God. She never...she never knew. Never really believed it could be like that—like it was with Elliot. That sex could feel that freaking good and special and breathtakingly intense. It was—*he was*—so much more than she'd ever hoped for...or dreamed of... or dared to imagine. He was everything to her. Heart, soul and future.

And yet, even as they lay there on the tangled sheets, wrecked with pleasure and gasping for breath, she couldn't help but feel that there was something—some unknown—still wedged between them. Something keeping him from being completely open with her. And it wasn't in the way he touched her. It was more...more of a shadow that would cross his eyes. A roughness in his deep voice, as if there was always something waiting on the back of his tongue that needed to be said, but that he fought back. That he refused to set free.

He'd taken her with him when he'd eventually rolled back over, murmuring that he didn't want to crush her. As she lifted her head from his chest, ready to ask him about the things churning through her thoughts, he caught her gaze with his heavy one, one hand stroking over her hair as he watched her and said, "I know there's still so much I need to learn for you—so that I can do right by you—but you already make me feel so amazing,

Skye. Like I was born for *this*. To give you pleasure. To make you laugh…and smile…and fall apart in my arms."

Emotion moved through her in a warm, huge swell, her mouth trembling as she tried to hold back a hot rush of tears. "Oh, God, Elliot. You're too much," she whispered, wishing she were brave enough to just come out and tell him that she loved him.

He tilted his head a bit as he studied her expression. "But in a good way?"

"Oh, yeah." She gave him a wobbly smile, and leaned up, pressing her lips to his. "In the best of ways."

He caught her behind her neck, holding her there so he could flick his tongue between her lips, the low sound that he made while he tasted her telling her he enjoyed it.

"You know," she said, when he lowered his head back to the pillow, one of his big hands cupping the side of her face like she was something endearingly precious to him, "if you keep this up, you're going to spoil me completely rotten."

A sexy grin kicked up the corner of his mouth as he stroked his thumb across the curve of her cheek. "Fine with me, baby. I happen to think you deserve some serious spoiling."

"Well, that goes both ways," she told him, loving his gaze like that, so hazy and warm with pleasure. "I…I want to make you happy, too." She paused to take a careful breath, needing a moment to dig deep for her courage. It wasn't easy, but he was worth it, damn it. He was worth…anything. *Everything.* So she looked him right in the eye, and said, "And if we're really going to do this thing—if we're going to…be together—then I want to help you…and be a true partner. I may be human, but that doesn't mean I need to be coddled. I'll learn what I need to know to make it here, and I'll be here for you to lean on when you need it. *Whenever* you need it."

He'd kept his gaze locked on hers as she spoke, though he'd smoothed his hand from her face, down the side of her neck, until he reached the start of her shoulder. Then he'd found her hammering pulse at the base of her throat with his thumb, stroking the sensitive skin as he listened to her, his eyes growing brighter and heavier, until they smoldered with heat. With preternatural fire. And a breathtaking look of awe.

Voice low and even huskier than before, he smiled at her and said, "You beautiful, surprising girl. What the hell am I going to do with you?"

She arched her brows at him. "Um, that was probably a rhetorical question, but I can actually think of all kinds of awesome things."

"Oh yeah?" His deep, rumbling laugh had her shaking on top of him. "You know," he added, stroking his big hands down her sides, "between our two dirty minds, we might never leave this bed."

"I could live with that," she said with an embarrassingly girlish giggle, and then as quick as her laughter had come, a sudden flare of guilt choked it off.

"What's wrong?" he asked, instantly picking up on the shift in her mood.

With a slight wince, she admitted, "I just… I can't help but feel guilty. I mean, Viv is out there with Max and they won't tell us what's going on, and I'm… I'm feeling so grateful to be here with you. It just…none of it seems fair."

"Skye, Viv is going to be fine," he assured her. "I promise you that Max won't let anything happen to her."

"But he refused to let you send help to him."

"Yeah, and I won't lie and tell you that it doesn't worry me. But I trust him. I know he wouldn't do this on his own unless it was the right call to make."

She sighed and lowered her head back to his chest. For a few breath-filled moments, she silently fought with herself about whether she should just keep her mouth shut, or go ahead and ask her earlier question, since she'd already spoiled the lighthearted moment. She came up with a hundred different reasons for why she should and why she shouldn't, and then she finally just blurted it out in a quiet, breathless rush: "What else aren't you telling me?"

"What? You mean about Max?" he asked, and she swore she could feel his body tensing beneath her.

Sliding onto her hip beside him, she braced herself on a straight arm, placed her other hand against his chest, over the heavy pounding of his heart, and slowly shook her head as she brought her worried gaze to his. "No. It's something…something about *you*. I don't know what it is…and before you say it, it's not about the connection. I might have freaked out at first, but I'm smart enough to be happy as hell about it—that it's *me* you're meant to be with. But I…I still can't help but feel that there's something you're still holding back from me."

"There's nothing," he told her, as he sat up and braced his back against the headboard, her hand trailing down to rest on one of his hard thighs. But she didn't believe him…because she was starting to realize that Elliot had a tell when he lied. He licked his lips.

And that's exactly what he'd done just now, before he told her he had nothing to hide.

Quietly, but with conviction, she said, "You're lying to me."

He opened his mouth, no doubt to argue, but nothing ever came out. His gaze had locked with hers, and it was like she could watch the fear and frustration as it built inside him. She could definitely feel it in the way his body stiffened, all those lean, ripped muscles hardening to stone.

Dreading the answer, she asked, "Does it have anything to do with why you think we need to wait before you claim me?"

His jaw tightened, and she could see the muscle that began to pulse there. One tick…two…*three*. And then his lashes lowered, and he slowly asked her, "Are *you* ready?"

She blinked, wondering where he was taking this. "Am I ready for what?"

He quickly shifted away from her, swinging his long legs over the side of the bed. When he turned his head and looked back at her over his broad shoulder, there was an almost cruel curl to his lips as he demanded, "Are you ready to open a vein and spill everything about yourself? Just lay it all out there? For *me*?"

She had to swallow a few times before she could whisper his name. *"Elliot…"*

"No?" he grunted, one dark eyebrow twitching. "Yeah, that's what I thought."

Drawing the sheet up around her, she cleared her throat, and managed to choke out a quiet "I wasn't trying to fight with you."

"Could've fooled me," he rasped, surging to his feet and reaching for his jeans. As he pulled them on, he flicked her a dark look from under his lashes, and muttered, "You just want something you're not willing to give me in return."

"That's…not true." Her throat ached, tight with the

fear that she was ruining everything. And yet, she knew this could never work unless they were both completely honest with each other. "I just… I'm not… I'm *trying*, Elliot. And I'm giving you every part of me."

"Not every part," he ground out. "Not your past. Not those deep, dark secrets you're still holding inside."

She flinched, but somehow managed to find the courage to say, "Only…only because I don't want you to judge me."

A harsh, bitter laugh burst past his lips as he shoved both hands back through his hair, his gaze colder than she'd ever seen it. "Yeah, well, back atcha, babe. I know exactly how you feel."

Her brows lowered as she gave him a quizzical look. "You're afraid I'll judge you?"

He smiled, but there was no humor in it. Just a hard, chilling reality. "I'm not afraid, Skye. I'm fucking terrified."

Panic was making it difficult to breathe, but she moved up onto her knees, desperate to make him believe her. "You don't need to be, Elliot. Not with me. I… I lo—"

"Hold that thought," he snapped, cutting her off, and she could feel his frustration being shaped into something ugly and raw, his muscles so sharply defined beneath his skin, he looked like he'd been carved with an artist's chisel. "Whatever you're getting ready to say, just…*don't*."

More than anything in the world, she wanted him to come back to the bed, lie down with her and hold her through the night like he was never going to let her go. Like everything would be okay, and they didn't have a mountain of secrets standing between them.

But he didn't. He dragged his hand roughly over his mouth, and then he turned his back on her.

With burning, tear-filled eyes, she watched him walk right out of the room, shutting the door behind him.

She waited…listening…and when the front door opened and closed a few moments later, Skye lay down, burying her face in the pillow that still smelled like Elliot, and cried herself to sleep.

Chapter 13

Elliot spent the better part of the following day doing everything he could to avoid Skye, and he hated every moment of it. But he didn't know what else to do. The last time they'd talked… Yeah, that had been gut-wrenching, and he didn't have anyone to blame but himself because he was the one who'd acted like an idiot.

After he'd stormed out, he'd spent his night prowling around the Alley until well after midnight, before finally creeping back into the cabin. He'd tried to catch some sleep out on the sofa, but had mostly just tossed and turned. He was up bright and early with the sunrise, and managed to get out to the meeting at Mason's before Skye even woke up.

He'd hoped the meeting might finally clarify some of the questions he had for the mercs, since they'd been so less than willing to discuss the wargs, as they called

them, in front of Skye. And it had, to a point. He just
hadn't liked what he'd learned. And he hadn't been able
to get anything out of the mercs about whoever might
have helped him up at the safe house. There was definitely something there they weren't telling him about,
and he was getting damn sick of the secrets.

And, yeah, the irony wasn't lost on him.

Before everyone had headed out, Mason had pulled
him aside and warned him to tread carefully with
Skye. Apparently their argument had been overheard
by a bunch of their neighbors, and the others were worried about him screwing up the best thing that had ever
happened to him. Then Mase reminded him about the
Christmas party they were throwing for the pack's pa-
trol scouts up in Shadow Peak that evening, and he bit
back a groan, thinking a party was the last thing he
felt like going to. Especially when he and Skye weren't
even talking.

The only bright spot in his day had been when he'd
run into Sayre on his way back to the cabin, and even
she'd given him a hard time, after he admitted that he and
Skye were fighting about his refusal to discuss his past.

"Elliot, you just need to tell her what happened to
you," she'd told him, sounding as frustrated as she did
sad. "If you don't, it could end up costing you everything. And I hear this girl is not only awesome, but that
she's freaking crazy about you. Don't you want to claim
her and marry her? Make a future with her? A family?"

"God, yes. More than anything. It's just that…"

"It's just that there's still a part of you that doesn't
feel like you deserve it," she'd finished quietly for him.
"Is that it?"

His throat had tightened with emotion. "Yeah."

"You can't think that way," she'd murmured, giving him a look that said she didn't know quite what to do with him. "How do you think it would make Mason and Torrance feel if they knew that's how you still saw yourself?"

"They don't have anything to do with this," he'd muttered, fully aware that he was talking himself into a corner.

Her pale brows had arched. "So the people who care about you don't matter?"

"Christ, Sayre, just drop it. You know I'm not like them. Like the rest of you."

"You know what Cian's past was like," she'd said in a low voice, looking as if she'd like nothing more than to shake some sense into him. "The people he killed when he was younger and still allowing his brother to influence his life—there were so many of them, Elliot. And yet, do you look at him today and think that he doesn't deserve to be happy?"

"No," he'd admitted, scrubbing his hand over his face. "Cian…he's a good man. One of the best I know."

"And yet, you can't say the same for yourself?" she'd pressed him. "Not even when the things that happened to you were beyond your control?"

Damn near growling at her, he'd said, "I didn't have to go to that Simmons asshole for help."

Sayre had nodded. "True. But you did it with the right intentions, Elliot. And if you explain that to Skye, she'll understand."

He'd blinked down at her, his next words falling from his lips like broken pieces of glass. "And if she doesn't?"

"Then *she* isn't worthy of *you*," had been his friend's

vehement response. But he knew that wasn't true. There was no one in the freaking world worthier than Skye.

Needing to change the subject, he'd forced a grin onto his lips, and said, "Enough about me, witch. Your guy told me you have some news to share. And from your scent," he'd drawled, "I'm guessing we'll get to meet this 'news' in about nine months, yeah?"

The smile on her lips had been unreal, her soft laughter filling the glade as she'd placed a slender hand on her still-flat stomach. "Cian's so excited, he can't stop talking about it."

Elliot could easily believe it. Cian Hennessey had taken to being a husband and father like he'd been born for it, and there was no one, not a single person, who knew him who didn't see how completely devoted he was to his wife and daughter. How he thought the sun and the moon hung with their happiness.

As if she'd read his mind, Sayre had looked at him and said, "You know, you'll be an amazing dad one day too, Elliot. Just like Cian is. It's something that you *both* deserve."

With her words spinning around in his head, nearly making him dizzy, he'd given Sayre a hug goodbye, and told her that he'd bring Skye by to meet her later. Then he'd headed back over to his cabin, and though he could hear Skye moving around inside, he kept himself busy out in the back. He replaced some of the weathered panels at the base of the back porch, and even did a bit of painting with the supplies he kept in a small shed.

He knew she could hear him, but she never came out to talk to him. He'd meant to head inside at some point and grab some lunch, but when he finally glanced down at his watch, Elliot was surprised to see that it was already after four.

It took him nearly a half hour to get things cleaned up and put away, and then he made his way around to the front. As he came into the cabin, he instantly spotted Skye, who was curled up in a corner of the sofa with his battered copy of one of James Patterson's first Alex Cross books. Her shuttered gaze skittered away from his, and he could all but feel the goddamn walls building between them.

It was absolute hell, not being able to cross the room and pull her into his arms, frame her beautiful face with his hands, and let his thumbs tilt her jaw up so that he could cover that pink, delicious mouth with his. She looked so damn sad and tense and pissed off, and when she glanced up at him again, she seemed almost surprised by his appearance. He figured he probably had paint smeared on his face, and his hair had to be sticking up in about twenty different directions, since he hadn't been able to stop stabbing his fingers through it all day. Then she just looked back down at the book, and he realized he'd been dismissed.

Shit. Just...shit.

With a hard swallow working its way down his throat, Elliot turned and headed into the kitchen. But instead of making himself something to eat, he found himself just standing there, hands braced on the counter as he hung his head forward and squeezed his eyes shut, his conversation with Sayre still looping its way through his brain on a constant replay.

Did he have the guts to just do it? And how the hell did you confess something like that to the woman you wanted to spend the rest of your friggin' life with?

He didn't know.

Then you need to figure it out, his wolf rumbled in a low, deadly voice, and Elliot could feel the animal's regret for what had happened all those years ago. Could feel its rage at being manipulated as sharply as if it'd only just happened. He gave another hard swallow, and could have sworn he felt the young woman's blood pouring down his throat, thick and rich and warm.

"Shit!" he cursed under his breath, gripping his head in his hands and squeezing, as if he could force out the macabre memories and somehow make himself clean.

And then Skye was there, in the kitchen with him, silently walking past where he stood and grabbing a bottle of water from the fridge. Before he could think of what to say, she turned around, and started to walk right by him again, and he couldn't take it. Lurching away from the counter, he blocked her path with his bigger, much taller body, and had to curl his hands into fists to keep from grabbing her. "Jesus, Skye. Can you at least talk to me?" he rasped, breathing hard as he stared down into her beautiful, troubled eyes.

"I've been right here, in this cabin, the entire day," she said sharply, crossing her arms over her chest. "You're the one who ran. Like a child."

"I know. And I'm...sorry," he choked out, finding it difficult to get enough air. "You have every right to be pissed at me. I should have... I should have stayed and... and talked things out with you."

She sighed, some of the stiffness in her posture easing as she looked away from him, seeming unsure what to say next. "Did you learn anything at your meeting this morning?" she asked, after several moments had passed and she finally brought her gaze back to his.

He thought of the things the mercs had told him and the others—things not even everyone in *his* world believed in—and decided that sharing something like that right now would be a bad idea. So he licked his lips, and muttered, "Not really."

She smirked, as if she'd seen right through him, and started to go around him again.

"Wait. Please," he begged, backing up and shifting a little to the right, so that he could stay in front of her. Stabbing his fingers back through his hair, he sounded desperate even to his own ears as he said, "I know things seem really weird between us right now, but if you'd just tru—"

"Don't!" she snapped, fisting her empty hand at her side as she glared up at him. "I swear to God, Elliot—if you say something stupid, like I should *trust you*, I will freaking scream!"

He ran his hand over his mouth, and this time when she went to move around him, he didn't try to stop her.

Well, hell, he thought, slumping against the counter as he heard his bedroom door open and shut. That hadn't exactly gone well.

Making his way back out to the living room, he dropped down onto the sofa just as his phone signaled a text. He pulled it out, scowling at the automatic reminder his calendar had sent him about the party, when he'd been hoping the message was from Max. He *needed* to hear from the guy, because he knew that his partner was definitely…off. And while he hadn't been lying when he'd told Skye that Max would do whatever it took to keep Vivian Jackson safe, what he hadn't told her was that Max hadn't sounded good—or at all like himself. And that was worrying the shit out of him.

Just as he was slipping the phone back into his pocket, it started to vibrate, and he was surprised to see that the call was from Monroe, since he'd talked to the guy just that morning. His conversation with the Fed was short and to the point, but it left him seething with fury.

According to Monroe, a young couple who'd been out hiking near one of the state parks, down in the nearby human town of Wesley, had been massacred. The Fed's gut told him the wargs had followed them to Maryland, and were responsible for the gruesome killings, and Elliot agreed. So far, Monroe's unit had managed to keep the media from learning about the murders, but the longer the wargs were left to roam through Wesley, which sat at the base of the mountains, the greater the chance that they'd catch the attention of the local police—and that would only cause trouble for the Silvercrest pack.

So, yeah, it was important they were dealt with as quickly as possible. But the fact they were there for Skye—for *his* woman—was the driving force behind every decision that Elliot made.

When Monroe asked if he'd fill in the others and let them know what was happening, he told him he would, then ended the call.

Moving to his feet, Elliot realized that the first thing he had to do was deal with Skye. At the meeting that morning, Mason had made it clear to everyone that if the safe house had been on the wargs' radar, then they would be stupid to assume the bastards didn't know about the Alley, as well. Seeing as this was where the Runners' families lived, their security levels were already high, but Mason had put plans into motion to have the security around the Alley and Shadow Peak made even tighter. So even with most of the others heading up to the party,

the woods would still be teeming with patrols, and Elliot knew the wargs wouldn't be getting anywhere close
to this place.

They had to know it, too. Which was most likely the
reason why they'd made the kills down in Wesley look
like a rogue feeding—because they were trying to draw
Elliot out, and to use him to get to Skye.

He was getting ready to walk back to the bedroom to
talk to her, needing to feed her a story so he could slip
away, when she stuck her head around the end of the hallway and told him that she hadn't slept well the night before, so she was going to skip dinner and go to bed early.

"Are you… Will you be here tonight?" she asked, giving him a curious look.

"I need to run out for a meeting," he murmured, licking his bottom lip, "but then I'll be back."

"All right," she said, pulling her own lip through her
teeth as she nodded. "Just…be careful."

With that, she turned and headed back down the hallway, and it took everything Elliot had not to call out to
her. Or better yet, simply follow her into the bedroom,
lie down with her and do everything he could to reestab-
lish their connection. But he didn't have the time, damn
it, because there was too much to do if he was going to
pull this off.

Thankfully, he wasn't flying completely blind. Ever
since Skye had agreed to come to the Alley with him,
he'd had an idea brewing in the back of his mind. All
it'd taken earlier that morning was a quick call up to
Lindy, one of Max's friends who lived in Shadow Peak
and who worked for one of the pack's security teams,
and she'd told him she was more than happy to help.
That he just had to let her know when she was needed.

So Elliot quickly pulled up her number on his phone, and asked her to meet him at the gas station that sat right at the foot of the mountain, on the main highway. Then he called Lev's number, and told the merc how he wanted this to go down.

Seeing as how his fellow Runners were all family men now, he didn't want to pull them into this mess until it was absolutely necessary. And the mercs would be more than enough backup. They were ruthless and deadly fighters, and they already had a good handle on what this group would bring to a battle. Hell, they knew more about the wargs than any of them did.

Plus, they could cry off from the scouts' party by simply saying they'd had something come up, since they still took work that had nothing to do with the Runners or the pack.

"How are you getting out of the scout thing?" Lev asked, when Elliot explained that he didn't want the Runners to know anything about his plans.

"I'll text Mase and tell him Skye isn't up for it. That she's still coming to grips with being here, and we just need to spend some time on our own."

The merc didn't say anything for a moment, and Elliot knew the guy was running it all through his head.

"You sure you want to do it this way?" Lev finally asked, after giving a rough sigh. "Mason and the others are gonna be seriously pissed when they realize what you've done."

"I'll handle Mason. You just get the other mercs together and set up close enough that you can reach us when we need you. We're gonna be in the parking lot behind the Grayson Industrial Center in two hours."

It would be dark by then, and all the businesses in the

center had closed down the year before, giving them the privacy they needed. Plus, with the rear parking lot backing onto one of the town parks, it would be a believable place for a werewolf like Elliot to take his girl for a walk under the stars. Not that he'd ever be stupid enough to do such a careless thing, when they were in danger, but he was banking on the wargs simply thinking he was an arrogant bastard who thought he could do as he liked.

"You know," Lev muttered, "you should just let us go and track these assholes down, while you stay here with Skye."

"This is *my* responsibility," he argued. "No way in hell am I passing it off."

Ending the call, he shoved the phone into his pocket, confident that his plan would work. The only thing that didn't sit well with him was keeping Skye in the dark. She deserved to know what was going on, but he couldn't risk her talking him out of it. Not when he knew this was his best shot at taking out—if not all—then at least a good portion of Chiswick's thugs.

Wanting to check on her before he left, Elliot quietly moved down the hallway and opened his bedroom door. She was already asleep on the bed, and he wasted precious minutes just soaking in the beautiful sight of her, his heart aching for everything he was so afraid they were going to lose. They'd slammed into a massive brick wall so hard he was still reeling, and he didn't know how to get around it without losing her.

Because despite what Sayre had said, he was still so goddamn terrified that Skye wouldn't be able to accept the truth.

Knowing he was short on time, Elliot forced himself to leave the room, quietly shutting the door behind him.

He grabbed his tactical gear from the locked closet in his office, then the keys to Skye's car and a few other things that he needed, and headed out through the back door to his Jeep.

When he met up with Lindy, who was similar to Skye in appearance, he gave her his mate's sweater and jeans that he'd taken from the dirty laundry, and waited while she used the ladies room to change. By the time the wargs realized Skye's scent was coming from the clothes, and not the woman herself, it would be too late. He'd have already drawn them out, and with the mercs' help, the bastards would be destroyed.

Leaving Lindy's car at the gas station, they headed into Wesley, and drove straight to the site of the murders. Lev had called to say that he and the other mercs were on their way and would be in position soon, but Elliot tried to stay calm, knowing they could have a long wait ahead of them.

Asking Lindy to stay in the Jeep, he made a show of getting out and speaking to the guys Monroe had guarding the site, making sure that he was seen by anyone who might be running surveillance. After about twenty minutes, he got back in the Jeep, and he and Lindy headed to the Grayson Industrial Center.

"What now?" she asked, as he pulled into a spot in the rear parking lot and cut the engine.

"Now we wait," he replied, scanning the tree-filled parkland that butted up against the lot.

She checked the clip in her gun, then slipped it back into her waistband. "Do you really think they'll take the bait?"

"I think they're too desperate not to," he said, turning

his head to look at her. "Just stay sharp, and if it turns to shit, you take the Jeep and get out of here."

She narrowed her brown eyes at him, clearly insulted. "What the hell, Elliot? I can fight."

"I know you can, Lindy. But these assholes aren't like anything you've ever gone up against. I won't have your death on my hands. You understand?"

"Yeah," she huffed, crossing her arms over her chest as she slid him a dark look. "But when I get to meet this girl of yours, I'm warning her that you're a bossy ass."

With a gritty laugh, he turned his attention back to the dark parkland, anxious to get things started. The plan was for the mercs to set up close enough that they could reach them quickly, but without being detected. The guys had said that wargs weren't known for their sense of smell, so he was counting on them being unable to pick up the mercs' scent until it was too late.

Pulling his phone out, he called Lev. "You in position?" he asked, when the merc answered.

"Yeah," Lev murmured, and he could hear the guy opening his truck door. "We're about a block down the road. Sam and James have gone to run some recon on the area. When they get back, we're gonna..." He paused, then made a rough sound of surprise. "*Well, shit.* Look who we have here." Another pause, and then, "Elliot, man, you're not going to like this. But we had a stowaway in the back of the truck, hiding under the tarp. And she definitely belongs to you."

Chapter 14

Elliot's pulse started to roar in his ears like a goddamn freight train, and rage unlike anything he'd ever known swept through his system, along with the kind of cold, bone-chilling fear that could make you stupid.

"Hey, man," Lev said into the phone. "Did you hear me?"

"Where. Are. You?" he bit out, the words feeling like gravel in his throat.

"Just off of Kane Street, behind the dry cleaners."

"I'm on my way," he grated, cranking the Jeep's engine. "Fucking lock her down and don't take your eyes off her."

He shoved his phone back in his pocket, ignoring Lindy's questioning look as he reversed out of the parking space so quickly the tires spun, then tore out of the place. When he pulled into the lot behind the cleaners and spotted the mercs' trucks, Elliot slammed on the brakes, jumping out from behind the wheel while the Jeep was still rocking.

As he headed toward the group standing beside one of the trucks, his phone started going off like crazy in his pocket, but he ignored it. His breaths kept coming in rough, uneven bursts, until Lev shifted to the side and he spotted Skye, and then a visceral, animalistic growl rumbled up from his chest. Christ, he didn't think he'd ever been this furious in his entire life.

"Please don't be mad at me!" she cried, suddenly rushing past Lev and Kyle, and throwing her arms around his waist. She squeezed him so tight it made his heart clench, and Elliot had never seen her skin so pale, or her eyes so wild with fear. Lifting up on her toes, she pressed her lips to the stubble on his clenched jaw, then tried to kiss his lips, but he set his hands against her shoulders and pushed her back.

"What the hell are you doing here?" he demanded, glaring down at her.

She flinched at the guttural sound of his voice, but didn't back away from him. "I...I knew something was up when Monroe called you. I didn't mean to, but I heard you on the phone with him."

"So you faked being asleep?"

She nodded, the way she lifted her chin telling him she didn't regret it. "Yes, and I kept the bedroom door cracked open while you were talking to Lev. I heard you planning...all this. You freaking lied to me. Again!"

He licked his lips. "I didn't lie."

"You sure as hell didn't tell the truth!" she shot back, cutting a sharp look over toward his Jeep, where Lindy was waiting off to the side...dressed in Skye's clothes. *Shit!*

Refusing to go on the defensive, he pointed a finger toward Lev's truck. "And what do you call this stunt you've pulled? Do you have any idea what you've done? How much danger you've put yourself in?"

"I don't care." She trembled as she drew in a deep breath, and he could have sworn she looked even paler as she pushed both hands into her hair, her gaze focused on the patch of dirty asphalt that stretched between them. Hands falling to her sides, she said, "I just... I couldn't stand the thought of you facing off against those monsters because of me and not being here to help."

He made a thick, rude sound that had her flinching again. "And what the fuck can you do to help, Skye?"

She swallowed, but didn't back down. Instead, she squared her shoulders and lifted her head, glaring right back at him. "I've got a weapon. I took it from your cabin."

His eyes bulged when she drew the handgun he'd taken from the safe house in Pennsylvania from the canvas purse that hung across her body. "Do you even know how to use that thing?" he roared. He could see the two mercs looking on with worried expressions, but warned them to stay back with a single glance.

"I wouldn't have taken it if I didn't know what I was doing," she muttered.

"How, Skye?"

She slipped the gun back into her purse, and he could hear the frustration in her low voice as she told him, "I didn't exactly have the best childhood. And, no, this is *not* the time to get into it. But I've been in danger before. I know how to be smart."

"Nothing about this is smart," he snarled, grinding the heels of his hands against his burning eyes. "Christ. What was it you said about stupid girls that first night I met you? That they end up dead?" Dropping his hands into fists at his sides, he closed the space between them with a single step, so pissed off he was damn near breathing fire. "It doesn't get more stupid than this shit!"

With her head tilted back so that she could look him in the eye, she asked, "Are we just going to keep hurling insults at each other?"

"No. You're not doing anything but getting the hell away from here."

"Elliot, I know you don't understand. But the thought of you in danger... I couldn't..." She pulled in another deep breath, and then slowly let it out as she kept her watery gaze locked tight on his. "I know you're angry about what I've done, but please try to understand that it's only because I...I didn't have any other choice."

He could have sworn there was something important she was trying to tell him, but he was too angry at the moment to figure it out. And then he caught sight of James and Sam coming around the back corner of the building on his right, and he knew the situation had just taken a turn for the worse.

Both mercs were carrying a body over their shoulders, and from the scent of the corpses, Elliot could tell they were wargs.

"Well, hell," Kyle muttered, as the mercs dumped the bodies into one of the truck beds. "Didn't take you guys long to find trouble."

"Tried to question them," Sam muttered, wiping his bloodstained hands on his jeans, "but the assholes wouldn't stop trying to kill us."

Lev snorted like a smart-ass. "You definitely put an end to the conversation."

"Were there any others?" Elliot asked, curling one

hand around Skye's upper arm as he headed over to the truck.

James shook his head. "Not that we saw."

Scrubbing his free hand over the bottom half of his face, Elliot stared down at the bodies through narrowed eyes, as if they were somehow going to give him the answers he needed. "There have to be more of them."

"Yeah," Lev muttered in agreement. "But this would be a shit location to face off against them. There's a crowded bar just down the road. If we get caught here, we won't be able to use any tactical weapons without the risk of drawing unwanted attention."

"Then let's get out of here," he grated, knowing the entire goddamn night was a bust. "The important thing is that we get Skye back up to the Alley. I'll find a way to deal with these assholes later."

Everyone nodded their agreement, and then Kyle said, "I'll tell Lindy we're calling it a night. If you want, Lev and I can give her a lift back to her car. Then we'll follow behind her and make sure she gets home safe."

"Thanks," he grunted, feeling the heat of Skye's gaze burning against the side of his face. If she'd listened in on his conversations earlier, then she knew he'd only been using Lindy as bait. But it still felt wrong to be caught out with another woman. Especially when everything between them was so screwed-up.

"Elliot, talk to me, please," she whispered, when he turned and started walking her over to his Jeep.

"Can't," he scraped out, the quiet word nearly carried away by the freezing wind. "Right now I just need to get you out of here."

"Before we leave, there's something I need to tell you."

"This isn't the time," he started to say, when one of

the mercs shouted a gruff warning. Instantly on alert, Elliot shoved Skye behind him as he did a quick visual sweep of the area, his heart damn near jamming into his throat when he realized they were suddenly surrounded.

With a quick look over his shoulder, he saw the mercs, as well as Lindy, taking up protective positions around Skye. For that right there, they'd earned his eternal gratitude. Not that he didn't already feel that way about this group. They'd proven themselves so many times it wasn't even funny.

But as grateful as he was, he still had a sick feeling in his stomach. Behind him, Skye had her hands fisted in his Henley, and she sounded completely terrified as she kept muttering "Come on, hurry!" over and over again.

There must have been nearly thirty wargs closing in on them from all sides of the parking lot, along with several men whose scent definitely marked them as pure-blooded Lycans. The wolves were no doubt part of some "bad guys for hire" scheme, which was something he and the other Runners saw too much of these days. Just as he was getting ready to quietly ask Lev if he had any brilliant ideas, one of the Lycans stepped forward and lifted his arm, signaling the others to halt. Elliot narrowed his eyes on the dark-haired, good-looking bastard, thinking he seemed vaguely familiar, though he couldn't for the life of him place where he knew the Lycan from.

Then a creepy smile tugged up a corner of the guy's wide mouth, and he said, "You don't look like you remember me, but I definitely know you, Elliot." Shoulders shaking with a gritty laugh, he added, "Oh, yeah. I've seen you at your finest."

Confusion creased his brow, while a nauseating wave of panic started to coil its way through his insides.

"Funny as hell that you're a Runner now," the Lycan drawled, and it was clear from the silence in the group that he had everyone's attention. "I've heard they call you and your partner the Wild Wolves or some shit like that. Laughed my ass off at that one." Lifting his brows, he said, "I mean, isn't the other guy a turned human? But you... Yeah, you I've seen get pretty wild."

"Who the fuck are you?" he demanded in a harsh shout.

"Nine years ago. A cave where Simmons and his groupies got up to no good." The asshole slid him a knowing smirk. "Ring any bells?"

Behind him, he thought he heard Lev curse under his breath, but his pulse was roaring in his ears too loudly to be sure. He sucked in a sharp breath and blinked, hoping he might wake up and this would all turn out to be just another twisted, horrific dream. But then the asshole started talking again, and he knew the nightmare was only just beginning.

"My name's Lopez," the Lycan said, keeping his dark eyes locked on Elliot. "But that's not something you would have ever known. I'm just someone who happened to be in the right place, at the right time. And I gotta admit, you put on quite a show that night." Whistling low, he pulled a pack of cigarettes from his pocket, took one out and lit it with a silver lighter, before saying, "Talk about a massacre."

Skye gasped, and Elliot felt every single ounce of blood drain from his face, unable to believe this was happening. "Shut the fuck up!" he roared, while inside he was dying, wondering why he hadn't explained everything to her when he'd had the chance. Because no matter what, this wasn't how he wanted her to learn. From some goddamn psychotic son of a bitch.

"Tell us the story," one of the wargs called out, leering like a jackass. "It sounds like a good one."

"And don't leave out any of the juicy details!"

"Yeah, come on, Lopez. Let's hear it!"

He felt Skye start to shake behind him, the pain in his chest from how hard his heart was beating nearly bringing him to his knees. Or maybe it was just the organ breaking, shattering into pieces. He supposed it'd been inevitable—given his work—that he would one day encounter someone who had been there that night. But, Christ, he'd never imagined it would be like *this*.

"The Lycan here, he was just a teenager, raging with his hormones, and this rogue wolf named Simmons found him a pretty little thing to pop his cherry," Lopez started, and Elliot made a sound that was raw and dark and deadly, but there was nothing he could say to shut the asshole up. And he couldn't attack him. Not when it would mean leaving his life-mate. And the mercs and Lindy were in the same position, each one standing with their back to Skye, ready to protect her when the time came.

Lopez took a long drag on his smoke, then slowly exhaled. "So there's a huge group of us in this cave, and Simmons has a red-faced Elliot take this stacked little blonde into the back, where there's this curtain hanging to give them privacy. He even had a bed set up for them and everything."

"You're a sick shit," Lev muttered, growling at Lopez.

But the bastard just smiled. "So there we are, listening to them get all worked up. And then Elliot finally gets to the good stuff, only to find out that the girl was a virgin, too. And there's blood. Too much of it for the young Lycan to handle."

"Oh, God," Skye whispered in a broken voice, tightening her grip on his shirt. "No...no...no."

"So we hear the girl scream bloody murder, and Simmons is wearing the biggest fucking smile as he rips the curtain down, allowing us all to see what's happening. He'd planned the whole thing, setting this little bastard up, and damn, it was a hell of a show." Grinning at Elliot through a cloud of smoke, he laughed as he said, "You fed on that girl like she was a juicy steak being offered to a starving dog."

More details followed, the words like a buzzing, lacerating pain in Elliot's head. The Lycan told them everything, even revealing parts that Elliot hadn't been able to fully recall until that moment. But it was all coming back to him now, the cold sweat on his face and the bile rising up the back of his throat warning him that he was about to be ill.

Skye... Oh, God, Skye. She knew everything now. Well, *almost* everything. And it was breaking his goddamn heart.

Tossing his cigarette butt on the ground, Lopez jerked his chin at Elliot, his grin widening as he said, "I think I'll enjoy doing the same to that pretty little morsel hiding behind you."

Over my dead body, Elliot thought, releasing his fangs with a deadly hiss of sound. But before he could issue his warning to the bastard, one of the wargs that he recognized from the safe house growled, "Not tonight, Lopez. That's not what we're paying you for and you know it."

The Lycan looked toward the long-haired warg and laughed. "Raze, you paid me and my men to back your pathetic ass up, because you're terrified of failing your boss man again. But don't delude yourself into thinking you call the shots here."

"Fuck you!" the warg snarled, getting right in Lopez's face. As the two continued to argue, the rest of the wargs and Lycans began to shift into their preternatural forms. The wolves only shifted the top halves of their bodies, while the wargs took on a change unlike anything Elliot had ever seen.

Earlier that morning, Lev had told the Runners that the wargs were "soldiers" that had been created to serve things that came from hell itself, and watching them now, he could believe it. Though they still had their basic human shapes and faces, their limbs bulged with thick muscle, and their jaws were elongated, ears pointed at the tips, with an eerie crimson hue to their skin. And just like the ones he'd fought at the safe house, they had claw-tipped hands and lethal fangs.

Glancing over his shoulder, he saw that the mercs had taken off their shirts and were already shifting their upper halves as well, while Lindy remained in her human form, but held a wicked-looking blade in each of her hands.

After the things Lopez had just revealed, shifting was the last thing he wanted to do in front of Skye. But he didn't have any other choice. Looking forward again without even making eye contact with her, Elliot ripped his Henley off, and allowed his own change to wash over him. Though his fur had been more golden in color when he'd been younger, it had darkened over the years, and it rippled over him now as his torso expanded, transforming into the deadly shape of his beast, while his head became wolf-shaped, complete with a fang-filled snout.

Whoever had helped him before, up at the safe house, clearly wasn't making an appearance tonight, and he couldn't help but wonder if that was because the mercs were there. Then he didn't have time to think about anything but keeping these bastards away from Skye, because they came at them hard and fast, their solid black eyes gleaming with violence.

And, yeah, he could see it now. Could understand what the mercs had been trying to explain to him and the others at the meeting that morning. The wargs...they weren't of this world. If you knew what you were looking for, you could see the shadow cloaking them. The evil that had followed them straight out of hell.

He'd been able to handle them in smaller numbers, but like this, they were damn near rabid, and he knew their viciousness came from a pack mentality. As ruthlessly as he and the others were fighting, there were simply too many of the assholes.

"Get her out of here!" he shouted over his shoulder, as soon as he'd downed another one. "All of you. I've got this!"

"What?" Skye screamed from just behind him. "Are you trying to get yourself killed?"

With James moving in to cover him, Elliot turned to face her for the first time in his partial wolf form. Unable to make himself look her directly in the eye, he flicked his tongue across his lips, then forced his words through the beast's muzzled snout. "It'll be okay. I'll be right behind you."

"You're lying!" she shrieked in a voice that was thick with tears. "You always lick your lips before you lie. It's your goddamn tell! Even when you look like this!"

He blinked, surprised by that revelation, since he'd never realized it before. But, shit, she was right.

"Just get her back," he snarled at Lev, who was moving to her side. "Now!"

"Wait, damn you!" she screamed. "Help is coming!"

"Help?" he grunted, wondering what the hell she was talking about. *Please God,* he thought, *don't let her have called the police.* Because if she had, they were screwed.

Swiping at the tears on her face, she said, "I found everyone's numbers written down in your desk. So I called him when we first got here."

"You called who?" he demanded, his brow furrowing as he stared down at her.

"Mason!"

Shit! That's why his phone had started going crazy earlier. And he couldn't even be pissed about it, because they needed the help.

Behind him, he could tell there was a definite shift in the battle, and Elliot knew his fellow Runners had just joined the fight. With a sharp look at Skye, he growled, "You stay the hell down."

"I've got her covered!" Lindy shouted, moving in close to his life-mate, the blades in her hands dripping with blood, while her dark eyes burned with determination. "I won't let these bastards anywhere near her."

Satisfied that Skye was in good hands, he turned and took in the welcome sight of his friends. Yeah, they were a badass-looking bunch, and he knew they would fight for him like they were fighting to protect their own families. Despite the fact that his intentions were good, he'd been wrong not to tell them what he had planned, and he definitely had a serious apology to make. But not right now.

Right now, shit was about to get real.

"Any of you warg assholes actually end up surviving this night," Mason called out in a deep, rough-edged voice, "and, let's face it, you'd have to run like a coward for that to happen. But if you do, be sure to let Chiswick know that every Bloodrunner in the Silvercrest pack will stand with Elliot Connors and go to battle for him. So if Chiswick wants war, he'll have war. We protect what's ours, and we're gonna be coming after him."

Before Elliot could so much as get a word out, he found himself facing off against one of the Lycans working with Lopez, and he quickly got him on the ground, then went in for the kill. All around him, the enemy was being taken down with lethal, brutal efficiency, and he could only imagine what Skye must be thinking of the carnage.

From somewhere off to his left, he heard one of the mercs shout that Raze was making a run for it, and James instantly retook his human shape so that he could go after him. Driven by the sole purpose of protecting his female, Elliot kept fighting alongside the others, until nearly all the remaining wargs and hired Lycans had been dealt with.

Using his forearm to wipe the blood and sweat from his eyes, he took a quick look over his shoulder just to assure himself that Skye was still okay. Lindy hadn't left her side, and as he turned his attention back to the battle, he saw that Lopez was the only adversary left... and Kyle and Jeremy had the asshole cornered.

"Get away from him," he bit out, stalking closer. "This bastard is *mine*."

Kyle lifted his claw-tipped hands. "All yours, Connors," the merc drawled in his slow Southern accent, while he and the Runner stepped aside.

As Elliot approached, Lopez stared back at him through cold, hate-filled eyes, and he knew this last fight was going to be anything but easy. But it would sure as hell be *satisfying*. Giving the jackass a sharp, deadly smile, Elliot charged as Lopez sprang forward, and they crashed together with a meaty, visceral sound, each of them snapping with their jaws.

His side stung as the Lycan's claws grazed him, and Elliot twisted with a powerful roundhouse, cracking his booted heel into the asshole's chest. Then he struck him again, even harder, and Lopez fell. Fueled by the anger burning through his veins, he came down over the bastard and straddled him, pinning him to the ground with one claw-tipped hand pressed hard against his throat.

"You think you know what you're dealing with?" Lopez wheezed, eyes bulging with rage as he tried to free his arms—but Elliot had them trapped against his sides. "You don't know shit, Runner. Before this is over, everyone you know and love is gonna *burn* and die."

"You first," he scraped out with another sharp smile. "And you're just gonna bleed."

He'd never enjoyed the feeling of his fangs and claws tearing through flesh as much as he did in that moment, the taste of the bastard's blood feeding that feral, destroyed part of him that was still howling in outrage over everything it'd undoubtedly lost, now that Skye knew the truth about him. The beautiful life that had *almost* been his. The way she'd looked at him, like he was her goddamn hero. The way she'd kissed and touched him, as if he were already something she...loved.

"Elliot, man, he's dead," Lev muttered at his side,

the merc's deep voice somehow reaching down into the blood-soaked chaos of his thoughts and bringing him back. "You're done. It's over."

He hung there over the body, feeling like he'd been on one of those carnival rides that just went round and round, until you didn't even know which way was up when you stumbled off, nauseous and disoriented.

And then he suddenly remembered where he was, and he felt Skye's penetrating stare before he even lifted his head...and locked his glowing gaze with her dark, shadowed one.

Hello, sweetheart. Meet your monster, he thought, knowing damn well that she must be horrified by what she'd seen. What she was looking at right then.

All those seconds and minutes and hours he'd done his best to be good for her. Sweet. Tender. Loving. He'd just killed them as brutally as Lopez's earlier recounting of the night Elliot had taken his first life.

Pushing himself sluggishly to his feet, he realized the other Runners had all retaken their human shapes and were talking to him, and he struggled to focus on what they were saying as he did the same. Since the sight of her pale face and tortured eyes was destroying him, he forced himself to look away from Skye, and narrowed his gaze on the guys around him instead.

"We'd already figured out something was up," Cian was muttering, as he used the T-shirt he'd shoved in his back pocket to wipe the blood from his chest. "Your girl just saved us the time searching."

Mason gave him a hard look. "You owe us an explanation, Elliot."

He exhaled a harsh breath, and stabbed his bloody

fingers back through his hair. "We'll talk later. Right now, just get her back."

"Wait. What did he say?" he heard Skye ask in a broken voice, from where she stood beside Lindy.

He turned his head and looked back over at her. His chest lifted with another ragged breath, and though he tried to force out some kind of explanation, he couldn't. So he ended up just shaking his head.

Tears poured down her face like a stream. "Elliot, please. Talk to me. Don't do this!"

Turning away from her again, he looked at Mason. "Make sure she's locked down in my cabin. I don't want her setting foot outside of the Alley until this nightmare is over." Shifting his attention to Lev, he asked, "You think he'll send more?"

"He'll think twice about sending any of his men down here again," the merc replied, rubbing his jaw. "At least not until he's had a chance to regroup, and that'll take time. But it means he'll probably go after Max and Vivian even harder now. A guy like Chiswick—he won't like losing."

"Shit," Brody and a few of the others cursed, their rough voices overlapping.

"I know he's your partner," Lev added, "and I know he's asked for time, but enough's enough, Elliot. The guys and I, we should go after him."

Even though he knew Max was going to be pissed, he jerked his chin in agreement. Because Lev was right.

"I looked over the notes you made for Mason and wrote down the towns where Vivian has family," Lev was saying, "so we'll start there. Just don't warn him until we've managed to track him down, yeah?"

"Yeah," he agreed as he felt for his keys in his pocket,

before remembering that he'd left them in the ignition. Looking at Kyle, he said, "Don't forget to make sure Lindy gets home safe."

"Where will you be?" the merc asked, giving him a wary look. Hell, they were all looking at him that way.

He managed to scrape out one single, throaty word: *"Home."*

"You're going back to the Alley?" Cian called out.

But Elliot had already turned his back on the group, and walked away, without ever answering the question.

Chapter 15

Two days. Almost two entire freaking days.

That's how long Elliot had left Skye down in the Alley, stewing over all that had happened.

She'd been put under guard that first night, thanks to Mason and the others. They were all afraid she would do something stupid that would result in her getting herself killed...or captured. And she'd been so desperate to find Elliot that she just might have tried it.

Throughout that long, painful night, she'd been so incredibly heartbroken for him, and for the boy he'd been, unable to get the shattered look that'd ravaged his handsome face out of her head. She'd finally collapsed in exhaustion on his sofa, and when she'd opened her eyes the next morning, her pain had morphed into an even darker, uglier anger. She'd been pissed at everyone and everything. At the bastard responsible for hurting Elliot all those years ago. At Chiswick and his asshole wargs for screwing with her and Vivian's lives.

And most of all, at Elliot, for walking away from her and leaving her there. Alone. Without him.

That seething, made-her-feel-like-she-was-being-flayed-alive mix of fury and pain had ridden her hard the entire day, until she'd finally just burned out. She'd crashed on the sofa again, waking up late in the morning, and three hours later, she was still just lying there. Drained. Broken. So exhausted she could barely move. She'd spent the last hour just watching the dust motes, scarcely aware of the sun's shadow moving across the wall, as she stared blankly into space.

Finally, she somehow found the strength to get up and eat a sandwich. Then she caught sight of herself in the stainless-steel surface of the fridge, and realized a shower was something she needed. Badly. Like forever ago.

An hour later, after she was clean, dressed in a fresh pair of jeans and a black sweater, and at least looking halfway human again, she started to head into the kitchen for a drink, when someone knocked on the front door. Skye was tempted to ignore it, since the last thing she wanted was to talk to Elliot's friends, much less socialize. But for all she knew, they had keys and would just let themselves in.

Shuffling toward the door, she opened it and found a group of women standing on the porch, with Torrance at the front, a determined expression on her pretty face. Accepting that she wasn't going to get out of this—whatever *this* was—Skye stepped aside and let them in. She'd already met all of them her first night there, except for the beautiful strawberry-blonde, and Torrance introduced her as Sayre Hennessey. Then they all gathered together in the kitchen, and Sayre—who she knew was a good friend of Elliot's—helped her put on some coffee.

Skye was grateful no one asked her how she was doing, since it had to be fairly obvious. Instead, Elise started things off by saying, "The men are so pissed that Elliot tried to leave them out of the fight."

"I'm sure he was just trying to protect them," she murmured, pulling some mugs down from one of the cupboards.

"Of course he was," Carla offered with a delicate snort. "But they don't need it."

Sayre winced. "That's Elliot's problem right there. Always thinking he knows what's best for everyone."

She nodded her head in agreement, even though she didn't really know *what* he was thinking at the moment. She just missed him like crazy. And was so freaking disappointed that he hadn't come to talk things out with her.

When the coffee was ready, they took their steaming mugs over to the table and sat down.

Carla leaned forward in her chair, crossed her arms on the gleaming wooden surface and locked her dark gaze with Skye's. "I might be wrong, but I'm pretty sure I know where he is."

Her hands started shaking so badly she had to set her mug down. "Where?"

Looking around the table, Carla said, "I think he might have gone up to his parents' old house."

Elise's long red hair slipped over her shoulder as she nodded. "I think Carla's right. The house sat empty for a while, but Elliot bought it once he became a Runner."

"But he's never lived there," Sayre added. "I mean, not since he was seventeen."

"I told him not to do it," Torrance said, the concern she felt for Elliot etched onto her pale face. "It's not healthy, holding on to that place. Not when his parents were so horrible to him."

"What did they do?" she asked, dreading the answer.

Torrance sighed as she shook her head. "I know this is Elliot's story to tell, but I...I think you need to understand as much about his past as you can, if you're going to fight for him." She paused and gave Skye a deep, searching look. "Are you?"

"Of course I'm going to fight for him." She sat up straighter in her chair, hoping the other woman could see just how much she meant those words...as well as her next ones. "He's... I'm in love with him."

Carla grinned and smacked her hands against the table. "I knew it!"

"Please," she rasped, needing someone to answer her question. "What happened with his parents?"

"They're assholes," Elise muttered with disgust.

In a gentler voice, Torrance said, "When all those awful things happened to Elliot, he was basically just a boy. He needed their help, their support. *Anything.* But when Elliot finally went and tried to talk to them, they told him to leave. That was the last thing they ever said to him. I think it's why he was so terrified of you learning the truth about what had happened."

"Oh, God," she breathed, her gaze skittering around the room, as if she were suddenly going to find him there. "I need to see him. To talk to him. Try to make him understand that I'm not going to do the same thing. That I'm not going to turn my back on him."

Carla gave her a small smile. "It won't be easy, honey. If he's anything like Eli, he could be getting completely hammered up there. That's what my boy did when things went to shit."

"No," Torrance murmured, shaking her head again. "Elliot's too worried about losing control. He won't be drinking."

She frowned, thinking that couldn't be healthy. To always be so on edge. Always worrying about how tightly he was reining himself in. Is that how he'd always felt with her? Like he always had to be careful?

If so, then that crap was stopping now. She wasn't a china doll, and he damn well didn't need to treat her like one. He just needed to treat her like *his*.

Tucking her hair behind her ear, she looked at Carla. "I don't care what Elliot's doing. I just need to get to him. But I think he took the keys to my car. And when the guys left me here, they said the Alley was being monitored." Looking around the table, she asked, "So how the hell am I going to get up there?"

With a slow smile curling her lips, Sayre said, "You just leave that to us."

Elise lifted her brows with interest. "What are you thinking, little witch?"

"I'm thinking we hide her in the back of my new truck. I've been carting around everyone's Christmas trees and wreaths, so there's no reason to think I wouldn't be taking a few more up to Shadow Peak. We'll just toss a blanket over her, and put a few lightweight wreaths on top."

"Ooh, good idea," Carla purred, rubbing her hands together. "I love it!"

Giving them a worried look, Skye said, "Won't Cian and the others be pissed when they realize what you've done?"

Sayre gave a low, wicked laugh, and waggled her brows. "I hope so. Makeup sex with my Irishman is *always* fun. We might end up with another broken bed, but it's worth it."

"Mmm, Eli's the same way," Carla murmured, flashing a wide grin. "I'll drive up with you guys, and that way he can get his feathers all ruffled, too."

"If we all go, they'll know something's up," Elise said with a disappointed sigh, setting her mug down on the table. "So I'll stay here with Torrance, and we can ask a bunch of them to help us get things ready for the sled races the kids want to have later. That should keep them distracted for a while."

Voice thick with emotion, Skye told them, "Thank you so much for helping me."

"I'm just glad he found someone so lovely and sweet," Torrance said, reaching over and giving her hand an encouraging squeeze. "After everything he's been through, that boy deserves the very best."

Too choked up to respond, Skye got up and threw her arms around the little redhead, giving her the biggest hug she could, which had everyone looking emotional when they finally broke apart, both of them teary-eyed and smiling.

Less than a half hour later, Skye was getting her first look at Shadow Peak as she sat in the backseat of the truck Sayre used for her gardening business. Once they'd made it out of the Alley, Sayre had pulled over onto the side of the road, and Skye had joined the witch and Carla up in the cab, thankful to no longer be freezing her ass off back in the bed, buried under three Christmas wreaths. The plan to sneak her out of the Alley had worked so well, she didn't doubt for a moment that the guys were going to be seriously bent out of shape when they realized how easily they'd been tricked. She would have to be sure to ask her new friends for all the juicy details when she came back with Elliot.

And, yeah, she was definitely returning with him. She wasn't taking no for an answer.

It didn't take them long to drive through the picturesque mountain town, and she knew which house was Elliot's childhood home the moment they turned onto the quiet residential street, because it was the only one without a single Christmas decoration or twinkling light.

"He must have parked his Jeep in the garage," she murmured, when Sayre pulled her truck up to the curb. Skye had thought she'd be nervous as hell, but her hands were steady as she opened the door and climbed out, her voice calm as she turned and thanked the women for their help.

"Give him hell," Carla said with an encouraging grin.

"And remember," Sayre told her, "you've totally got this."

She gave them a brief smile, then turned and made her way up to the front door. She didn't bother knocking, but simply reached for the doorknob. It turned easily, which didn't surprise her. Elliot didn't seem like the type to worry about his own safety—just everyone else's.

The downstairs was quiet and bleak, without a single piece of furniture, and so she headed up the staircase, figuring she'd find him in one of the rooms on the second floor. And she did. In fact, as she stood in the open doorway of the third room on the left, she knew she was looking into Elliot's childhood bedroom, and it broke her freaking heart. Because while his asshole parents had cleared the rest of the house, they'd left this room untouched, as if they hadn't wanted to take a single reminder of their son with them.

He was sitting in a chair by the window, staring out at the backyard, and she drank in the sight of him as she stepped into the room, thinking he was the most beautiful thing she'd ever seen. Even in his wrinkled clothes, and with those dark shadows under his eyes, the sunlight only making them more pronounced when he quickly turned his head in her direction. He'd obviously been buried so deep in his thoughts, he hadn't even realized she was there until that exact moment.

"Skye?" he croaked, running an unsteady hand over his face as he pushed to his feet. "What the hell are you doing here?"

"Seriously?" She shook her head as a soft, humorless laugh fell from her lips. "It kinda pisses me off that you even have to ask me that."

His shock was wearing off, and in its place she could see his defenses building. His fear of what this visit meant. He stared back at her like he was gearing up for a confrontation, his hooded gaze dark and measuring… and wary as hell.

Pulling in a deep breath, she slowly exhaled, and knew she needed to start talking. "At first," she said, walking a little farther into the room, "I was so angry at you. Pissed that you hadn't trusted me enough to tell me the truth. But then I realized I was being a hypocrite. I mean, it's not like I've completely trusted you, either."

"Skye—" he started, but she cut him off before he could say anything more.

"I know how guilt can eat you alive. God, do I know." She swiped at the stupid tears that were suddenly slipping over her cheeks, but forced herself to continue. "And there are so many stories that I could tell you about my childhood—so I will, if you want to hear them. Stories like the one about how my mother named me after her dealer, Matthew Skye, because she thought it was funny, seeing as how she'd been high on some coke he'd given her when she got pregnant with me."

"Fuck," he muttered under his breath.

"My, um, dad was out of the picture really early on," she said in a low voice, walking across the room and sitting down on the foot of the double bed. Bringing her gaze back to his, she went on. "And one day, my mom just took off, leaving me and my older sister, Lara, with our grandmother. But when she realized that Lara was also into drugs, she told us to get out."

His brows were drawn with concern, and she could tell there were so many questions he wanted to ask her. But he choked them back, giving her this chance to explain.

"So, long story short, we heard that our mom died from an overdose about a month after she left. By that time, Lara had managed to get us a tiny apartment, and we were trying to get by. But I…I knew she was in danger of ending up on that same path."

Holding on to the edge of the bed with a white-knuckled grip, Skye pulled in a quivering breath, then made herself keep talking. "She would work to keep herself clean for a few weeks, but it never lasted, and she was already an addict by the time she was eighteen. When what little money we had ran out, she started bringing men back to our crappy little one-bedroom for sex. She was…hooking in order to feed her addiction, and I… I hated her for it. Hated the things I would come home from school and see. Hated the guys that would try to corner me, thinking I would put out for money, too."

"Jesus Christ," he rasped, taking a jerky step forward, as if he felt the magnetic pull between them just as strongly as she did.

"And the…the thing about my past that I didn't want to tell you," she said, forcing the husky words from her tight throat, "is that there was this guy who had a thing for Lara. He was a big-time drug dealer in the area, but I…I didn't know that at the time. I just knew that he'd always been nice to me whenever I ran into him."

She could see the dread that spilled over his face, and knew he was headed down the wrong path, so she rushed to explain.

"He didn't hurt me, Elliot. But… I saw him one day in town, and when he said he was worried about Lara and wanted to talk to her—that he had this amazing job opportunity for her--I…I brought him back to our apartment with me."

She blinked when Elliot suddenly started pacing with a restless, edgy energy, as if he could no longer just stand there and listen. But he didn't look away from her, not even once, and she drew strength from the powerful emotion she could see burning in his dark, beautiful eyes, her voice a little stronger as she said, "When we got to the apartment, my sister was with a…a client who was old enough to be our dad, and the dealer lost it. He and the guy fought, and he ended up getting rid of the creep." She gave a hard swallow, swiped at the tears on her cheeks, and with her pulse rushing through her ears, she heard herself say, "Like a stupid little twit, I had hoped everything would be okay then, so I left. But it…wasn't. Once I was gone, the dealer tied my sister up, raped her, and gave her a lethal dose of heroin. Then he crawled into bed with her, and did the same to himself."

Stopping in the middle of the floor, Elliot quietly cursed as he shoved both hands back through his hair, his tension like a raw, visceral thing there in the room with them, so thick she felt like she could breathe it into her lungs.

Clearing her throat, she told him the rest. "When I came back to the apartment hours later, the cops were there. They told me what had happened, and I said that I would go to stay with my grandmother, since she was still my legal guardian."

He kept his troubled gaze locked tight with hers. "But you didn't."

Shaking her head, she said, "I got on a bus, and my money ran out in Charity. I lived on the streets there for two days, until I got lucky and someone told me about the shelter. And then I met Viv and her family." A brief, poignant smile tugged at the corner of her mouth, because she knew she'd been saved that day. "When her mom finally got an apartment, Viv and I moved in with her. We said that Viv's mom was my aunt, and so the school Viv went to didn't give me any hassle when I registered. We finished high school together, graduated and then moved out on our own to give her mom and brothers some more room."

Taking another deep breath, she said, "So that's my story. And now that I've opened my veins and spilled all that ugly shit, I need you to talk to me, Elliot. I *need* you to trust me enough to know that there's nothing you can tell me that will make me look at you any differently."

He gave her a hard, guarded look. "Lopez already took care of that, Skye. What more is there to tell?"

"Your story, damn it. Do you think I care what that asshole had to say?"

She watched a flat, emotionless smile twist the corner of his mouth. "He didn't lie."

"I didn't say that he did. But he wasn't the one it happened to. You were. So all I care about is what *you* have to say."

He stabbed his fingers into his hair again, his frustration so raw and real, she could *feel* it pressing against her skin. "What I did... *Christ*, Skye. I was such a little idiot." With a grim set to his jaw, he looked around the room, and slowly shook his head. "I never came back here, except to get my things."

Softly, she said, "Torrance told me about your parents. What they did—it was wrong. They should have been there for you."

A low, bitter sound tore from his chest, and he brought his dark gaze back to hers. But he didn't say anything.

"Elliot, talk to me. *Please*."

"The reason I went to Simmons was because of this girl. I'd met her at a concert, and I...I wanted to ask her out. But she was human." He paused, flexing his hands at his sides, and his breath left his lungs in a jagged, shuddering burst. "It's ironic when you think about it," he rasped. "I mean, my parents thought it was my lack of control that landed me in such a shitty mess, when it was control that I had hoped Simmons could teach me." A harsh laugh fell from his lips, and they twisted just a little on one side. "Though I know my old man meant control over *everything*. In his eyes, it was wrong to want her. To want something that wasn't meant for me."

"He sounds like a complete asshole."

"You have no idea." His voice turned even rougher,

like he'd swallowed something gritty. "So after I ended up with the Runners, Simmons…he took the girl. Her name was Marly."

"Oh, no," she whispered, understanding so much more now. About how he thought. About the mountain of guilt he'd carried with him all these years.

"Yeah. The son of a bitch killed her, in the worst way you can imagine, Skye. And it's on *me*. All of it. That's why I don't deserve you."

"No!" she snapped, surging to her feet as she crossed the floor to him. "That's not true, Elliot. Don't you see? We *both* made mistakes by putting our trust in the wrong people. But that's what they were. *Mistakes*."

"It's not the same," he argued, scowling down at her. "You have no goddamn blame in what happened to your sister."

"I do. I have just as much as you," she said desperately, clutching on to his powerful arms. "But it doesn't mean we're bad people. We were both victims of manipulation, but only because we were hoping for something better in our lives. You would never have intentionally harmed that girl in the cave or put Marly in danger, just like I would have never led that dealer to our apartment if I'd known what he would do. But it happened to us, and now we have to move on. We can either let it destroy the best thing we've ever found, or we can tell it to go to hell and make the future *ours*. We can make it whatever we want it to be."

He sucked in a sharp, stunned breath, and she reached up, cupping the sides of his handsome face in her trembling hands. "And I know what I want," she told him, hoping he could see just how much she meant each husky word. "I want *you*. Every beautiful, protective, perfect-for-me part of you. The rest is just details that don't really matter, as long as I have you in my life."

His eyes went glassy with tears; his expression one of complete awe, as if he couldn't believe this was happening. "Are you... Are you serious, Skye?"

"Why else do you think I'd come here and do this?" she whispered, giving him a watery smile. "I'm *begging* you to be with me. To share your life with me."

"I love you," he suddenly growled, yanking her into his arms and crushing his mouth against hers. "I love you so goddamn much. And I should have told you before. But I just... I *love* you."

Oh... Oh, God. That was the sweetest freaking thing she'd ever heard. "I love you, too," she cried against his lips, unable to hold the torrent of tears inside a second longer.

His own tears were falling as he drew his head back, his hands buried in her hair. "You know, the whole begging thing—all you did was beat me to it."

"What do you mean?" she asked, unable to get enough of the way he was looking at her, as if she were the most precious, most meaningful thing in his entire world.

"I mean that as shit as I felt about you getting stuck with me," he admitted, pressing his forehead against hers, "I wasn't going to let you go without one hell of a fight."

"But you came up here and...stayed." *Away from me. Without me.*

"Just to get my thoughts straight," he said in a low voice that was hoarse with emotion. "Christ, Skye. I've been racking my brain for the right arguments to make, so that when I headed back down to the Alley tonight, you wouldn't have any choice but to realize that staying with me was, *is*, your only option." Cupping her wet face in his hands, he rubbed his nose against hers, then looked her right in the eye, and said, "Unless, of course, you wanted to leave me as a poor, pitiful wreck of a man who would spend every damn day of his life missing the hell out of you. Aching for you. *Craving* you."

"You know," she murmured with a warm smile, "for a guy who everyone says is usually so quiet, you have a hell of a way with words."

"Only 'cause it's you," he groaned, brushing his lips across hers, while his big hands moved down her back, pressing her in tight against him. "Only 'cause this matters. More than anything."

With her hands braced against his powerful biceps, she arched back a little, until she could search his dark, molten gaze. "And you…you were really going to fight for me? To…beg for me?"

"Damn straight I was. And if it meant getting down on my knees, then I'd have stayed on them till they bled."

She gasped in response, completely undone by his words, and then his mouth was claiming hers—truly *claiming* it—and they were lost in a kiss so wild and hot and passionate, Skye didn't know how she managed to stay in one piece. One moment they were in the middle of the room, and in the next, he had her pushed up against the nearest wall, her legs around his waist and his hands under her ass as he ground his rigid erection against that most sensitive, needy part of her.

"I know I can be difficult," he muttered against her wet, sensitive lips, feeding the husky words into her mouth. "That I can be too quiet at times, and I'm no partier. And I'm sorry as hell that I didn't tell you everything when I had the chance. That you had to learn the way that you did. But I will *worship* you, Skye. Every single day, I will do whatever it takes to make sure you know how important you are to me."

"Shh," she whispered, pushing her hands into his hair. "Just shut up and take me to bed now, Elliot. Or the floor. Even this wall. Hell, I don't care. Just get inside me!"

He was kissing her again before the last syllable left her lips, and they were both smiling as they tore at each other's clothes, desperate to get to hot, slick skin. Then they fell onto the double bed together in a tangle of limbs and greedy, clutching hands, breathless with excitement, and she knew without any doubt that she'd never wanted anything more in her entire life than *this*. Than *her man*.

With his heavy-lidded gaze deep and dark and burning with emotion, he slammed every inch of himself inside her, and she realized that this time would be *different*. That he was no longer holding back on her. Their walls had been fully destroyed, and they were finally free to lose themselves in each other, and the breathtaking power of their connection.

It was a raw and rough and brutally aggressive joining, but so damn *real*, their fingers gripping hard enough to bruise, skin so damp with sweat they were sliding against each other, his hips slamming into her so hard it was crashing the bed into the wall in a loud, banging rhythm. And this time, when she came, he crashed over that blinding, shattering edge with her, their hearts pounding against the other, and she swore she could taste his happiness in the rough, sexy-as-hell growl that he fed into her mouth. Hoped like crazy that he could taste hers, too.

Hours later, after they'd made love so many times she'd lost count, and they were still lying there in the tangled bedding, wrapped completely around each other, he put his mouth against her ear, and said, "You're gonna marry me, Skye."

She'd decided somewhere around her fifth or sixth orgasm that her new motto went something like: *Stupid girls might end up dead—but only a crazy woman would ever say no to Elliot Connors.* So with a wide smile on her lips, she squeezed her arms and legs around him, and murmured, "Of course I am."

"You promise?" he rasped, and she could see the excitement gleaming in his beautiful brown eyes as he drew his head back and took in the I'm-so-freaking-happy, gonna-love-this-man-till-I-die look that was on her face.

"I know some people might think this is crazy, but I don't care. We've crammed a freaking year into a matter of days, and I trust how I feel, Elliot. I trust it in a way I've never trusted anything in my entire life." She leaned forward and nipped his sexy lower lip with her teeth, loving the way he growled and pulled her closer. "So, yeah, I will marry you and keep you forever."

"Damn straight you will," he groaned against her mouth, kissing her like a man who had finally found his happiness. And when the moon had risen high into the night sky, he released his fangs, and made what he'd told her was the most important bite of his life.

He made her *his*, for that moment...and for all the days and nights and moments to follow.

And though she didn't have his Lycan genes that would enable her to do the same, Skye didn't give a damn. No way in hell was she going to let that stop her. Wrapping her arms around her man, she told him again how much he meant to her, and claimed him back just as thoroughly…and powerfully…and everlastingly…

With her love.

Epilogue

Christmas day

Christmas in Bloodrunner Alley was a beautiful thing. Elliot and Skye had awakened just after seven to the sight of snow falling past the bedroom windows, and the sound of children's laughter ringing out through the glade, as the little ones took everything from their new sleds to soccer balls out into the snow to play.

With a huge smile on his face, he'd carried his mate out to the living room, laid her down under the tree they'd put up together, and made love to her until he had to cover her mouth with his own to stifle her screams of pleasure, before burying his primal growl against the side of her throat, his tongue lapping possessively at the bite he'd made there.

The one that marked her as his...forever.

With a gift like that, he didn't need anything else. And yet, she'd still spoiled him rotten with a beautifully decorated bookshelf that had been a complete surprise. She must have worked on it when he'd been in meetings with Mason and the others—they'd been trying hard to come up with a plan for how they were going to deal with Chiswick—and he couldn't believe she'd managed to make something so awesome in such a short amount of time. It was freaking kick-ass and he loved it.

The shelves were painted a dark, midnight blue, with moons and stars, and on both sides there were handwritten quotes from the Chilean poet Pablo Neruda. Poignant passages about the power of moonlight, as well as love, commitment and passion.

It was by far the most amazing, meaningful gift anyone had ever given him, and Elliot knew the cell phone and designer bag he'd gotten her didn't come anywhere close, but she'd still loved them.

At noon, they'd done a quick gift exchange with everyone over at Jeremy and Jillian's, and there had definitely been a theme to the presents he'd been given. Goddamn peanuts! He'd unwrapped everything from peanut butter and brittle to peanut-decorated boxers. And Skye, the little imp, had laughed her head off the entire time.

Now it was close to dinnertime, and they were heading over to Mason and Torry's for Christmas ham and all the trimmings. He knew his friends were going to take one look at the huge, lovesick smile on his face and give him a hard time. But he didn't care. He'd never had or enjoyed a Christmas like this in his entire life, and the knowledge that they could *all* be like this... Yeah, that pretty much wrecked him. But in a good way. In the best of ways.

Just as they were about to climb up the first porch step, his phone vibrated in his pocket. He pulled it out, took one look at the name and said, "Skye, it's a text from Max."

"Seriously?" she gasped. "What's it say?"

They hadn't heard from Max since the night Elliot had told him that Skye was his life-mate, so he could understand her surprise. Hell, he was feeling pretty surprised himself. Starting to read the text, he said, "Damn, he knows Lev and the guys are looking for them. He says…to call them off. That he's… Holy shit, he says they're headed back."

"They're coming here?" she asked. "To the Alley?"

"Yeah. He says they'll be here by the end of the week."

"Yes!" she squealed, throwing her arms around his neck and pulling him down for one of the sweetest friggin' kisses he'd ever had. He could feel her smile against his lips, and he was so damn happy that his girl was happy…and that his partner would finally be where he could keep an eye on him.

Thankfully, there hadn't been any new abductions, but they knew they were playing a waiting game. If Chiswick wasn't going after his next victims, it meant he was still focused on Skye and Vivian. It would have driven Elliot insane, if he hadn't been secure in the knowledge that she was safe in the Alley. So they'd set some basic ground rules. She wouldn't do anything foolish, like try to sneak out, and would only leave the safety of the glade when Elliot could organize a group to go with them.

For Elliot's part, he'd promised her he wouldn't sneak off to confront Chiswick and his men without telling her. James was still tracking the one named Raze, who'd run, and the merc seemed confident that he might get a lead on how to find Chiswick and the women he was holding captive.

Typing in a quick response to Max, Elliot slipped the phone back into his pocket. Then he grabbed his girl's hand and pulled her up the steps with him, putting all that crazy shit out of his head for the night, determined to keep it from casting a shadow over their first holiday together.

Just as he lifted his free hand and started to knock on the front door, in the center of the festive wreath that hung there, Skye tugged on his other hand to get him to look at her. With a warm, sexy smile on her gorgeous lips, she said, "By the way, I have one more present for you."

Elliot lifted his brows. "Oh, yeah?"

"Mmm-hmm." She caught her lower lip in her teeth, then slowly let it go. "But it's one I can't give you until we get home tonight, because I'm wearing it."

He froze midknock, his imagination going wild over what kind of provocative wisps of lingerie she could be wearing under her clothes.

Grinning up at him, she whispered, "Looks like you're going to have to unwrap me."

"Yeah," he breathed, already picturing in his head *exactly* how he wanted to do it. Tightening his grip on her hand, he said, "Come on. Let's go home. Now."

Her head went back as she laughed, the husky sound shredding what was left of his control. "We can't do that. This is a special meal with your family." Green eyes shining with humor, she added, "And Katie would probably just track us down anyway."

"Fine," he muttered, turning back to the door, since there was a strong chance he would just toss her over his shoulder and start running if he kept looking at her. "We'll eat, and have coffee, and then we're getting the fuck home."

With another soft laugh, she asked, "Where's your Christmas spirit?"

"The second we're through our front door," he growled, "you're going to be drowning in it."

"Mmm. Sounds fun."

"Hell," he groaned, knowing that he *had* to kiss her now. So he pulled her into his arms, and he did. Until Mason finally opened the door and let out a rough bark of laughter.

"Damn, Elliot," the Runner drawled. "You could at least let the poor girl come up for air."

He smiled against her mouth, and whispered, "Oops, we just got busted."

They were both laughing as they went inside and quickly found themselves surrounded by their friends, and their family, in the truest sense of the word.

Beside him, she whispered, "I love that dimple, boy," and he was surprised to realize he was smiling so wide his face hurt.

He leaned down and whispered something dirty in her ear, loving the way she blushed. And as she started to talk with the people around them, he thought back to all the years he'd felt so alone, even when surrounded by this wonderful crowd. Christ, he didn't even know how to describe how blessed he felt now. Because Skye wasn't just a good woman—she was the absolute finest. And she was *his*.

He loved a girl who was his everything. Who challenged him and supported him, and had taught him how to accept his past and to look forward to his future. She was his lover, his mate, his best friend and his heart. She was all of those things…and *more*.

As Katie came running over and launched herself at Skye, Elliot couldn't help but imagine one day holding a little girl of his own in his arms—one who had his woman's beautiful hair and eyes and breathtaking smile. Her heart of pure gold…and more courage than any Lycan he'd ever known.

He knew, without any doubt, that it would be the best damn day of his life.

And he couldn't wait for it to get there.

* * * * *

MILLS & BOON®

**If you enjoyed this story,
you'll love the the full *Revenge Collection*!**

**Enjoy the misdemeanours and the sinful world
of revenge with this six-book collection.
Indulge in these riveting 3-in-1 romances
from top Modern Romance authors.**

Order your complete collection today at
www.millsandboon.co.uk/revengecollection

'The perfect Christmas read!' - Julia Williams

Jewellery designer Skylar loves living London, but when a surprise proposal goes wrong, she finds herself fleeing home to remote Puffin Island.

Burned by a terrible divorce, TV historian Alec is dazzled by Sky's beauty and so cynical that he assumes that's a bad thing! Luckily she's on the verge of getting engaged to someone else, so she won't be a constant source of temptation... but this Christmas, can Alec and Sky realise that they are what each other was looking for all along?

Order yours today at
www.millsandboon.co.uk

MILLS & BOON®

Why shop at millsandboon.co.uk?

Each year, thousands of romance readers find their perfect read at millsandboon.co.uk. That's because we're passionate about bringing you the very best romantic fiction. Here are some of the advantages of shopping at www.millsandboon.co.uk:

* **Get new books first**—you'll be able to buy your favourite books one month before they hit the shops

* **Get exclusive discounts**—you'll also be able to buy our specially created monthly collections, with up to 50% off the RRP

* **Find your favourite authors**—latest news, interviews and new releases for all your favourite authors and series on our website, plus ideas for what to try next

* **Join in**—once you've bought your favourite books, don't forget to register with us to rate, review and join in the discussions

Visit **www.millsandboon.co.uk**
for all this and more today!